The First Time Ever

The First Time Ever

Ted Darling crime series

'original, character-driven crime fiction'

L. M. Krier

Contents

About the Author

L M Krier is the pen name of former journalist (court reporter) and freelance copywriter, Lesley Tither, who also writes travel memoirs under the name Tottie Limejuice. Lesley also worked as a case tracker for the Crown Prosecution Service.

The Ted Darling series of crime novels comprises: *The First Time Ever, Baby's Got Blue Eyes, Two Little Boys, When I'm Old and Grey, Shut Up and Drive, Only the Lonely, Wild Thing, Walk on By, Preacher Man.*

All books in the series are available in Kindle and paperback format and are also available to read free with Kindle Unlimited.

Contact Details

If you would like to get in touch, please do so at:

tottielimejuice@gmail.com

facebook.com/LMKrier

facebook.com/groups/1450797141836111/

https://twitter.com/tottielimejuice

For a light-hearted look at Ted and the other characters, please consider joining the We Love Ted Darling group on Facebook.

Discover the DI Ted Darling series

If you've enjoyed meeting Ted Darling, you may like to discover the other books in the series:

The First Time Ever
Baby's Got Blue Eyes
Two Little Boys
When I'm Old and Grey
Shut Up and Drive
Only the Lonely
Wild Thing
Walk on By
Preacher Man

Acknowledgements

I would just like to thank the people who have helped me bring Ted Darling to life, beta readers: Jill Pennington, Kate Pill, Karen Corcoran, Jill Evans, Alison Sabedoria, Emma Heath, Police consultants – The Three Karens, Martial arts consultant – Nathan Pill.

Special thanks to Kate Pill for nobly agreeing to be the guinea pig to ensure all the martial arts moves described in the book are realistic and feasible.

To Karen

Thanks for helping to keep it real in police terms

Author's Note

Thank you for reading the Ted Darling crime series. The books are set in Stockport and Greater Manchester in general, and the characters use local dialect and sayings.

Seemingly incorrect grammar within quotes reflects common speech patterns. For example, 'I'll do it if I get chance', without an article or determiner, is common parlance.

Ted and Trev also have an in joke between them - 'billirant' - which is a deliberate 'typo'.

If you have any queries about words or phrases used, do please feel free to get in touch, using the contact details in the book. I always try to reply promptly to any emails or Facebook messages.

Thank you.

Chapter One

Ted Darling was about to kill a man. For the first time in his life. He was twenty-nine years old.

He could hear the voice of his boss, Inspector Matt Bryan, through his earpiece. Calm, steadying, slightly roughened by too much tobacco, which was clearly going to be the death of him if the graveyard cough was anything to go by.

Bryan was old school, formal. He used Ted's call-sign, only rarely his first name. Usually he called him Sergeant.

'Right, Sergeant, on my order only, you will fire and it's code Fahrenheit. I repeat, code Fahrenheit.'

That was the shoot to kill order. Not unexpected. From Ted's vantage point on a high building, it was the only shot he could go for – a head shot – and even then it was at the limit of his considerable skill.

'Can you do it? Do you have clear line of sight?'

'I think so, sir.'

Bryan made a sound of annoyance.

'Think so is no good to me. It's my name on this and I need higher authority. It's the first question they're going to ask me. Can you do it or not?'

Ted sighted along the barrel of the Heckler and Koch tucked snugly against his shoulder. He was looking at a youngish man, on the brink of total panic. The man's left arm was around the throat of a young woman, his right hand alternately brandishing a Glock at anyone around him and holding it against his captive's head.

There were already two casualties of the armed robbery gone wrong. One inside the building, reportedly dead. The other was a young woman Police Constable outside, near to the armed man, and they had no information at present as to whether or not she was alive. She was down, motionless, and there was a lot of blood. But she was neither moving nor making any sound.

She hadn't even been a first responder. Just unlucky enough to be walking past at the precise moment the failed robber decided to try to make a break for it with his hostage when the whole situation had blown up in his face.

He seemed to be working alone. It made him even more dangerous. He would be desperate, with no one to help him or back him up. It made him capable of anything. They had no ID on him, no idea of who he was, whether or not he had previous form.

A trained negotiator was trying to defuse the situation, talking calmly and reasonably over a loudspeaker. The young man was getting more unpredictable by the minute. It was past the point where talking was likely to do any good, especially as the young woman he was holding on to as if his life depended on it was becoming hysterical. And he clearly realised that she was now all that was standing between him and a bullet.

Time seemed to have slowed to a crawl. Ted knew his boss would be seeking authority from higher up the chain of command to end this situation the only way which now seemed possible. There could still be thirteen rounds left in the Glock 19 the robber was using. An awful lot more potential casualties if the siege wasn't brought to an end soon.

Then Ted heard the gravelly voice in his ear once more, giving the order. This was what he was trained for. It was still the first time he'd had to do it and no amount of simulation could prepare him for the feeling of the real thing.

He could almost swear he saw his bullet make its leisurely way through the air as he watched anxiously. Had he got it right? Had he made enough allowance for the angle? The life of the young woman hostage was in his hands as much as that of the robber if he had made even the smallest error.

Then he saw the man's head explode like a watermelon, watched the young woman fall to her hands and knees and start to crawl away from the nightmare scene, her mouth open in one long anguished scream. Physically, she was safe, unharmed. The psychological effect could be a different story altogether and could well stay with her for the rest of her life. But at least she was alive.

'Good work, Sergeant,' Bryan told him briefly through the earpiece, a disembodied but reassuring voice.

Ted went into autopilot mode. He made his weapon safe, breathing slowly through his mouth to counteract the effects of the sudden adrenaline hit which invaded his body. He was numb for the moment. Whatever feelings the incident provoked in him would come later, once the formal side of things was out of the way. After he'd sunk a few glasses with the team at the end of the shift. Probably not until he'd got back home to his dad's house and dealt with whatever might be awaiting him there.

Down below him the scene burst into activity. Two green-clad paramedics were rushing to the fallen officer. Ted was anxiously awaiting news of her condition as well as confirmation of the state of the other reported victim. Authorised Firearms Officers were encircling the robber, although there was no chance of him moving, not ever again. Medical crew and police officers were swarming into the building, led by more AFOs, to check on those inside.

Matt Bryan came stumping slowly up the steps to the roof space where Ted was waiting. His hacking cough echoed in the concrete stairwell, the climb clearly challenging his smoke-ravaged lungs. One of Ted's own squad came with him, looking anxious about his sergeant.

'You all right, Skipper? Bloody good shooting, though.'

Ted nodded, not trusting himself to speak. He was starting to come down from the first buzz and realise all the implications of what had just happened. Even though he was acting under orders, there would need to be an immediate full inquiry, especially with such a high profile operation. He'd been too caught up in his job to notice, but he was sure the local press and media would be down there in force.

He knew his ticket would be pulled immediately as a matter of routine and he'd be driving a desk until all the ramifications had stopped rumbling. He hoped the boss wouldn't ground the rest of his squad as well, though he might do. They operated as a unit and a tight one, at that. With their Skipper in dry dock until the outcome of the enquiry, they may also be desk-bound to keep him company.

Ted would be driven mad by the inactivity and there would be worse to come – the obligatory offer of counselling. Ted hated talking about himself and his feelings. There were dark inner thoughts he kept locked away deep inside and had never spoken about to anyone. And that's how he preferred it to remain.

He'd had to cope with all that stuff when he'd applied for the additional training to become a Specialist Firearms Officer. He'd had to undergo security clearance and to pass written psychological tests before he'd even been accepted for the course.

He would try to resist now but he knew he would be obliged by regulations to go and see someone, if only to explain in person why he felt fine. He'd just done the job he was trained to do, albeit for the first time. He'd had to shoot to wound before but this had been his first ever killing shot. He didn't feel in any way psychologically scarred by the experience. At the moment he felt nothing but a strange detachment from reality. He just wanted to get back to his squad and his job.

'Murphy, take the sergeant's gun, follow procedure and

piss off back to the vehicle. Then wait to drive him back,' Bryan told him. 'We'll all meet back at the nick for a debrief as soon as I'm cleared to leave the scene.'

AFO Declan Murphy snapped partially to attention with a sharp, 'Sir,' and did as he was instructed. Inspector Bryan was a good boss but a proper bastard if anyone got it wrong. He certainly didn't want to get on the wrong side of him on a day which was already fraught for all concerned.

Bryan perched against the balustrade, his hand instinctively going to his pocket in search of his packet of fags. He wouldn't smoke one, not on duty and in uniform, but his body was craving nicotine so he clamped an unlit one between his lips and sucked greedily on the unfiltered end. Close to, Ted noticed that the rattle from his lungs was audible every time he took a breath. He was just recovering from yet another bad bout of bronchitis and clearly hadn't allowed himself enough time to recuperate.

'All right, Ted. Just you and me now, so no bullshit. Are you all right? Really all right?'

'Fine, boss, no worries. It's just a job.'

'Well, for god's sake don't go saying that to the bloody shrink. They don't like officers who enjoy killing or aren't affected by it. You won't get your ticket back with that attitude.'

'I didn't say I enjoyed it, boss. I was just following orders, doing my job.'

'That's what they all said at Nuremberg,' Bryan grunted. 'We'll have half an hour together back at the nick, after the debrief, to make sure you get your story straight. I know you're good at talking your way out of trouble but you need to get it right on this one.

'Is there any news of the officer down, boss? Did she make it? Any more casualties?'

'Early reports are that she's alive, but only just. The person inside was not so lucky. I'll update you on the officer as soon as I hear anything. But you certainly saved a few more lives, the way the situation was developing.

'Right, so, paperwork next, for all of us. Fully detailed reports. Let's cover our arses thoroughly on this one. You know there'll be red tape and hoops to jump through. Then I expect you'll want a drink with the lads. I'll call in for a swift one with you all, if I get a minute. Got anything planned after that?'

'I'll need to get back to my dad, boss. Make sure he's ok. If any of this has been on the telly, he'll only worry.'

If he's sober enough to notice, Ted finished silently to himself. Things weren't good with his father at the moment. He drank far too much and Ted didn't know how to deal with it. He could understand his frustrations at being disabled, wheelchair bound, but adding to them with excessive drinking was more than he could comprehend. He tried to be understanding, but sometimes it was hard. There was only Ted and his dad. Had been for years since Ted's mother had walked out on them both a long time ago.

Ted's mobile rang. He looked to the boss for permission before reaching for it. Bryan nodded.

'The boyfriend? I suppose he'll be worried too. He's bound to have heard about it, with his connections. I'll leave you to it, but get yourself back to the nick without delay.'

Philip's voice was breathless with anxiety, his words falling over each other as soon as Ted picked up the call.

'Oh, my god, are you all right, my Darling? I've just heard the news. Were you there? Were you involved? Oh, heavens, please tell me it wasn't you who did the shooting?'

'I'm fine. Honestly. Don't fuss. I'll tell you all about it when I see you.'

'Can it be tonight? I'll be worried sick until I can see for myself that you're really all right.'

'Not tonight, Phil. I've got all kinds of shit to sort out at work now. Then I'll need to get back to my dad. He'll be worried, too. I'll probably get a couple of days enforced leave so maybe, if you're free, we could do something?'

'If you're being put on leave then it was you who shot him, wasn't it? Oh my god!'

There was no fooling Philip. He was a Crown Prosecutor with the CPS. He knew all about police procedure.

'Honestly, I'm fine. Look, I've got to go now or my boss will be after me. I'll call you as soon as I know what's happening.'

Ted cut short Philip's protestations of affection. He didn't feel the same way. He was fond of him, but that was all. And right now, he was far more worried about the prospect of an enforced break from the job he loved doing and the squad in whose company he was happiest.

Chapter Two

Four months earlier

'Right, settle down you lot, for god's sake. This is a briefing, not the kindergarten.'

Inspector Matt Bryan was seldom a morning person. Today he seemed tetchier than ever and it didn't help that his team members were restless. They'd had a quiet couple of weeks without excitement. Routine plodding round the city's streets in case anything happened. Training sessions. Desk jobs to be cleared up. Dashing off to answer a shout which turned out to be nothing for them. They were itching for a taste of some real action.

'First off. Sergeant Darling, you and your merry band get straight off to court. Your special skills are required there. And I don't mean your knack for pissing off senior officers with backchat.'

There was a ripple of laughter from all the Firearms officers present. Ted had recently had a stand up confrontation with an officer who outranked him considerably over deployment of his squad. He'd had to call up his own boss to sort it out.

'I haven't got time today to come over to muzzle you and put you back on a lead if you start getting arsey with a senior officer. There's a remand hearing, with a possible terrorist connection. The defendant will be coming under his own armed guard, of course, but we've been asked to provide some back-up. There's been a tip-off there may be an attempt to spring him and it's being taken seriously, hence the request for extra officers from us.

'You take your squad there, you report to the officer in charge,' he paused to check his notes, 'Inspector Rawlings. You deploy where he tells you to, you watch for any suspicious activity and you keep your gob shut. Clear?'

'Clear, sir,' Ted replied meekly.

Although he knew he wouldn't. If some officer with no firearms experience ever tried telling him how to do his job, putting Ted's squad members at risk, he would never keep it zipped. It had got him in trouble on more than one occasion but it had kept his team safe and that's all Ted cared about.

'Well, what are you waiting for? Shift yourselves.'

Ted's three squad members were in high spirits as they headed for their black van, fully tooled up and ready for the prospect of a bit of action at last.

'The boss's got your measure, Skip,' AFO Declan Murphy laughed. 'You don't take crap from anyone. That's why we love you.'

'Shut up, Dec,' Ted told him, but his tone was good natured.

They were a good team, driven by a mutual respect. Ted was the only Specialist Firearms Officer in the unit. He'd done an additional eight-week training course to qualify and did refresher training whenever he could. He could easily be serving with an elite unit somewhere, doing exciting stuff on a regular basis.

But Openshaw suited him just fine. It meant he could carry on living at home in Stockport with his dad, a disabled ex-miner with a serious drink problem who needed a lot of attention. His dad was the reason he'd not taken a gap year before going to university and the reason he was still living at home. When he had to be away for training, Ted paid for a live-in carer to keep an eye on him. It was also why a lot of his relationships tended to be brief. He was not about to move in with anyone and that sometimes put a damper on things.

Ted was the shortest Firearms officer in the division. That, coupled with his unfortunate surname and his being gay could have caused him a lot of trouble. Once any other officers he had to serve with discovered his specialist skills included black belts in four martial arts, they treated him with plenty of respect.

The area around the court building was taped off when they arrived, with a highly visible police presence. The black van was waved through. Scott Hardwick, Ted's second in command, was driving and slid the vehicle into a space indicated to him by a uniformed constable. The four armed officers got out and, with Ted leading the way, went to find the officer in charge, Inspector Rawlings.

Ted hadn't encountered him before, but he was used to the kind of look the inspector threw his way. Ted always had to resist the urge to tell officers who didn't know him that yes, he was a trained Firearms officer and yes he did have a letter from his dad saying he could be out on his own. Even at nearly thirty, his short, slight stature and floppy, dirty blonde hair gave him the look of a schoolboy.

'You deploy as you see fit at the front of the court building, Sergeant. You're the expert.' Rawlings told him, which was better than Ted had feared. 'But no one unidentified or in any way suspicious-looking – and I do mean no one – gets into this building without thorough vetting. Any doubts at all, you contact me. We've got intel which we're treating as serious for now that some of this bloke's friends may just be planning to break him out and they won't be too fussy as to how they do it. Can I safely leave that in your hands?'

'Yes, sir.'

After his initial recce, Ted decided that he and Scott should take posts outside the building, leaving the other two inside as back-up should it be needed. Rawlings had told him there would be plenty of other Firearms officers covering the rear vehicular access, the way in which the defendant would be brought and led into the building.

If whoever was involved in any attempt to spring the prisoner was audacious enough, they might just try walking straight in through the main doors to see how far they could get. They could even try that tactic as a distraction to whatever else might be going on elsewhere.

Security was tight and anyone wanting to go into the public galleries was being routinely searched, an increasingly common occurrence in many major cities.

Ted was letting practised eyes survey the comings and goings on the street in front of him. His peripheral vision was particularly acute with all the martial arts training he did, where it was vital when fighting more than one assailant at a time.

From the corner of his eye he saw a blur of movement, whirled on the balls of his feet, instantly bring up his Heckler and Koch to point at a man hurrying towards the court. The man was in a dark blue suit. His head was down and one hand was fumbling in the open briefcase he held in the other hand.

'Armed police! Stand still!' Ted barked sharply.

For an instant it appeared that the man had either not heard him or had not realised that the shout was directed at him. It was only when Ted repeated the order, louder this time, that the man looked up. He visibly jumped, his face draining of colour.

'Stand still!'

There was nothing about the man's appearance to suggest a real and present threat. He was an IC1 male, perhaps forty. Smartly dressed in a good suit and tie. But Ted didn't like that hand inside the case. Not when he didn't know what it was holding or what it might be about to pull out.

Again Ted spotted movement out of the corner of his eye, then he heard a voice he recognised, puffing, out of breath,

11

sounding worried.

'Ted! Ted! It's all right.'

It was the voice of one of the court ushers, a man called Dick, rushing up to him, his black gown flapping around him, making him look like an anxious hen.

'Don't shoot him, Ted. It's Mr Grenville. From the CPS. He's new.'

Ted relaxed fractionally, though he did not yet lower the muzzle of his gun.

'Put the case down on the floor, please, sir. Very slowly, and very carefully.'

With visibly shaking hands, the man did as he told him.

'Without moving your hands, can you just tell me, yes or no, do you have any identification on you, sir?'

'Honestly, Ted, he really is all right. He's a new Crown Prosecutor,' Dick told him, still not getting his breathing back under control, as much from tension as exertion.

'I think you can both understand why I need to check that for myself,' Ted said levelly. 'Do you have any ID on you, sir?'

'I do. It's in the inside breast pocket of my jacket.'

Ted had never yet met a member of the legal profession who could answer a question with a simple yes or no. Even when facing the barrel of a firearm, it seemed.

The man's voice was shaking almost as much as his hands. People were stopping to look at what was going on. Ted knew that Scott would have his back and would be communicating with the rest of the squad in case they were needed, so he took no notice of what was happening to the rear of him.

'Then with just one finger and thumb, moving very slowly, could you please open your jacket to show me where it is? Without making any move to touch anything.'

The man complied. Ted could see the material of his trouser legs was moving and rightly guessed that his knees were trembling.

At that moment, two wigged and gowned barristers appeared round the corner and stopped in their tracks at the spectacle in front of them. One of them knew Ted by sight, having cross-examined him in court on one occasion. He seemed to find the matter amusing.

'It's probably not your smartest career move to shoot a Crown Prosecutor within the courtroom precincts, Sergeant,' he called out cheerfully.

Ted was starting to realise that he was in the process of making a complete idiot of himself on full public display. The trouble was he was now so far in that he couldn't quite see a way to extricate himself whilst maintaining any shred of dignity.

Scott muttered to him quietly.

'Skip, I think you've dropped a bollock.'

Ted had one more attempt to sound as if he knew what he was doing.

'If I could just check your ID please, sir? Just take it out slowly and carefully.'

It was a ground opening and swallowing moment when the man cautiously produced what Ted could see, even at a distance, was perfectly valid identification.

'Thank you, sir. I apologise for the error.'

'Oh, please don't apologise, officer. It was my fault entirely. I was on the last minute. I should have thought about what it looked like, me rushing up to court fumbling in a bag, on a day like today,' the man's words were tumbling over one another in his relief that the situation had been defused. 'I wonder if you would perhaps allow me to buy you a drink at some point, as my way of an apology?'

Ted hid his surprise well. As chat-up lines went, it was definitely a new one on him.

'It really isn't necessary, sir. I apologise once again.'

Trembling even more with the relief, the prosecutor hurried on his way. Scott was chuckling, just behind Ted.

'He so fancies you, Skip. Get your coat, you've pulled.'
'Shut up, Scott.'

Luckily, Inspector Rawlings seemed to find the whole affair amusing, to Ted's surprise. He was expecting a bollocking when debriefing, at the least, but Rawlings laughed it off.

'At least it shows you were on the ball, following my orders. He's new, you weren't to know he was CPS. I imagine Grenville will be too embarrassed to make a fuss, but get your report written up as soon as possible and copy me in, just so we're covered.'

It was a different story the minute Ted and his team got back to their own station. Ted had barely walked through the door when Matt Bryan flung open his own door and barked, 'Sergeant Darling, get your sorry arse in here, now, and explain yourself.'

The boss was sitting back down when Ted went in and stood in front of his desk, not quite sure how much trouble he was in. He started to explain carefully exactly what had happened. Then he heard a strange rasping noise he couldn't immediately recognise. He finally realised his boss was laughing. He couldn't ever remember hearing it before.

'You were probably right in your instincts. Most lawyers are crooks in my experience. Just write your notes up carefully, in case he makes any waves.'

He was still making the strange sound as Ted left his office.

Ted was just clearing his desk at the end of his shift ready for a drink with the team before he headed home, when his desk phone rang.

'A Mr Grenville, from CPS, asking to speak to you personally, Sarge. Will you take it?'

'Thanks, yes, put him through.'

He doubted the prosecutor would speak to him directly if he was going to make a complaint so he wondered what he might have to say to him.

'Sergeant Darling? Philip Grenville here. I just wanted to apologise again. And to see if I could take you for a drink, or perhaps even a meal, to make amends? Would you be free this evening, by any good fortune?'

'Unfortunately not, Mr Grenville.'

Ted hesitated before continuing. He wasn't with anyone at the moment. The lawyer hadn't seemed like his usual type. But then he hadn't been having much luck of late with his usual type. Perhaps it was time for a change. He decided to chance it.

'I might be free tomorrow though, if you'd like to give me your phone number so I can contact you?'

Scott Hardwick was nearby, clearly listening to Ted's side of the conservation and guessing the rest.

'I told you you'd pulled, Skip. His tongue was hanging out.'

'Shut up, Scott.'

Chapter Three

'Ted, this is Trevor. He's just joined the club and wants to upgrade to black. I said you'd be the best possible person to help him improve his technique. He's very good, just needs some tidying up and fine-tuning.'

Ted had been doing his usual warm-up routine at his local judo club when the coach, Bernard, approached him and spoke. He stopped what he was doing and looked up into the bluest eyes he could ever remember seeing. They belonged to a young man – barely out of his teens, Ted thought. He was smiling at him, his expression eager, standing next to Bernard at the edge of the mat. He was wearing a brown belt. Judo was just one of the martial arts in which Ted held black belts.

'I'd really be grateful for any help you could give me. I know I still have a lot to learn.'

He was well-spoken. Posh was the word that instantly leapt to Ted's mind. He tried to think of something to say in reply but found his mouth had gone dry. So he bowed formally. He couldn't think of anything else to do.

'I'll leave you two to get on with it then,' Bernard said as he withdrew.

Ted really wished he hadn't put it like that. It took all his self-control and professionalism to bring his mind back into instruction mode. He felt awkward and uncomfortable about having to touch the young man. But clearly he was going to have to. Martial arts were physical, intimate. Judo more so than some of them.

Ted decided to stick to fast work, standing. He wasn't sure if he trusted himself down on the mat in groundwork with someone so attractive.

Trevor was good. Fast. A quick learner. But some of his attacking moves were naive. Ted saw them coming a mile away. Despite the difference in height, with Trevor being around seven or eight inches taller, by Ted's reckoning, Ted could still throw him effortlessly. It wasn't long before they were both sweating and out of breath. Ted called a halt.

Trevor bowed to him at the end of their session. His blue eyes were twinkling as he straightened up and looked down at Ted.

'Thank you, *sensei*. That was really helpful. Perhaps we might be able to do more of the same next week. Maybe even take it a bit further?'

Ted felt a flush run up his neck to his face. He wasn't sure if he was being flirted with or teased. Or perhaps a bit of both. He'd never felt quite so tongue-tied. Or so stupid. His discomfort was only relieved when Bernard came back over to them.

'How did you two get on? How was your pupil, Ted?'

Ted was self-confident in his work setting, used to leading a team, able to stand his ground with senior officers. He'd never been more acutely aware of his accent. Lancashire roots blurred by many years in Stockport. He felt like a complete idiot.

'Yes, fine, good. He worked well.'

'Trevor, a few of us usually go for a jar when we've finished here. You're very welcome to join us, if you'd like to. Ted, you'll come as usual, will you?'

'Not tonight, Bernard, I'd better get off. Stuff to do. You know, work stuff.'

He wondered if he sounded as stupid as he felt. Bernard was looking at him curiously. He'd never known Ted turn down going for a drink before, not unless he had a shout from work. He looked from one to the other and the penny dropped. Poor Ted had clearly got it bad. Before even either of them knew anything about young Trevor.

Ted decided he needed to get away in a hurry, to sort out his feelings. He didn't even stop for a shower, just changed quickly into his outdoor clothing, stuffed his judogi into his kit bag, slung it over his shoulder and ran, fast, all the way home.

He stowed his bag in the hallway, went into the lounge and dropped on to the sofa next to where his dad was watching television. He looked reasonably sober, for once. He was absorbed in some political debate, which would usually hold his attention enough to limit his alcohol intake. His eyes were bright, focused, as he looked hard at his son, who was still breathing heavily and dripping with sweat.

'What's got you grinning like the Cheshire cat? Have you met someone?'

'Don't be daft,' Ted retorted, slightly too quickly. His dad may have been an alcoholic, but he was still astute. He knew his son well and could read his moods and his body language.

'You have. You've met someone,' Joe Darling insisted. 'Bloody good for you. I hope it's someone worthy of you.'

'I haven't. I just had a good session at the dojo, that's all, and I decided to run home, for a training run. Anyway, I'm with Philip.'

His father gave a snort of derision.

'Philip? That bloody old man? He's no good to you. No, he's more like an old woman. And he'll make an old woman of you too, Ted lad, if you stay with him. What do you even have in common? Apart from sex, and I can't imagine that's anything to write home about.'

Ted and his dad had always spoken frankly, even back when Ted was a small boy. He'd had to be both mother and father to his son, growing up, and he'd done the best he could to fill both roles, despite his own problems.

'Philip's great, if you'd only take the time to get to know him better. We get on well together. I like him.'

Another scornful noise.

'You liked rice pudding when you were little. But it didn't make you smile like treacle pudding and custard always did. What interests do you share?'

'Lots. We go walking together.'

This time Joe laughed out loud.

'Walking? That wet weekend is tired out after once round Roman Lakes. You could run up and down Snowdon twice before breakfast. And he doesn't put a soppy grin on your face like the one you were wearing when you got back home. I really do hope you've found someone to make you look like that, son. You deserve to. You're a good lad, and you always have been.'

Inevitably, although he was relatively sober, Joe quickly became tearful and reached for his whisky glass.

'I'd love to see you settled with someone nice, before I die.'

'You're quiet tonight, my Darling. And you've hardly eaten a thing. Tough day at work?'

Philip Grenville loved the fact that his boyfriend's name was in itself an endearment. He had to confess to himself to having strong feelings on everything to do with Ted Darling. He'd admitted to Ted that meeting him at the other end of a high-powered firearm had been the most erotic experience he'd ever had.

The food was good, as ever. Philip liked gourmet food. It was French, expensive, and he was enjoying a bottle of excellent red wine with it. Ted was mostly just pushing his round his plate and had hardly made a dent in his half of lager.

'Work was all right today. Nothing exciting, just routine stuff. It's just ...' Ted hesitated, putting his fork down. 'I think we need to talk.'

Philip also dropped his cutlery. He looked stricken.

'Oh, please, Ted, no. Not here. Not anywhere, preferably, but certainly not here. Not the "it's not you, it's me" speech. If you must do that, can we not at least do it in private? Leave me some shred of dignity, please.'

'I'm really sorry, Phil. It's just something my dad said yesterday.'

The noise Grenville made was not unlike those Ted's father had produced the day before.

'Your father has never liked me. He looks at me as if I'm something that got caught on the wheel of his chair. He doesn't think I'm good enough for you.'

'But it's me who's not good enough for you. I'm just a miner's son from the Lancashire coalfields. Look at us. You're good wine and fine dining. I'm a snakebite with the lads and a takeaway on the way home sort of person. We don't really have all that much in common, do we? I just think it's time we admitted that it's not going anywhere.'

Of all the reactions he'd expected from Philip, the sudden look of cold fury on his face was not one he had anticipated.

'Get out!' the prosecutor spat. 'Go on. If you're going, go. Don't drag this out any further or make it any harder. It's not what I want but if you're intent on leaving then just do it.'

Ted got to his feet, awkwardly reaching for his wallet.

'At least let me pay for the meal ...'

'You're breaking my heart, Ted. You're killing me. So whoever it is you're leaving me for, I hope you deserve each other. Now just go.'

Chapter Four

'Right, ladies and gentlemen. Operation Flytrap. The action takes place tomorrow, subject to any last minute hitches thrown up by this briefing or by the final recce this afternoon.'

Ted and his squad were at the force Headquarters for the briefing, together with another firearms squad from Openshaw, with their boss, Inspector Matt Bryan. This operation was a big one, with the Drugs Unit in charge, but they'd requested Firearms back-up plus the expert input of an SFO. That was Ted. He was the one with the specialised method of entry training. It would be his role to advise on the swiftest way to gain access to the target premises while at the same time minimising risk.

The Drugs Unit had had a production factory, housed in a unit on an industrial estate, under observation for some time and were keen to get it closed down as quickly as possible. Their intelligence showed that it was churning out some particularly nasty stuff which had already been responsible for at least three deaths on their patch. They also knew the people involved were professional, ruthless, and not averse to using explosives to protect their operation.

'For those who don't know, Inspector Bryan here,' Chief Inspector Rod Halliwell indicated the man sitting next to him, 'is kindly lending us Firearms support, which includes an SFO to advise on means of entry.'

He was looking round at the assembled officers, clearly expecting to see someone looking like a cross between Rambo and Jack Reacher. He couldn't keep the surprised look off his face when Ted raised a hand and said, 'That would be me, sir. Sergeant Darling.'

Halliwell recovered his stride quickly enough. He was the senior officer on this operation, working with a lot of officers he'd not seen before.

'Right. I see. Thank you, Sergeant. You'll forgive me for saying but you don't look like what I was expecting. No offence intended.'

'None taken, sir,' Ted replied mildly, thinking that if he had a fiver for every time someone had said that, or similar, to him, he could have retired by now. Taken his dad to live in the sunshine on some tropical island. Not that it would have appealed to either of them. It was just a pipe dream.

'We've had the unit under observation for some time, of course, but I thought you might like a final walk-through yourself before we go in. And we have the perfect cover for you. The industrial site in question has security patrols, men with dogs, from a local company. We've got a police dog for you and a jacket similar to the ones their blokes wear, although it might be a bit on the big side, now I've seen you in the flesh. So you can go and have a stroll round, without anyone taking much notice, and report back here to debrief at the end of the day.'

'Sorry sir, but I'm not very good with dogs.'

Halliwell raised his eyes skywards and sighed theatrically, then looked at Matt Bryan.

'I thought you said he was a Special? It's a trained police dog, for god's sake, Sgt Darling. It's not going to eat you.'

'He's special, all right,' Matt Bryan muttered, then addressed Ted directly. 'It will be fine, Sergeant. Just do it. I agree. It's the perfect cover.'

'Sir.'

Ted still didn't sound convinced. He generally found he didn't need any cover. He looked so different to most people's idea of what a policeman should be like that he could usually go in anywhere without raising suspicions. But this wasn't his operation and he knew better than to make too many waves early on.

Halliwell went on, 'And we've been planning this operation for months. I'm not going to let it go tits up because you're windy about handling a dog.'

He was looking round at the assembled officers.

'Where's the dog handler? Can you reassure Sgt Darling?'

A constable waved a hand as he said, 'Here, sir. Constable Rosser. Sarge, you'll be fine with Regan. He's a great big soppy thing. He lives at home with my kids. He's also trained to pi...' He was about to say piss then thought better of it, not knowing what Halliwell was like, so he corrected himself. 'He'll pee on command, too, so you can stop wherever you want to. His command is City.'

There was a small ripple of amusement round the room. Rosser was clearly a United supporter.

'The site has several security lights around it, some of them up on poles,' Halliwell took over once more. 'Conveniently for our needs, there's one just near the unit we're interested in. So when you're walking past there, Sgt Darling, you command the dog to piss up that post and you have a good look at the point of entry. Do it more than once if you have to. There's nothing unusual about seeing a dog cock its leg up a post. It won't draw attention to you.'

'Sir.'

Once Halliwell had wound the briefing up, the dog handler, PC Rosser, came over to Ted.

'I've got Regan outside in a van, Sarge. I thought you might like to have a try with him here first. You really will be fine with him, he's as soft as butter.'

Ted didn't want to offend him by telling him he'd rather handle a poisonous snake than a dog. He'd never trusted dogs and he had no idea why. He couldn't remember ever having been bitten and he had no scars from a bite. He'd always preferred cats. He didn't have one at present because of his hours and because his dad wasn't wild about them. It was Ted's mam and her mother who'd been the cat people.

When Rosser opened the back door of the unmarked white van and got the dog out of its travel cage, Ted couldn't help taking a step back at the sheer size of it. He reckoned he was going to look stupid marching about with a thing that enormous and trying to pretend to be in control of it.

Rosser was handing him the end of the lead and telling him what to do.

'Walk him on your left, Sarge, keep him on a short lead. You'll only need three commands, heel, sit, and City. Don't worry, he can tell the difference.'

At the sound of the last command, the dog towed Ted to the nearest tree and obligingly cocked its leg. Ted was busy trying to work out how he could avoid getting pulled over if the big beast decided to ignore everything he said. But with Rosser's patient input, after a couple of trial circuits of the car park, Ted and the dog were, if not yet quite a bonded unit, at least singing from the same hymn sheet.

Rosser drove to the industrial unit, parked up in a far corner of it and got the dog out. Ted had been studying plans of the site on the way over, so he knew where he was going and what he was looking out for.

'One more command that might come in useful, Sarge,' Rosser said cheerfully. 'If anything goes wrong, just drop the lead and tell him "go find Dad" and he'll come and get me.'

Ted fervently hoped it wouldn't come to that as he took the lead and set off, the big dog walking calmly close to his left side.

'Nice boy, Regan. Good dog. Heel.'

He was saying it more for his own benefit than the dog's. He could have sworn the animal gave him a pitying look, clearly realising it was in the hands of an amateur.

But as soon as Ted got near to the unit they were interested in, his professional instincts kicked in and he found he could almost ignore the dog and do the part of his job he was trained for. The building was all on one level so he wouldn't need to abseil down an outside wall and in through a window, which was another part of his training as an SFO.

He reached the lamp post and, without much confidence, gave the command, 'Regan, City.'

He was impressed when the big dog gave a cursory sniff then obligingly cocked its leg to empty its bladder.

Nothing could have looked more natural than a man in dark clothing, with a logo across the back of his jacket, patrolling the estate with a great brute of a guard dog, even in the daytime. As Halliwell had said, the jacket was too big on Ted's slight frame but even though several people passed him, none of them seemed in any way suspicious of him. Several of them exchanged an 'all right, mate?' with him.

Ted made several passes round the site, particularly anxious to get a look at the rear of the unit. He had one anxious moment when someone came out of the target building on one of his trips past it. The dog seemed to sense something as for a moment it strained forward against the lead, raised its hackles and gave a bark which worried Ted almost as much as the man, although he was careful to hide the fact.

'Regan, sit,' he told the dog, trying to sound masterful, grateful when the dog immediately did as it was told.

'Glad you've got it on a lead, mate,' the man called out as he headed back inside. 'Bloody great big bugger of a thing.'

'Aye,' Ted agreed, 'but at least you know you're getting the security patrols you pay for.'

The man laughed as he disappeared, clearly not in the least concerned.

Despite his success, Ted was relieved to hand over custody of the animal to Rosser when they got back to the van. He didn't risk trying to pat it in thanks. Things had gone better than he'd feared so he wasn't going to take any chances now.

Rosser and his dog had finished their shift for the day so he dropped Ted off at Headquarters then went home.

As soon as Ted started to present his findings at the end-of-day briefing, he sensed a change in Halliwell's attitude towards him. If he'd previously dismissed him as a jumped-up short arse, probably picked as a token gesture to having vertically challenged officers, listening to him now, he realised that he was the specialist in what he was talking about.

Ted went carefully through the plans for gaining access, making suggestions for some slight modifications to what had been planned, based on his own observations. What he said made sense and he said it with an authority that meant that no one, not even the Chief Inspector, questioned or challenged him.

'Right, everyone, an early start tomorrow, remember, but if all goes well, we should have you all home to your nearest and dearest at a decent time, once reports have been written. And with a good result to show for it. Thank you all.'

Ted went for a drink with his team mates before he headed home. He didn't want to make it a late one, because of his dad and because he suspected he would be sinking a few pints the next day, if all went well.

The day after the operation was his judo night and he was looking forward to it more than ever. He'd be seeing Trevor again. He still didn't know where he stood. He just couldn't read him well enough to know if he would be making a complete prat of himself if he made a move. And with such an age gap between them, he was afraid of getting it badly wrong.

After their first encounter, they now trained together most weeks and had both been out for a drink afterwards in the same crowd. But that was as far as it had gone and Ted was still uncertain of how to proceed. He just sat there, gazing at him across the bar whenever Trevor was not looking at him. When he did, Ted's drink suddenly became irresistibly fascinating.

He needed to get his dad cleaned up again when he got home. It was getting to be a regular thing, his incontinence. It wasn't pleasant for either of them. Ted had talked about it with his dad's case worker but her solution of incontinence wear was not one he even dared to broach with his dad. He could talk to him about almost anything. But not that.

At least he wasn't too drunk this time, Ted thought, as he took him, changed into fresh clothes for the night, back to the kitchen to try to get him to eat something. Half the problem was that he didn't eat anything like as much as he should, which didn't help with the high alcohol consumption.

'I might be late tomorrow night, dad.'

'Going out with your old woman again?'

'I finished with Philip, remember? I told you.'

Joe Darling's blood-shot eyes turned beady as they fixed on his son.

'So you are seeing someone else?'

'No, I'm not,' Ted told him patiently as he started to put together some supper for the two of them. 'But I thought about what you said and I realised you were probably right. We didn't have all that much in common so it was probably best to end it before either of us got in too deep.'

'Well, I just hope I live to see you settled with Mr Right, son. You deserve someone really nice, after all you've done for me.'

Joe Darling never did live to see his son settle down. When Ted got back late after a resounding success on Operation Flytrap, followed by a round of celebratory drinks, which somehow turned into at least three rounds, he found his dad stiff and cold on the floor and proceeded to get himself thoroughly drunk to numb the pain, guilt and intense loss he was feeling.

Sitting there, next to his dad, he found he was able to talk to him about his feelings. Ted had spent a lot of his life blaming himself for his mother leaving. Even as a small boy he'd always thought it was in some way his fault that she'd gone. He'd grown up idolising his dad, always so grateful for everything he did for him.

'I'm so sorry, dad. I'm sorry I was a rubbish son to you. You were a brilliant dad. You were always there for me, when I was a kid. After mam left. Even with all your own problems. You never let me down. I should have done better for you.'

He missed morning briefing because he was too drunk to wake up, never mind on time. He got himself a bollocking from Matt Bryan when he phoned to find out where he was, but was given some time to sort things out, including himself. He'd woken up with the mother of all hangovers which, coupled with a warning from his boss, had made him swear off the drink for ever more and be determined to get himself on track.

There was a lot he needed to sort out. The specially adapted house in Offerton was let to his dad through a miners' welfare scheme and Ted had no right of tenancy. He'd need to fix himself up with a new place to live as soon as he could. They wouldn't exactly throw him out on the streets, but they would be keen to repossess the property for someone else in need and Ted understood and expected that.

It had been an upheaval for the family to move there after the mine explosion which broke Joe's back and left him partially paralysed. Joe and his wife had jumped at the offer of a house in Stockport as her mother already lived in the area and would be essential help and support for her daughter after her husband's accident.

Once he'd sobered up enough, Ted made a few phone calls to agents to try to find a flat to rent until he got himself suited. He was keen to stay in Offerton if he could. It was only half an hour for him to go to work and it was near the dojo he'd been going to since he was a boy. He also made a quick phone call to Bernard, from the judo club.

'I won't be there tomorrow, Bernard, sorry. My dad died yesterday so I have stuff to sort out. Please will you pass on my apologies to Trevor and tell him I hope to see him next week.'

Chapter Five

It seemed somehow fitting that the day of his dad's funeral was chilly, damp and dismal, Ted thought. That about summed up how he was feeling.

He'd arranged a cremation at Stockport. His dad would have no truck with graves, claiming they were an iniquitous waste of land which could have provided valuable space for social housing. Nor were there going to be religious trappings of any sort, Joe having turned his back on any form of deity a long time ago.

Ted had tried to let everyone he could think of know the date and time of the funeral. He'd put an announcement in the local paper in case anyone he'd forgotten about might be interested. His dad hadn't had many friends of late. It was difficult. Not all of them could cope with him going from rantings at social injustice and the oppression of the working class to self-pitying tears followed by inevitable loss of bladder control. It took true friendship to stick with someone through all of that.

Ted was surprised and touched when his boss, Matt Bryan, turned up at the crematorium. Bryan had met Ted's dad on a few social occasions, like the shooting competitions where Ted inevitably took home at least one trophy to add to his collection. He insisted on keeping them hidden away in boxes in the attic, but his dad was always so proud of his success.

Arthur also came, Ted's old firearms instructor from his Claytonbrook days. Arthur was long retired but was still always there to support old friends for all the competitions. He'd got to know Ted's dad through them, as Ted tried to take him to watch him compete whenever he could, both at shooting and at martial arts. Arthur had become the nearest to a close friend Joe had and had asked to be able to say a few words.

A few older friends from Joe's mining days had made the trip over from Wigan, fewer in number these days, a lot of them broken men like Joe had been. There were a couple of his home carers, too, turning up to pay their respects. It didn't amount to much after a lifetime, albeit one cut relatively short. His dad had no family of his own still living and had cut off any contact with his wife's family when she'd left him and Ted.

Absolutely no hymns. Joe Darling would turn in his coffin if anyone had even suggested such a thing. Ted had one of his dad's favourite tunes played, then Arthur stood up to say his bit.

'Goodbye Joe, you Bolshie commie bastard,' he began and the tension was immediately broken by laughter.

Ted smiled. His dad would have loved that.

'Thanks for all the heated political debates. The hours spent putting the world to rights. Above all, thanks for giving the Force your Ted. He's a Bolshie little sod himself. Takes after his old man. But he's a good man and a good officer. You were proud of him and rightly so. We are too. So don't you worry. We'll take good care of him now you're not here to keep an eye on him.'

Ted swallowed hard past the lump in his throat. His service friends were his family now, with his dad gone. He sat and listened to the rest of Arthur's speech, which was perfect. He recounted anecdotes of his meetings with Joe and glossed skilfully over the more difficult aspects of how he'd been in recent times as the alcohol got the better of him. He made everyone laugh but at the same time Ted noticed he wasn't the only one who needed a hanky to wipe his eyes a time or two.

After the coffin had disappeared through the curtain, Ted went to the doorway to thank everyone for attending. Looking out into the drizzle, he could see the rear view of a woman, hurrying away along the drive leading to the chapel doors. There was something vaguely familiar about the way she moved. He imagined it was probably another of the carers. Ted knew his dad's relationship with at least a couple of them had gone beyond the professional and he was glad of that. At least Joe had had some comfort after his wife had left him.

'Thanks for coming, boss,' Ted told Matt Bryan as he shook his hand. 'I appreciate it.'

'Your dad was a good man, and I'm sorry for your loss,' he said and barely took a breath before he was back in work mode. 'Now, are you sorted? Got somewhere to live? Don't forget to get your file updated with your new contact details.'

'Yes, boss. I've got some drinks and sandwiches sorted at the pub just down the road, if you want to join us for one?'

Matt Bryan was surprised to see Ted order ginger beer for himself while he was getting drinks in for everyone else. He knew his sergeant could put it away with the rest of them, sometimes too much. But perhaps he was driving somewhere afterwards.

'Not drinking, Ted?'

For once, he was being informal. The occasion called for it.

'Given up, boss. For good. When I saw what it did to my dad, I thought it was time. Besides, I'm driving this evening. There's somewhere I need to be.'

Ted was hurting, more than he wanted to show. And when he was in any kind of emotional pain, there was only one release that worked. He was driving over the Pennines to a dojo where he could work out, hard, at the most extreme of his martial arts, Krav Maga. He would risk getting the stuffing kicked out of himself but he knew he would feel better for it.

He left a tab behind the bar so everyone present could carry on giving his dad a good send-off while he slipped quietly away and headed for the M62 motorway, eastbound.

Then tomorrow evening, if he got away from work in good time, he could go to his own club for his judo training, and there he would see Trevor again.

Nine years earlier

'That was some very good shooting today.'

Ted Darling was nursing half a lager as he sat at the bar in the hotel. He looked at the older man who had slid on to the barstool next to his.

'Thank you,' he replied guardedly.

'You're good,' the man continued. 'You could be a lot better with some proper coaching.'

It wouldn't be the first time Ted had been chatted up by an older man in a bar. And it wouldn't be the first time he'd left with them, if the evening panned out as Ted suspected it might.

'Good enough to take the trophy,' Ted pointed out, his tone neutral.

He was away from home, taking part in a shooting competition. He'd waltzed home in the Under-21s class. His dad hadn't come with him this time. He was going through a bad phase and he didn't want to cramp his son's style.

'My name's Arthur,' the man said, holding a hand out to Ted, who shook it warily. 'I'm a police Firearms instructor. Hence the critical interest.'

'Ted. And I'm planning on joining the police.'

'Are you now? Firearms?'

'I haven't decided which branch yet.'

'Why do you shoot?'

'Because I'm not bad at it. Because I like it.'

Ted remembered the first time he'd discovered he was not a bad shot. He was only a kid at the time. His dad had taken him to Blackpool as a treat for his birthday. His dad didn't drive. As a boy, Ted always assumed it was because of his broken back. As he got older, he realised it was because of the drinking. Joe relied on lifts from friends or took taxis. He'd fixed up with an old mate of his from his mining days, Meurig, to drive him and Ted to Blackpool.

When Ted saw the shooting galleries and their prizes, he wanted to have a go. His dad tried telling him they were all rigged, nobody ever won anything. But Ted was determined. He had the same stubborn streak as his father. His first efforts were a disaster. The gun seemed ridiculously big in Ted's small hands. Only his sheer determination kept him trying, with his dad, as ever, happy to keep putting his hand in his pocket to indulge his son. Joe had received a decent compensation payout for his industrial injury. What didn't go on carers went on drink for himself and for anything his son wanted.

And keep on trying Ted did until he won a prize. Then another. Then another one. Eventually the stall-holder refused to let him have any more goes, saying he was cleaning him out of prizes. The three of them went on their way, Joe and Meurig laughing loudly, Joe's wheelchair piled high with a collection of cuddly toys.

Joe had been so proud of his son that day. Even more proud when Ted had asked if they could give the toys to children in hospital.

'Have you left school yet?' the man was asking him now, jerking Ted back to the present.

Ted looked much younger than his years. People always took him for a schoolboy, although he was in his second year at university.

'I'm at university. In Manchester.'

'Graduate entry, then? Looking for fast track promotion? Why did you choose that route?'

'When my dad took me to ask about joining, they said it was a better option.'

'And what are you reading at uni?'

'Politics with criminology.'

Arthur threw his head back and laughed out loud at that.

'That sounds about right. Most politicians are crooks, it seems to me. And you've not decided which branch takes your fancy? Shooting as well as you do already, you could do really well in Firearms. And if you stay in Manchester, I might well be your instructor.

'I have to be frank with you though, Ted. I saw on the results board that your name's Darling. That and you not being a big chap probably won't give you an easy ride, although I wish I could say the force was better than that these days.'

'I'm gay, too,' Ted told him candidly. 'But I generally find that when people know I've got three martial arts black belts and I'm in training for a fourth, they don't tend to give me much trouble.'

This time Arthur let out a bellow of laughter and clapped Ted on the back.

'Well, that should keep you out of a lot of trouble. And seriously, Ted, with that lot already under your belt, or under all three of your black belts, you should consider going for Specialist Firearms Officer. They do all the exciting stuff. Could you see yourself killing someone if you had to and you were ordered to?'

Ted took a swallow of his lager and considered his response carefully before he spoke.

'I don't see how anyone could answer that, until the first time it happened.'

'Good answer! Perfect, in fact. The ones they don't accept are the ones who say they could easily kill. We don't need psychos like that. Look, here's my card. If ever you decide you might consider firearms or you want any help at all, feel free to contact me.

'Oh, and in case the thought crossed your mind, I'm not gay so I wasn't chatting you up. I was genuinely impressed by your shooting and I just wanted to tell you so.'

With that, he slid off the stool, wished Ted good night and went off to his room. Ted headed for his, too, anxious to phone his dad. They'd arranged a night carer for while Ted was away. Joe could do quite a bit for himself but once he'd had too much to drink, he couldn't even get himself to bed without a lot of help.

'Dad? Are you all right? Yes, I won the Under-21s. I've got one more class tomorrow. You'll never guess what, though. I got chatting to a man in the bar ... no, not like that, not this time. Only he's a police Firearms instructor. He got me thinking.'

Chapter Six

'Well, if you're not going to ask me, I'll just have to ask you. Will you come for a drink with me?'

Ted was gobsmacked. He was still plucking up the courage to ask Trevor out. It had already taken him weeks and would probably have taken a lot longer still. Now the tables were turned and here he was, the one who was being asked.

Trevor had waited a respectable time after Ted's dad's funeral before asking him. Ted still couldn't work out whether it was just a thanks for his mentoring or something else. Trevor's eyes always shone with such a hint of mischief he found him impossible to read.

The first time they'd seen one another after Trevor had heard about his loss, Trevor had laid a hand on his forearm as he'd offered his condolences. It felt like a static electrical jolt which almost took Ted's breath away.

'We're all going for a drink as usual, I think,' Ted said awkwardly.

'I meant just us two,' Trevor explained patiently. 'You know, like a first date.'

The evening turned into a bit of a train wreck. Trevor asking him out like that had unsettled Ted even more and he just couldn't find a way to have any sort of meaningful conversation. He was used to being the younger man, going out with older men. This time he found himself acutely aware of the age difference between them.

'What do you do for a living, Ted?'

'I'm a policeman.'

'I never expected that.'

'Because I'm short? Everyone says that. There's no height restriction now.'

'No, not at all. It's just not what I'd have guessed. I think I'd have expected you to be a teacher. You're brilliant at mentoring me.'

It wasn't helping that Ted was on soft drinks. He could have done with a bit of Dutch courage, but he'd made a pledge to himself that he was off the drink for good and he was a man of his word.

'What about you? Are you studying? What subjects?' Ted asked once he'd recovered from a coughing fit caused by pouring his ginger beer down the wrong way in his discomfort.

'I'm training as a motorbike technician. I've got the chance of an apprenticeship so I want to make sure I'm up to speed.'

His answer surprised Ted. He'd assumed someone like Trev, as he'd said he preferred to be called, would be at university studying something more academic. Ted found he'd run out of things to say and there was an awkward, prolonged pause before he resumed.

'Look ...' he began, before Trev interrupted him.

'Oh, no, not the dreaded "it's not you, it's me" speech already? And it was all going so well.'

He was smiling as he said it.

'No, not that. It's just ... I'm seriously rubbish at sitting here making small talk. I'd really like to get to know you better but I'd rather talk outdoors, out in the open. Do you like hillwalking? We could perhaps go out to the Peaks one day?'

Trev wasn't a hillwalker although he sometimes ran to keep himself fit for his martial arts, and he played several racquet sports when he got the chance. His interests had always centred on bikes or horses in the past. But he wasn't going to miss out on an opportunity to spend more time with Ted in a setting in which he felt more relaxed, so he accepted. As long as Ted wasn't planning on scaling any high rock faces or doing a twenty-mile forced march, he reckoned he would be fit enough to keep up with him.

At least Ted plucked up the courage to kiss him fleetingly during the picnic. But that was as far as it went, although they did, finally, start to talk properly to one another, to share parts of their life stories.

The hill walk was the first of several days out together. Ted always timed the trips so the question of staying over anywhere never arose. He wouldn't have known how to cope, what to suggest by way of accommodation.

Ted was starting to get stick at work, at his judo club and now at karate club too, since Trev had joined the same one and was again being coached by him. People were noticing a change in his behaviour. He kept laughing it off as him being off the booze, but no one believed him.

One morning at work, as the different teams were down in the garage getting into their vehicles for the day, Ted's three squad members suddenly donned dark glasses and started hamming up Madness's *Lovestruck*, big time, to the amusement of all present, except Ted who was mortified.

They were good, too. They only stopped when Matt Bryan appeared, growling at them all to 'bloody well get on with the job the tax payer expects you to do,' although Ted noticed even his lips were twitching upwards in what might have been a smile.

It was even worse the morning after Ted and Trev had finally slept together for the first time. Even that had been at Trev's instigation rather than Ted's, although he desperately wanted it to happen. Trev hadn't stayed over afterwards. Ted was still worried about rushing things so had watched him ride away on the ancient and irascible Honda he was doing up.

Going into work the next day surrounded by coppers, and observant ones at that, Ted knew he had zero chance of keeping his private life to himself, which was what he preferred to do.

In the end it was the old Honda which moved their relationship up to the next level. Ted walked to the curbside with Trev in the early hours of one morning as ever but the bike refused point blank to start, despite all Trev's best attempts.

'Do you think it's trying to tell us something?' Trev laughed, aiming a kick at his mutinous mode of transport.

'I didn't want to rush you into any kind of commitment or anything, but you can stay here any time you want to. I'll give you a key. And this place is only temporary. I've just rented it for another couple of months. I had to get out of my dad's house and this was the best that was available. I was thinking of looking for somewhere to buy. Perhaps ...' he hesitated again, unsure of his ground. 'Well, perhaps you could at least help me look?'

It made sense. Trev was spending more and more time at Ted's flat. His own flatmates had almost forgotten what he looked like. Ted didn't know where this relationship was going, if anywhere, but perhaps this was a way to find out.

Trev had had great fun prowling round the modest accommodation as he spent more time there, finding out more about Ted by looking at his music and DVD collection and peering into the flowerpots on the minuscule patio to which Ted had right of access through the French windows.

'Lilies and Dolly Parton? Seriously, Ted? Could you possibly be any more camp if you tried?' Trev had laughed when he made the discovery.

'What's your taste in music, then?' Ted tried not to sound defensive.

'Queen, of course,' Trev told him, then threw his head back to belt out the familiar opening:

'Each morning I get up I die a little, Can barely stand on my feet.'

Ted knew by now that Trev possessed a wicked sense of humour. He thought this was just a part of it. It was possibly the most tone deaf performance he had ever heard. He was astonished. He already knew that Trev was fluent in several foreign languages. When they'd been out for meals to different restaurants he'd seen waiters react in delight to his exchanges with them in French, Italian and Japanese. He realised, with dawning horror, that Trev was blissfully unaware of how truly awful his singing voice was. How to defuse the situation without hurting his feelings?

'Camp, am I?' he asked, taking Trev's arm and pulling him towards him. 'Perhaps I'd better put that myth to bed straight away.'

'Right, shut up and listen. We're being asked to assist with another fun operation. With the Serious Crime Unit this time. Porno film making. The worst kind. Involving kiddies,' Matt Bryan told the assembled officers at morning briefing.

'It's planned to go ahead next week. The whole place is under close observation and is being listened in on. There's a big cheese who's behind the circulation of the stuff who's due to visit. Clearly we want to catch the whole gang but him in particular. All this is happening in a tower block flat so this time, Sgt Darling, you get to do your Spiderman impersonation.

'There's intel to suggest these people may be armed, though they're not thought to be particularly dangerous. But they are computer savvy. The minute anyone goes in through that front door, someone is going to hit a button which will immediately trigger rapid deletion of everything on the computers. So we need to prevent that happening through the element of surprise. Someone needs to go in fast, hard and armed through the window, where they're least expecting it and stop that happening. By extreme measures if necessary.

'All of which timing falls very nicely as, if I'm not

mistaken, Sgt Darling, it's this weekend you go off to practise your rope tricks with your friend from the special forces.'

'It is, sir. Abseiling update and fast rope skills refresher, amongst others.'

'Well, try not to fall off any cliffs. We need you in one piece for this one. And for all those of you involved in this, just a word of caution. It's not going to be a pleasant one for those going in first. There is a strong possibility that there will be children inside, children being abused. We're going to get this gang, every last one of them. But we're going to do it properly and professionally. There will be no, I repeat no, mishandling of suspects. No rough stuff. Nothing which could come back to bite us on the arse when it comes to getting a conviction.

'I will personally deal, in the strongest possible way, with anyone who can't keep a lid on it and jeopardises the operation. Is that abundantly clear to you all?'

There was an obedient chorus of 'Sir' from all present. They all knew that you didn't mess about with Matt Bryan when he issued a warning like that.

'Today's little challenge shouldn't present too much of a problem, even for the Ruperts among you.'

Mr Green's tone was, as ever, scathing, especially when he used the British army slang term for officers. He himself was a retired Warrant Officer who'd served in both the Parachute Regiment and the SAS. He now earned a living teaching special skills courses, with a sideline that Ted preferred not to think about.

Ted had trained with him several times previously. He'd even earned as much grudging respect as Green ever showed anyone. The first time they'd met, the course included some basic martial arts training. Ted took a huge gamble by turning up for the first session in his own judogi and judo black belt. It marked him out as the highest graded person on the course. Green looked him up and down in open contempt.

'Did you think you'd impress me by borrowing your dad's kit?'

'No, sir. This is mine, not my dad's. My dad's a paraplegic and I don't think they have any wheelchair martial arts yet. Sir.'

There was some muted sniggering from the others around Ted as he stood there, chin lifted defiantly. He couldn't see Green's mouth for the thick, bristling moustache he wore but he thought he detected a glint of amusement in his eyes.

'Today's lesson is Krav Maga basics. It's based in part on judo and karate. So you, Darling, get to be guinea pig for demonstration purposes. And don't call me sir. Call me Mr Green.'

'Yes, Mr Green.'

Ted wasn't trying to show off. But he did have three black belts and was already training in Krav Maga. Once he had successfully blocked an attacking move from Green in a purely reflex action, the man proceeded to comprehensively wipe the floor with him, to make a point. But from that moment, his attitude towards Ted softened by a degree and the nickname he soon awarded him, Gayboy, was almost affectionate, compared to what he called some of the other victims of his training. Ted didn't parade the fact that he was gay but there was little privacy, sharing cramped accommodation with others and spending a lot of time with them on these courses.

On this latest course, Ted had no problems with the rope work. He always kept his training up to date and fared a lot better than some others. He also had no difficulty staying at the front on a punishing run to their next destination. But it was there that he found himself facing his biggest nightmare. He'd been lucky so far on the training courses. But this was the first time the particular scenario had arisen.

Green had assembled them towards the end of a lake and was pointing across to the opposite bank.

'Your objective is over there, on the other side of the water.

Your intel is that they are armed and alert and are holding a hostage. Your task is to get over there and defuse the situation. It goes without saying that you keep your powder dry in the process. Now get on with it.'

The other course members were launching themselves into the task. Some paused to remove boots and hang them round their necks. They were soon on their way, using side-stroke, allowing them a free arm to hold their weapons aloft out of the water.

Ted remained frozen at the water's edge. He had never learned to swim. Deep, disturbing memories, flashbacks and vivid nightmares plagued him still, after many years, about the reasons why not. He couldn't do it.

'What are you waiting for, Gayboy? A written invitation? There's a hostage in danger over there.'

'I can't swim, Mr Green.'

Ted stood braced for the torrent of abuse. It never came. Green's tone was still contemptuous but nothing compared to what Ted feared it might have been.

'Who said anything about swimming? I thought you had a brain. Aren't you graduate entry? Well bloody well use it! What earthly use to anyone will any of those cretins be anyway by the time they've exhausted themselves trying to swim across. Now think, for god's sake. Consider your options.'

Ted was looking all around him in desperation.

'There's a boat ...' he began with relief, spotting the prow of a rowing boat jutting out from under the bank.

'Don't even think about it. That's for my use exclusively, when I have to row out there and pick up the dickheads who failed to do a risk assessment first. Think, damn it.'

Ted was thinking, and looking, with increasing desperation. Then he saw it. Not all that far away. There was a barrier across the end of the lake. A sort of dam, or a sluice. And there looked to be a path along the top of it.

Despite the earlier punishing run, Ted still had some energy left because he always kept himself fit. He was driven by the fear of being the only one to fail this part of the course. He could see that if he ran as fast as he was capable of, he could still probably reach the target before any but the fastest swimmers. As long as there were no nasty surprises for him on the dam.

In fact, without being hampered by extreme fatigue and weighed down by sodden clothing, he got there first. When the others started to flounder ashore, while Mr Green rowed out to rescue those in trouble, Ted was crouching calmly by the water's edge, his firearm pointing at those attempting to make landfall.

Green took him to one side afterwards. Ted certainly never expected praise from the man so he wasn't surprised that his only comment was, 'Never again dare to turn up on one of my courses without being able to swim.'

Lying next to Trev in his own bed in the flat after he'd got back from the training course, waiting for his breathing and heart-rate to return to normal, Ted tried to formulate how he was going to ask the question. Although he'd told Trev some of what had happened to him in the past, his inability to swim and fear of water was a source of shame and embarrassment to him.

'If I ask you something, will you promise not to laugh at me?'

Trev propped himself up on one elbow so he was looking down at Ted's face. His black curls were damp with perspire-ation at the temples.

'Of course I won't laugh. But if this is you fishing for compliments about your performance in bed, I can tell you that you have nothing to worry about on that score.'

'No, it's not that, but that's nice to hear. But do you think you could you teach me to swim? Please?'

Chapter Seven

Ted didn't mind heights. He wasn't too keen on flying, but that was because he was a control freak. Putting his life in the hands of someone he didn't know, who might have money worries or other issues which were preventing them from concentrating, was not his idea of a fun way to travel.

From his point of view, the target block of flats presented no problems for him to access via an outside window, even on the twelfth floor. It was an older block. No double glazing or toughened glass. He'd insisted of having a sample of the windows involved as part of his preparation. If the operation was relying on him giving them the element of surprise, there was no point him abseiling down the outside of the building then finding there was no way he could break in.

Even Matt Bryan knew better than to argue with Ted when he was making his preparations. If he wanted to smash up three lots of windows finding the best and quickest way to gain access, then the budget would just have to cope with it. Ted was a perfectionist. He left nothing to chance which was why his record was outstanding.

Trev sensed a change in Ted's mood in the run-up to the operation. They were spending most of their time together now. Not quite living together. Trev had made it clear early on that he enjoyed a drink, and the odd spliff. Ted had made it equally clear that that was none of his business, as long as it didn't happen in his presence. So sometimes Trev reverted to student mode and spent a night getting happily drunk and stoned with his friends. But he always came back to Ted.

He'd started to take over the cooking. Now Ted had discovered what an excellent cook his new partner was, he felt embarrassed at some of the offerings he'd served up. Trev was by nature a nurturer. He loved looking after Ted, making sure he always had a hot and tasty meal waiting when he got home.

'Is it something dangerous, whatever it is you're going to be doing?' Trev asked him one evening as they ate together in the poky flat.

Ted never liked to talk about work at home. He'd only spoken about his role in broad terms, although he'd had to offer some sort of explanation when he'd gone away on Mr Green's course.

'Not really. Not for me. I'm just doing stuff I'm trained to do. But I really can't talk about an operation like this before it happens. It's not that I don't trust you. It's just that I'm strictly not allowed to. Besides, I'm as superstitious as anything. If I tell you, I'll jinx it.'

He was trying to make light of it, but he could see that Trev was worried.

'Will there be shooting? Will you have to shoot people?'

Ted had told him he was in Firearms but had been vague about exactly what his role was.

'Not this time. I'm in charge of method of entry mostly. I don't shoot people every day, you know. It's a rare occurrence.'

For once, Trev's mood was serious.

'But you have done it, haven't you? And you might have to do it again.'

Ted had mentioned to him briefly the one time he'd had to make a fatal shot. Trev had asked him outright if he'd ever killed anyone and he didn't want to spoil their relationship with lies. He'd explained about losing his ticket until the enquiry was over. What he hadn't told him was how gutted he'd felt to learn that the man he'd shot was a first offender, driven to desperate measures to get money to pay for medical treatment for his girlfriend which was not available to her on the National Health.

Ted was up at silly o'clock on the morning of the planned raid. He'd already discovered that not much woke Trev in the mornings so he didn't have to be too careful about making any noise when he got up. He'd also found out that Trev slept spread-eagled over the bed taking up most of the space and hogging the duvet. If they were going to continue sleeping together, Ted would need to look at getting a bigger bed for his new home, when he found one, and a much bigger duvet.

He arrived at work before the rest of his squad to allow himself time to check all his equipment thoroughly himself. Looking after his ropes and harnesses, taking personal responsibility for them, before such an operation was something Mr Green had drummed into him and all those present on his training courses.

Ted's role was pivotal to the success of the whole operation. If he fluffed his entry and gave warning of the police presence, those inside the flat would potentially have time to start wiping computers and destroying other vital evidence. A bungled entry could also jeopardise the safety of any children in the flat.

His three squad members, Scott Hardwick, Declan Murphy and Jimmy Briggs, weren't all that long behind him arriving at work. They would be first in via the door as soon as their Skipper had breached the window. There was a bit of the usual banter between the team members but behind it they were deadly serious, checking their own equipment, fired up and ready for action.

'Hope you got plenty of sleep last night, Skip. Don't want you falling asleep sliding down the rope because your boyfriend tired you out.'

Ted let it go. It was harmless enough. He knew they would

all revert to professional mode, as if someone had thrown a switch in their heads, as soon as they got to the operation site and were being briefed by whichever senior officer was in charge. Ted just hoped it was no one he'd clashed with before. The last thing they needed today was any infighting before the operation had even got going.

Then they were piling into the black van, quieter now, more serious. Matt Bryan, was catching a lift with them so they kept it zipped with him in the vehicle. They were the only squad going for this one. The risk was assessed as low. Although this gang might panic when cornered, they were not considered likely to use weapons as long as the element of surprise remained in the favour of the teams going in.

They were going to hit early morning, around dawn, while it was nice and quiet. Their recent intelligence told them there were two small children in the flat who'd been there since the previous day. That part unsettled Ted somewhat. He was trying to prepare himself for what he might see, and also basing his risk assessment on getting those children out safely, whatever else happened.

Matt Bryan would be with the senior officer in the Command Post, in constant contact with all officers involved. He'd be watching Ted's descent, making sure he targeted the right flat. It would be easy to lose track, coming down the outside like that.

From Ted's point of view, the building was a dream. No balconies to worry about getting snagged on. Plain panelling between the windows which meant he would not be visible to the flat's occupants until the very last moment.

Once he reached the roof, he checked his equipment one last time then took his position at the edge, waiting for Matt Bryan's command. He was going to go down fast, hopefully before anyone had chance to see him and perhaps raise the alarm. It was just possible that the porn gang had lookouts outside, round and about, though none had been identified during days of close surveillance.

Bryan would coordinate Ted's arrival at the window with his squad members being outside the flat door with an Enforcer, ready to break their way in. Ted looked casually over the edge at the first early-morning workers setting off on their daily commute, looking like so many coloured ants.

Then he heard the familiar order in his ear and he was over the edge, rappelling fast, pausing for a fraction of a second to get confirmation that he was outside the right window and his lads were also in position.

Ted often referred to himself as a skinny little runt. But every inch of him was powerful muscle, especially his legs. He was glad he'd been thorough in his preparation and hadn't left anything to chance. He bounced away from the wall then swung in, feet first, bursting cleanly through the window, just as it had gone in training, already bringing up the Heckler as he shouted, 'Armed police! Stand still.'

His three lads were through the outer door at exactly the same time, also shouting. Right behind them were the two IT experts, ready to seize all the computer equipment there before anyone could do anything to disable it.

Scott and Dec were all over the flat like a rash, kicking doors in, rounding up suspects. Ted provided cover with his gun while Jimmy handcuffed everyone they found. Only when that was done were two women officers from the Serious Sexual Offences Unit, specially trained in dealing with young abuse victims, allowed to go in to see to two frightened small children who had been huddling together in the corner of a bedroom. Ted tried not to dwell on what might have been happening to them.

Ted heard his boss coming, wheezing and hacking, long before he arrived at the flat. Other uniformed officers were taking the suspects away. It was just Bryan's luck that the lift was out of order. He came into the flat behind a uniformed superintendent. Ted had seen Eric Haslam at the pre-operation briefings. He was senior officer in charge of the whole operation and he was beaming his pleasure at a successful result.

'Well done, everybody. Really very well done. That's what I call a result. It looks like we got everyone we wanted, and at least the kiddies are safe now. Impressive stuff, Sgt Darling. Thank you very much.'

'Sir,' Ted responded curtly. He hated any kind of fuss. As far as he was concerned, he was just doing his job.

Superintendent Haslam left the flat and Matt Bryan turned to his officers, his chest still heaving from the effort of climbing up twelve floors.

'Right, before you all start patting yourselves on the back, get back to the nick and get your reports written up. If you can manage that without too many spelling mistakes,' he was looking pointedly at Jimmy Briggs as he said it. 'And if nothing else comes up, you can take an early lunch then stand down for the day. And try not to get too pissed. I'll need to debrief here then I'll get a lift back to the station.'

'Yes, sir, thank you, sir,' the squad members chorused. They weren't going to turn down an offer like that. They didn't come around all that often.

For once Ted was home early, well before Trev arrived back. He decided to pick up something for them to eat on his way home, to save Trev having to cook. Something nice, a bit special. Now he'd tasted Trev's cooking, he knew his didn't compare.

He opted for a meal for two from a deli he passed on his way, with a bottle of wine for Trev. On the spur of the moment, he picked up some flowers to brighten the flat up, give it a better ambience for intimate dining. He nearly had second thoughts at the checkout, wondering if it was too much, too soon.

He had plenty of time to clean and tidy the flat before Trev arrived. He'd already discovered that sharing living space with Trev involved an awful lot of picking up after him. He smiled indulgently to himself. Trev was still barely out of his teens, after all, and a student at that.

On a whim, he called one of the agents he was talking to about finding a proper place of his own and arranged a house viewing for his next day off. It was time he sorted himself with something a bit more homely than the flat.

'Oh, wow, this is all very nice. I could get used to being spoiled like this,' Trev said in delight as he let himself into the flat.

He peeled off his motorbike helmet and leathers in the tiny entrance hall, leaving them in a heap on the floor as usual, smiling at the flowers on the table and the food smells coming from the kitchenette.

'Are we celebrating something special?'

'Not really. Just the operation went well this morning and the boss let us go early, so I thought it would be nice to make an evening of it. There's some wine, if you want some?'

'Mmmm, please. That sounds wonderful.'

Trev hugged him and bent to kiss him.

'Will the dinner burn if we're delayed somewhat?'

'I'll turn the oven down.'

Afterwards, they ate together then settled down to watch television, replete and contented in each other's company. Eventually, the local news came on. Ted was horrified to see film of himself abseiling down the side of the tower block and kicking his way in through the window of the target flat.

Trev immediately sat up straight and leaned forward, staring intently at the screen.

'Oh, my god! That's you, isn't it? Ted? It is you.'

'It could be anyone,' Ted said evasively.

'No it couldn't. Look at the scale. Unless those windows are huge, and I'm pretty sure they're not, that figure is small.

Smaller than average.'

He turned to look searchingly at Ted.

'Someone about the same size and build as my very own Pocket Rocket. It is you, isn't it?'

Ted shifted awkwardly in his seat. He wouldn't lie, but he would have preferred for Trev not to know about the kind of work he did.

'Yes, it was me. But it was nothing. Just routine stuff. No shots fired.'

He was trying to make light of it, not wanting Trev to worry. He made a clumsy effort to change the subject.

'I've made an appointment to go and look at a house on Saturday, if I don't get called in to work. Just a small semi, nothing grand. Perhaps you'd like to come with me?'

Trev was looking more serious than Ted had ever seen him.

'Are you asking me to move in with you? I mean, properly. Not like we are at the moment.'

'I'd like that. I really would. I think we'd be good together.'

Trev sat up straighter and took both of Ted's hands in his. Ted felt his stomach drop into his feet. He was totally smitten. He'd propose to Trev, for a civil partnership, if he didn't think it was far too soon and would kill the moment. But was he about to get the brush-off?

'Ted, look. I'm sure you must know by now, I'm really into you. I love you. You are the kindest, gentlest man I've ever met. Which makes you even more of an enigma, given your work role. You're an attentive lover. I feel safe with you. I know you would never, ever do anything to hurt me. I love that you finished with Philip before you'd even plucked up the courage to ask me out.'

'There's a but coming, isn't there?' Ted asked miserably. 'And I'm not going to like the but.'

'I'm just not sure I could live with someone whose job involves killing people.'

'It doesn't happen every day. It didn't happen today. Just a quick, clean arrest with no firearms involvement. I've only ever shot one person. I told you that and it's true.'

'I know that. I understand. I'm just trying to be honest with you, because I know you're always honest with me. You could have to kill again, in your line of work. I'm just trying to imagine what it would be like to go to bed with a person who's just killed someone and it seems so matter-of-fact to them.'

'Are you asking me to choose between you and my job?'

'No, Ted, I'm not. I would never do that. I'm just trying to explain. If you were a teacher, like I thought you might be, I'd move in with you properly tomorrow. But seeing you like that, seeing the other side of you, I just don't know if I could.'

Chapter Eight

'You bloody stupid pillock.'

Ted knew he was not going to get an easy ride from his boss. And he knew there was nothing he could do about it, other than stand there in front of his desk like a prat and take it.

'Seriously? You're packing in a good career in Firearms to go and listen to old biddies reporting their moggies missing? And for what? For a bit of a lad you've known five minutes? Are you thinking with your dick instead of your brain, Sergeant?

'It's not even as if it's some lass you've got up the duff and you're trying to do the decent thing. I could just about understand that. But why would you want to be with someone who expects you just to throw your career on the shitheap to be with him?'

'He doesn't expect me to, sir. He didn't ask me to. He doesn't even know I'm considering it. It was my choice. I want to be with him and he doesn't think he can live with me being in Firearms.'

Ted hated talking about his private life. But he felt he owed his boss some sort of explanation.

'Oh, please! Have you heard yourself? It makes me want to puke.'

Matt Bryan leaned back in his chair and looked up at Ted.

'Look, sit down, for god's sake. Let's talk about this sensibly. Like grown-ups. You're about to commit possible career suicide and I want to be sure you understand the full implications of what you're doing. And take that bloody stubborn look off your face. You're like a bloody mule with its ears back. Arthur was right. You are a Bolshie little sod. Sit.'

In all the time he'd served with Matt Bryan it was the first time Ted had ever been told to sit in his presence. Perhaps his boss was going to try the gentle touch. Ted was almost looking forward to his attempts. He'd never yet seen any hint of a softer side to him, apart from him turning up unexpectedly at his dad's funeral. And that might just have been because he thought it was the right thing for a boss to do.

'Right, what I tell you now goes no further than this room. Is that understood?'

'Yes, sir.'

'This smoker's cough of mine? It's lung cancer. Terminal. Typical bloody copper, always working so I left it too long to go and do anything about it. And now there's nothing to be done.'

Ted opened his mouth to commiserate but Bryan stopped him with an impatient gesture.

'Shut up and listen. That's not important. Shit happens. What is important is that I'd been talking to the powers that be about a replacement for me, someone to head up the section. I'll be going on extended sick leave shortly and I won't be coming back. I had suggested you.

'You've done your inspector's exams now, got good grades. You've done your time, too so it's time you moved up a rank. You'd have to do a promotion board, of course, but it should be a foregone conclusion with your track record. You have the experience. And where are they going to find another SFO happy to work in this role when they could be off doing something really exciting? There are no promises in this game, you know that, but the post's as good as yours if you want it. Plus the promotion and associated pay rise, of course.

'But what are you going to be doing instead? The odd burglary? Some shop-lifting? You may get lucky and get some drunk and disorderlies, if the excitement doesn't kill you. Jesus Christ, man, think about what you're doing.

'You could be shooting yourself in the foot, pun bloody well intended. Are you sure it's worth it? And before you say anything, believe it or not I do know all about this first love shit. I was like that with Jeanie when we first got together. But it doesn't last, Ted. Passion like that. It burns out. You finish up being comfortable with one another, if you're lucky. Are you sure it's worth the gamble?'

'It's time for a change, boss. Time to settle down.'

'Where are you going to go?'

'There's a vacancy coming up for a sergeant at Longsight. I've been asking around.'

'Longsight? Dear god in heaven! And you've started this already? Without talking to me first?'

'I was just getting a feel for what was available, sir. I've not even talked to personnel yet. Nothing official. Just getting an idea.'

'Well, that's bloody big of you. Look, if you've really made your mind up, I'm not going to beg you to stay. I'll give you a decent reference, of course, even if I do think you're a bloody idiot. Just promise me you'll think very long and hard before you do anything rash, because there's no coming back from this, if you make a mistake now.

'You'll finish up running round playing mother hen to a bunch of young likely lads for the rest of your life, if you're not very careful, and you're not a pen-pusher, Ted. It's not in your nature. You like the Action Man stuff too much. Yes, you'll be going out on patrols but seriously? It's not going to be like what you're used to, nor what you're trained for.

'Go for a pint with your team. Talk to them. They'll probably say the same as I've said. Just for god's sake weigh up all your options before you make a serious mistake.

'And remember, what I told you is in confidence. It goes no further. No one else in this nick knows, so if it gets out, I'll know where it's come from and I won't be pleased.'

'You're quiet this evening. Did you not like the house?'

Ted and Trev were walking back to Ted's rented flat after the viewing. It wasn't far and they both preferred to walk when they could. It was another way of keeping themselves fit for their martial arts training, which both took seriously.

'It's nice. It has potential. You could do a lot with it.'

'Perhaps we could. I'm a bit rubbish at decorating. I've got no taste. I hoped you might help.'

'You definitely want to stay in Offerton?'

'I like it round here. It's easy to get to the dojo and the karate club. Not far to go up to the Peaks when I want to blow a few cobwebs away. Besides, it's handy for Longsight. An easy commute.'

'Longsight? I thought you worked out of Openshaw?'

'Openshaw is for Firearms. When I go back to Uniform, I could be working out of Longsight. There's a vacancy coming up there for a sergeant. Not immediately, but coming up in a while.'

Trev stopped in his tracks and turned to look at him.

'You're leaving Firearms?'

'Well, if that's what you want. If that's what it takes for you to believe that I'm serious about this. About us.'

'Are you kidding me? You'd really do that for me?'

'Of course I'm not kidding. I'm trying to show you that I want us to be together. If it's what you want.'

'What I want,' Trev said, a slow smile spreading across his face, 'is to hurry back to the flat, rip all your clothes off and show you how much this means to me. And I promise you that you will never regret your decision because of me.'

'Three pints and I'll have a ginger beer please, Sue.'

Ted was getting the drinks in for him and the lads at the local pub they used often. They were well-known there, good customers. Sue, behind the bar, was only just getting used to not pouring snakebites for Ted now he was on the wagon. He was busy trying different soft drinks to find one he could tolerate.

'Do you want me to put some lime in that for you, Ted? It might perk it up a bit.'

'I'd prefer you to swap it for a snakebite but I've said I'm quitting so I will. Go on then, some lime and a bit of ice.'

'Sit down, I'll bring them over while it's quiet.'

Sue liked Ted. Even when he'd had a few in the past he was always the perfect gentleman, never any trouble. She'd had a go at flirting with him early on until she realised she was wasting her time.

Once Ted and the lads had their drinks in front of them and Ted had taken a big swallow of his – the lime lifted it a bit, but that was all he could say for it – he looked round at his squad members, Scott, Declan, Jimmy. He didn't imagine this conversation was going to go any better than the one with the boss had done.

'I wanted a quiet get-together, away from the nick, because I've got some news and I wanted you to hear it from me, before the rumour mill gets going.'

'You've turned straight and you're going to marry a woman, Skip?'

Scott, always the joker of the squad, spoke up first.

'Not quite, but my life is going in a new direction. I'm leaving Firearms soon and going back to Uniform. I've got the chance of a sergeant's job at Longsight.'

Scott nearly choked on his beer in surprise.

'Hey, I'm supposed to be the funny man on this team, and that's not even funny.'

'It's not a joke. I'm serious. I've enjoyed working with you all, you know that, but it's time for a change. I'm hanging up my holsters and going back to riding a desk.'

Ted was trying to make light of it but his heart was heavy.

He kept reminding himself why he was doing it. It was going to be worth it. He hoped it was.

There was a stunned silence from the other three then Declan spoke.

'Well, good luck, Sarge. I hope you'll be happy in your new role.'

Sarge. In their minds he was no longer one of them. No longer their Skipper so he didn't deserve the title. Him leaving them like that clearly felt like a betrayal.

Ted was at a low ebb when he drove home to the flat. He was suddenly confronting the reality and not at all sure he was doing the right thing.

As he let himself in through the front door, he could hear one of his CDs playing, one of the Kenny Rogers ones, and smell something delicious wafting from the small kitchen. Trev appeared, a tea-towel tied round his waist like an apron, and greeted him with a warm hug and a lingering kiss. And suddenly it felt all right again.

'Well, I must say, your CV is extremely impressive, Sgt Darling.'

Chief Superintendent Greg Pilling was a big man, powerful, with massive hands. He also had an unfortunate lisp which didn't entirely go with the physical image. He would be Ted's new Divisional Commander if he was confirmed for the upcoming post at Longsight.

Pilling had asked to meet him in person, clearly not believing his luck at getting someone with Ted's record. A graduate entry with an excellent degree, good prospects and an impressive set of arrests to his name. Someone like Ted didn't come his way all that often. But he was of a sceptical nature. He believed in the saying 'if something seems too good to be true, it usually is.'

There had to be a catch, somewhere.

'Very impressive indeed. One might just say you were

overqualified for the role you've applied for. What would you say to that, Sergeant?'

Ted had taken an instant liking to his potential new senior officer. He admired him for not trying to use sentences avoiding the dreaded S sound, as some would have done. He knew too that he was a good copper with an impressive record of his own. He also knew instinctively that he couldn't get away with bullshitting this man. He realised that his carefully prepared speech of needing to get back to real day-to-day policing might not ring quite true enough. He opted for frank honesty.

'My domestic circumstances have changed a bit, sir. I have a new partner, we're getting a house together, and he's not too keen on the Firearms thing.'

'I see. Well, it's not my place to pry into your private life. But I must just ask. Do you make a habit of letting it rule your work, your career prospects?'

'No, sir, I don't. This would be the first and only time. I think I can be just as valuable to the force in Uniform as I was in Firearms. I joined the police because I wanted to make a difference to how crime was handled. I think I have plenty to offer in this new role and I'm looking forward to the challenge.'

Pilling was looking at Ted's CV again.

'I see that you read politics and got a good degree. I think you would have made a good politician, being able to spin a line like that and make it sound convincing. But I'm impressed by your CV and I like what I've seen of you so far.'

He extended one of his big hands across the desk.

'Welcome to our humble division. I hope you enjoy your new role and find it challenging enough.'

Chapter Nine

June 1984

'Hi, dad, I'm back.'

Ted carefully hung up his school bag and put his martial arts kitbag away. He knew better than to leave anything lying around on the floor. It was hard enough for his dad to get about in the wheelchair without Ted turning the place into an assault course.

His dad paid for him to have martial arts lessons every week. He was learning judo, karate and jiu-jitsu. Ted was small and skinny, an easy target for bullies once he'd started school, especially with a name like Darling. Joe had vowed that no one would ever lay a finger on his lad. He couldn't teach him to defend himself, but he used all the spare cash he had to make sure experts could. The difference it had made to his son's self-confidence was worth every penny he'd paid out, and more besides.

Ted went into the living room where his dad was watching telly. The news was on.

'Just sit down quietly a minute while I watch the rest of this, Ted, there's a good lad.'

Ted sat down obediently on the sofa near to his dad's chair and looked at the screen. He couldn't quite work out what was going on. It looked like some sort of a riot. A lot of police officers and civilians fighting hand to hand, mounted police chasing after people on foot, batons swinging. Police dogs *barking and snarling and trying to bite anyone who got near to them.*

His dad was muttering to himself, the occasional swear word. Joe Darling hardly ever swore in front of his son and certainly wouldn't allow Ted to use bad language. Joe had his customary glass of whisky in his hand and Ted could see the level in the bottle nearby had gone down a fair bit since the day before.

Once the news item had finished and the scene had changed to something else which didn't interest either of them, Joe used the remote to switch the TV off then turned to his son.

'How was school, son? Was it judo or karate today?'

'School was ok. Karate was brilliant. Dad, why were the police on telly attacking people and hitting them like that? It must have been scary, them coming charging up on big horses.'

'Because they're bastards, Ted. Establishment lackeys.'

Ted was taken aback by the vehemence of his dad's tone, and the use of the strong language.

'This government wants to break the unions, lad, take the power away from working people. Look at me, stuck in this bloody thing. My union, the Mineworkers, had been negotiating with the management of the colliery where I worked for months, telling them it was dangerous and they needed a major overhaul of safety measures.

'But they were only interested in making money. To hell with the men down there, risking their lives. Those Lancashire coalfields are full of gas. Known for it. Some of the most dangerous ones to be worked. And then there was the explosion. You could say I was lucky, because I got out. Some of my friends didn't.'

'But I don't understand why the police were behaving like that. I didn't think they were supposed to hit people like they were doing.'

'They'll say the pickets started it, son, but it didn't look like

it to me.'

Joe spent some time patiently explaining to Ted what the strike was all about, the use of mass picketing, the police reaction and everything else Ted asked him about. He tried to keep his views balanced, not slanted by his own opinions. He was proud of his son, who was like a sponge for absorbing everything he told him. But Ted's reaction when he'd finished really shook him.

'Dad, I think I want to be a policeman when I grow up.'

Joe took a drink of his whisky before he replied.

'Why's that, lad?'

'Well, there must be some good policemen. They can't all be like the ones on telly just now. So perhaps if there were more good ones, things like that wouldn't happen. At least not so often.'

Joe carefully put his glass down on the small table next to his chair and held a hand out to his son.

'Come here, Ted, lad.'

For a moment, he thought his dad may be angry with him. Perhaps he'd said the wrong thing. Perhaps his dad didn't want him to be an establishment lackey, although Ted wasn't entirely sure he'd understood properly what that meant. His dad was never angry with him normally. He was always patient and kind.

'You're a very good lad, Ted. I'm proud of you. You'd be a very good policeman because you're intelligent and fair. And if that's what you want to do, I'll support you every step of the way. And we'll start by finding out exactly what you need to do if you want to join the force.'

The woman behind the desk looked over it at Ted, standing there in front of her, barely tall enough to see over it.

'Can I help you?' she asked, pleasantly enough.

'My dad's outside. He wants to talk to someone about me joining the police. Only he's in a wheelchair so he can't get in.

Is there someone who can talk to him, please?'

'You want to be a policemen? You might need a lot of porridge to grow big enough.'

Now Ted didn't like her tone. He didn't like anyone making fun of his small size.

'I'm only nine. I've not finished growing yet,' he told her, keeping it polite because that's the way his dad had brought him up. 'So is there someone who can talk to him, please?'

A police officer in uniform was just going past them. He stopped, looking at Ted.

'Can you help this little lad, Sarge?' the woman asked him. 'Says his dad is outside and wants to ask about police recruitment for him.'

'Did your dad not want to come in himself, son?' the sergeant asked him.

His tone was a bit kinder. Ted didn't like the woman calling him a little lad.

'My dad's in a wheelchair. He couldn't get in.'

'I can get him in round the side entrance. Shall we go and find him? What's your name?'

'Ted. Ted Darling.'

'Well, Ted, a name like that is going to get you a bit of teasing, but I suppose you're used to that already.'

'I don't get teased much about it. Not since I started taking martial arts lessons.'

'Good for you,' the sergeant laughed then, as he saw Ted's dad sitting in his wheelchair, waiting patiently, he went on, 'Mr Darling? Sorry for the inconvenience. I'll take you and Ted inside now and tell you all I can about joining up. I think you're going to do best to contact Chester House, our Headquarters, the recruitment section. But I'm happy to find you a cup of tea and I can at least answer any questions about what the job's like at the coalface.'

'Thanks for the offer, Sergeant, but I doubt that,' Joe Darling said dryly, although he was smiling. He sensed the

sergeant meant well. 'I was a coal miner, before this happened to me.'

'How did your first day go?' Trev asked anxiously as soon as Ted walked through the door at the end of his first shift back in Uniform. 'Were you bored witless?'

'No time to be bored. I go out on patrol, like a proper policeman. And Firearms isn't all action, you know. We used to do a lot of waiting around for something exciting to happen. My new Inspector seems all right. She's certainly a lot less grumpy than Matt Bryan. I've got a couple of new probationers to babysit. One lass was so nervous with me in the car, for some reason, she tried to go the wrong way up a one-way street.'

Trev put a hand on his arm, his expression worried.

'You hated it, didn't you? Be honest. I know you'll be brilliant at mentoring people, but it's so different from what you're used to.'

'It's fine, honestly, don't worry. It's a bit of a change but that's just what I need. We had some action today, at least. A young thug on a mountain bike, handbag snatching. We got him though, me and the nervous driving lass, so that was a good start.'

He was trying to make it sound exciting. He didn't want Trev worrying about the decision he'd made.

'Oh, and I got some good news today, too. The estate agent phoned. My offer on the house has been accepted so that can go ahead.'

It was his turn to look anxious as he asked, 'If you're still up for it? Moving in properly with me? In our own place. I don't want to rush you into anything, if it's too soon.'

'I'd love to. I can't think of anything I'd like more. I just don't want you to think I've pushed you into a career change you didn't really want.'

'It's going to be fine. I joined up because I wanted to make a difference. Now I'm going to be working with young officers from the time they first join. If I can't make a difference that way, there's no hope for me.

'I'll go and see someone about a mortgage. That should be fine. I've got a bit put by for the deposit. And I'll find a solicitor to do the conveyancing. I'll put the house in both our names. That way you'll at least have a house if anything ever happened to me.'

Trev laughed.

'That's a bit morbid. And is it just a way to find out my full name? It's Trevor Patrick Costello Armstrong, as it happens.'

'That's a bit posh. Is it double-barrelled?'

Trev smiled at him.

'Nothing so vulgar. Just two family names. So what about you? Is it just Edward Darling?'

'It isn't even Edward. It's Edwin.'

'Edwin? I like that. It's unusual. It suits you.'

'Clark? This assault on a young woman you attended yesterday.'

Ted was talking to a young PC, a tall, somewhat lanky lad with a shock of carroty hair. He wondered what had possessed Mr and Mrs Kent to saddle their son with a name like that, guaranteeing him the nickname of Superman for the rest of his life.

'Yes, Sarge?' Kent queried.

'You haven't flagged it up as of possible significance.'

Ted had been at Longsight for a good few months now, long enough to get to know the strengths and weaknesses of the officers on his shift. Anything that happened on his watch went across Ted's desk. It was his job to pick up anything out of the ordinary. Which was just as well as although young PC Kent tried hard, he wouldn't notice the nose on his own face, if it hadn't been a large one.

'I didn't think it was, Sarge. Just another prozzy getting a slapping from a pimp ...'

He saw the look on Ted's face and started to try to back pedal. He and the rest of them had rapidly discovered that Ted insisted on respect for everyone, however they made a living.

'I mean, it's not right, is that, of course. It's just that it's not that uncommon so I didn't think any more of it.'

'It's the third one across my desk this week, Clark, and the week's not yet over. I think it needs a bit more looking into, don't you? Just to make sure there's nothing going on that we should be aware of. You didn't really get much of a statement from her.'

'She just kept saying it was fine and she didn't want to press charges.'

'Clark,' Ted said patiently, 'you should know by now that it's not up to the victim whether or not charges are brought. We need to investigate this a bit further, try to find out who's behind it, look for links to the other cases, then take it from there.'

'So shall we hand it over to CID, Sarge?' Kent asked hopefully. It was starting to sound like rather a lot of work to him.

Ted brandished the report the young officer had filed.

'There's not enough here to hand over to anyone. Let's you and me go and see if we can find this young woman and ask her a few more questions. And while we're out there, we'll track down the other two victims and see what they can tell us.'

Ted was good at talking to people. It was one of his greatest strengths. Because he was short, polite and quietly spoken, he wasn't seen as a threat. And he was patient. He kept on asking questions, often the same one several times over, though couched in different terms, until he started to get some answers.

By the time Ted was back in to write up his own notes at the end of the shift, he was seeing a definite pattern starting to emerge.

He had no proof, just a strong hunch, that at least one of the girls they'd spoken to may have been trafficked into the country and was being forced into prostitution against her will. She clearly now had a drug addiction which made her dependant on her pimp for her supplies. With a lot of persuasion and reassurance from Ted, she'd finally given them a name for her pimp. It was clearly a nickname and it meant nothing to Ted, but it was a start.

It looked as if he would now need to pass this one over to CID. He didn't see the need to run it past his own Inspector first. He'd just look in and see if there was anyone in the CID room and at least ask them to check out the name he had for the pimp who could well also be behind the trafficking and the drug supply.

There were a couple of DCs at their desk when Ted went into the office. He hadn't yet had much to do with the plain clothes officers in this nick. A lot of them thought themselves a cut above the lowly Uniform lot and he could see from the look these two were giving him that they were in that same category.

He outlined what had brought him to see them. He could tell from the moment he started speaking that they weren't interested, just going through the motions so as to stay the correct side of impolite.

'Doesn't sound like much to me, Sarge,' one of them, DC Grieves, said dismissively. 'The street girls are always getting slapped around by their pimps. Shouldn't happen, of course, but it's one of the risks of the job. I don't think it's one that we could do much with.'

'Tell you what, Sarge,' the other one, DC McGowan said with a sly wink at his colleague, 'if you're worried about this one, you should take it to DCI Baker, at Greenheys. He's in charge of anything serious like this happening right across South Manchester, so this would come under his remit. Could be a feather in your cap if you've uncovered some sort of big trafficking and drug-running ring he doesn't know about yet.

'I might just do that, thanks.'

Ted wasn't fooled. He suspected he was being set up, but he wanted someone to take seriously what was happening to these young women. And the DCI might just be the person to do it.

'What a pillock,' McGowan said after Ted had left the office. 'Big Jim will eat him for breakfast and spit out the pips.'

Chapter Ten

'DCI Baker? Sergeant Darling here, sir, at Longsight.'

The DCI hadn't been in his office the previous day when Ted had tried calling him after his less than helpful discussion with his own station's CID officers. He'd made it his priority to call him first thing in the morning and had caught him at his desk.

'What can I do for you, Sergeant? Only make it quick, I'm just on my way to a meeting.'

Ted didn't know the DCI but he'd heard good things about him. He explained as succinctly as he could what he'd picked up from reports and why he thought it needed looking into.

'It's a sad fact of life, Sergeant, but this type of thing is all too common, and I've got limited resources to work on anything based on your hunch, excellent though it may well be.'

Ted could sense another brush-off coming and he wasn't having any of it. He was convinced there was more to this than met the eye. Now he just needed to persuade the DCI of that.

'Sir, with respect ...'

The DCI's voice was a low, warning grumble as he cut across Ted.

'Let me stop you right there, Sergeant. You and I both know perfectly well that as soon as someone says that, it means the very opposite. I really don't currently have the time or the resources to do anything. You'll just have to try a bit harder to get your own CID to take an interest.'

'Well, sir, with respect or without it, I think this may just be bigger than that.'

There was a pause in which Ted suspected he had probably crossed way over the line with a senior officer he didn't even know.

'Sergeant Darling, I have heard about you on the grapevine. About your tendency to be a bit of a cocky sod and not easily intimidated by rank. But you've clearly got some balls, I'll give you that. So here's what I'm going to do for you.

'I'll give you until this time tomorrow morning to put together a detailed report which will convince me why you're right and your own CID officers are wrong. And why I should take this case up and run with it. You write your report and you come and present it to me in person. Is that understood, Sergeant?'

'Yes, sir. Thank you, sir.'

Ted couldn't swear to it but he thought he heard a low chuckle as he ended the call.

Ted made another quick phone call before he went to join his shift for their usual morning briefing from the Inspector.

'I'm going to be late tonight, sorry. I've got extra homework to do to present a report to a DCI first thing in the morning.'

Trev laughed at the other end of the phone.

'Great minds, and all that. I was just about to phone you and say the same thing. The sodding bike died on the way into work just now and at the moment it's looking terminal. I had to push it the last half mile or so. Good job I work in a Honda dealership, eh? Geoff's kindly said I can stay on after we close up and see if I can't get it going again.'

Trev's training was with hi-tech bikes which needed a computer to put them right rather than a spanner and an oily rag. He still loved to tinker with the old classics, though, which was why he was happy to carry on struggling with the old

Honda. If he ever succeeded in getting it going again, it was a collectible so he should be able to sell it on and have money to put towards something newer.

'Do you want me to come and pick you up, if you can't get it going?'

'That's kind but don't worry. Geoff's got a part-exchange bike or two in so he's said I can borrow one of those if I need to. What about food?'

'I'll grab something at my desk. No idea how late I'll be. I want to get this right.'

DCI Baker started a cursory scan of the report Ted had painstakingly prepared the evening before, then he looked up from his reading to where Ted was standing in front of his desk. Even though the DCI was sitting down, Ted could see that he was a big man, bulky, with the dimensions of an American fridge.

'You prepared this yourself, or did you have input from anyone else?'

'No, sir, it's my work.'

The DCI dropped his head again and started reading carefully through every line. When he reached the account of Ted's interviews with the three victims of the assaults, he looked up again.

'And you got these girls to tell you all this just by having a chat with them, did you?'

'I did, sir. People talk to me. I don't look much like a policeman, even in uniform, so they tend to trust me and talk freely.'

Baker grunted as he carried on with his reading. When he got to the end, his expression, as he studied Ted, had changed.

'This is good work, Sergeant Darling. I've got experienced CID officers who'd struggle to prepare a report this good on such a short deadline. I think you possibly have something here. And I think you were right. This is something that needs looking at more closely.

'I'm going to pass this over to my team and get them to start looking at it immediately. And since you've already clearly made a connection with these young victims, I'm going to talk to your boss at Longsight to ask if we could perhaps borrow you, if necessary, to talk to them some more.

'I like that you clearly care about these girls, that they're not just another crime statistic to you. Do you have children, Sergeant?'

'No sir, I don't.'

'Well, I do. I have a teenage daughter. She's both the love of my life and the bane of my life. She's just at that age. But if anything like this,' he shook the report in one of his large hands, 'ever happened to her, I'd like to think a caring cop somewhere would do something about it.

'CID at your nick should have listened to you and they should have taken this up. I'll be having a word with them. But well done to you for having the initiative, and the balls, to come to me directly with it. Otherwise this could have kept going on and more young lasses could end up like this.

'Good work, Sergeant. I've a feeling we might work together some more in the not too distant future.'

Ted had told his Inspector he'd have to miss morning briefing as he'd been summoned to talk to the DCI. He didn't go into much detail of what it was about, just that something he'd been working on with young PC Kent had seemed to be more a case for Jim Baker's team so he'd been asked to go over and present his report in person.

He was surprised and pleased with how it had gone that morning. On the drive back he'd put one of his Willie Nelson CDs in the car's player, the Red Headed Stranger album, and sang along to it as he drove. He had a good voice, though he never let anyone else hear it, except occasionally Trev.

His good mood continued through the day when he caught

up with his shift. Things seemed to be going well and although he hadn't really expected to, he found himself enjoying his new role.

Once he got back to the station after being out on patrol, he headed for the gents before he started sorting paperwork at the end of the day. He was just using the urinal when the outer door burst open, almost springing off its hinges, then was slammed shut just as violently. DCs Grieves and McGowan stood there and they weren't looking pleased.

'You bloody creep!' McGowan spat. 'We just got a right bollocking because of you.'

Ted had to make a split-second decision. They might simply be going to mouth off. But with both of them there, they might decide to get physical. They knew Ted had come from Firearms. They may well not know about his Specialist training. He could either finish what he was doing, make himself presentable and try to reason with them. Or he could do what most trained exponents of Krav Maga would do in the face of a perceived threat.

Then the decision was made for him. McGowan was coming head-on, fists flailing. Ted took him down with a carefully controlled kick which knocked the wind clean out of his sails without doing him any serious harm. He simply had no breath left to pose any kind of immediate threat.

Seeing his oppo down seemed to enrage Grieves, who let out a roar like a maddened bull and launched himself at the much shorter Ted, swinging one arm to try to land a punch.

Ted side-stepped neatly, calmly grabbing Grieves' arm and pulling it up from the side. Then he brought his own spare arm down across Grieves's shoulder, keeping himself behind his attacker, forcing him down to a position from which he could use neither his arms nor his legs for further attempts.

It brought Grieves's face so close to the urinal that his nostrils were filled with the combined stench of urine and and the sickly sweet smell of a lemon channel block. Grieves was humiliated and powerless to move but made up for it with the increase in the amount of noise he was making.

'I'll let go of you once you agree that you'll just go quietly back to your desks and we'll pretend none of this ever happened,' Ted was just explaining patiently and calmly when, after the most cursory of knocks the door opened once more and Ted's boss, Inspector Michelle Williams, stood in the doorway surveying the scene with open distaste.

Ted immediately dropped Grieves' arm and took a step back, his hands raised to shoulder height in a gesture of appeasement. McGowan was just about recovering enough wind to speak and complained, 'This is the gents' bogs. You can't just come bursting in here.'

'What I think you were trying to say, Detective Constable, was, "You can't just come bursting in here, ma'am". Now, is someone going to tell me just what the bloody hell is going on here? And Sergeant Darling, I suggest you adjust your clothing, sharpish. You lot could be heard halfway round the station, which is why I came in. And I repeat. What exactly is going on?'

McGowan and Grieves were looking daggers at Ted, clearly daring him to say anything which would land them in even more trouble.

'Sergeant Darling, you're the senior officer among the three of you. I'm still waiting for an explanation. And it better be a good one.'

'Sorry, ma'am, just an impromptu demonstration of self-defence which got a little bit out of hand,' Ted replied blithely.

He never normally addressed her as ma'am. His new boss was informal, on first name terms as a rule and they got on well. He picked up his lead from her, in front of the two CID officers.

'And that necessitated shoving the DC's head down the pisser, did it? Well, let me just remind you all that this is a police station and not the school playground. It's not the sort of behaviour I expect from any of you. Get back to work, you two, and Sergeant Darling, my office, now. But please stop to wash your hands first.'

Michelle Williams was quite short, not much taller than Ted, and rather broad of build. But she managed to look imposing enough as she sailed off back to her office without a backward glance.

'This isn't over between us,' Grieves told Ted as he did as he was told, adjusting his uniform and washing his hands. 'You dropped us right in the shit. The DCI phoned our boss and complained.'

'Well, I'm sorry, about that, lads. I did come to you first but you gave me the brush-off, remember. In fact, it was your suggestion I went straight to DCI Baker, if I remember right. I think perhaps you thought I might get a different reception from him.

'And you probably weren't interested enough in a short-arse like me from Uniform to do any detective work about my background. I was an SFO, not an AFO, and I have black belts in four martial arts. That was a bit of Krav Maga but if you like, I'd be happy to show you some judo, karate or jiu-jitsu.

'Now, if you'll excuse me, I'd better go and see what my Inspector wants with me.'

He knew he'd just made a couple of bad enemies. It wouldn't be the first time. But he was fairly confident he could handle the pair of them, both together again if need be.

'So what the bloody hell was that all about really?' Michelle Williams demanded the minute Ted got through her office door and sat down as instructed. 'And don't spin me that old bollocks about a demonstration of self-defence or whatever crap it was you tried to trot out before.'

'Sorry, Shell,' Ted replied, reverting to informal now it was just the two of them again. 'Those two clowns tried to set me up into making a fool of myself with the DCI and when it didn't go quite according to plan, they came looking for revenge.'

'If you hadn't all been making so much noise about it I'd have left you to it. I'm sure you were quite capable of sorting those two arse-wipes out without my help. But you risked stirring up bigger fish than me and it might all have got a bit out of hand.'

Ted liked his new boss. She had a mouth like a fish-wife on her, called a spade a bloody shovel. But she was good at her job and she was easy to work for.

'And by the way, the DCI phoned me, too, singing your praises. Let me have a copy of that report you did for him. It must have been good. He seems to think you're the dog's bollocks now. We've not had you for very long but we're getting quite fond of you and your little ways. So if he thinks he's going to pinch you right out from under our noses, he can piss off.'

Chapter Eleven

It felt strange being back amongst friends and former colleagues from Firearms after being away for several months now. Stranger still to see his old squad, with Scott Hardwick now promoted to sergeant and heading up the team. Ted was pleased for him. He'd always been a good second and it was time he moved up.

There was a new fourth member to bring the squad back up to full strength. Scott introduced her as Lara. It seemed even stranger to hear her and the others addressing Scott as Skip. Ted was just Sarge to them now, except to Scott who slipped easily into first name terms now they held equal rank.

'Is the boss not here?' Ted asked, looking round the hotel bar for Matt Bryan.

'Haven't you heard, Ted? He's gone into hospital. Word is that he won't be coming out except in a box. A few of us are getting our best uniforms dry cleaned, just in case.'

He was making light of it but Ted could sense the team were worried about their boss. Ted would have liked to have seen him again but Bryan's farewell to him when he left Firearms had been frosty, to say the least. He was clearly convinced that Ted was doing the wrong thing.

They were meeting up with other Firearms officers for a shooting competition which involved Ted staying away from home. He'd made it clear to Trev that he was welcome to join him but Trev had been equally adamant that he was not keen on the whole Firearms thing, even when Ted was only shooting at targets.

Considering he had once accused Ted of being camp, Trev really could play the part sometimes and Ted never knew whether or not he was entirely serious. They'd moved into the new house together and the first time they had coinciding days off, Ted suggested they visit a DIY shop for paint to start changing the faded décor. Trev had looked at him in horror.

'When you suggested me helping with the decorating I rather saw myself reclining languidly in a steamer chair on the patio, with a Pimm's in one hand, flicking through some interior design magazines. Not actually getting my hands and clothing covered in paint.'

They did go to the DIY shop but all they came back with was two hardwood steamer chairs, with green striped cushions. It was a bit on the chilly side when they got them home and put them up but Trev was determined they should sit in them, surveying their new surroundings. The garden was only a modest size but it was still much more spacious than Ted's small patio at the flat had been. Trev was sipping wine, Ted enjoying a mug of tea.

As they sat, a small, young-looking cat wandered out of the thick bushes at the bottom of the garden and sauntered up the overgrown lawn towards them, tail erect, looking completely unafraid.

'Oh, look, Ted, isn't she gorgeous? I wonder who she belongs to.'

'How do you know it's female?'

'Tortoiseshell. Almost always female. She looks hungry, bless her. She's quite skinny. Should we feed her?'

'I'd better be a responsible policeman and try to find out if she belongs to someone. I'll go round and ask the neighbours if they know anything about her. If I draw a blank there, we should take her to the vet to see whether or not she's micro-chipped. If she'll let us handle her. Someone might be missing her. She might even have got left behind by the former owners.'

Ted had been lucky with the house. It had been repossessed by the mortgage provider because of mounting arrears. With no chain in place for Ted as the buyer, the sale had gone through quickly and smoothly.

The little cat, after sniffing at Trev, made the decision for them by jumping up, turning round and treading on his stomach then settling down, paws folded under her, purring at the top of her voice.

She was to become a third member of their household, inevitably called Queen. The neighbours hadn't known who she belonged to when asked and she had no microchip. Nor was there any response to the posters they put up around the area. She was clearly there to stay.

'Hello, Ted, they're still letting you compete, then? Despite being a traitor and deserting us all?'

Arthur greeted Ted at the hotel with a thump on the back but his smile was friendly enough. He didn't profess to fully understand why Ted had made the decision he had in switching career paths, but he was prepared to respect it.

'Yes, you don't get rid of me that easily. There's a special class for turncoats.'

'I hope you've been keeping up the practice?'

'Whenever I can. I go to my old target club from time to time as well.'

Arthur made a scornful noise.

'Bloody pea-shooters, no doubt. Still, any practice is better than none. We're relying on you to uphold our honour. Looking at the other entries, there's not much there to worry you. You've beaten most of them before, several times over.'

He pulled a piece of paper out of his pocket and jabbed a finger at one of the names listed in some of the same classes Ted normally competed in.

'Just watch out for this one, though. New to our area. An

inspector. Moved up from down south. Some sort of *wunderkind*, by all accounts. Don't look now, but that's her over by the bar, talking to the bloke.'

Ted looked first at the list to see if he recognised the name. "Caldwell, D." followed by the division she was from. It meant nothing to him; not someone he'd encountered before. He took a casual glance towards the woman by the bar. She didn't look much older than Ted so she was clearly something of a high-flyer. She was perched on a bar stool but he could see, even though she wasn't standing up, that she was tall and slim, black hair pulled back into a casual pony-tail.

'She's fearsome with a handgun but you should have the edge over her at long distance, if you keep your focus. And above all, if you stay sober.'

Ted picked his glass up and waggled it in front of Arthur.

'Ginger beer and lime. That's about as exciting as it gets these days. I promised myself I'd give up for good when my dad died and I haven't fallen off the wagon since.'

'And it's working out all right for you? The new job? You and the lad?'

'Trevor,' Ted told him patiently.

He knew Arthur struggled with the whole idea of Ted moving in so soon with someone so much younger than him, although he'd known him long enough to accept his sexuality.

'And yes, thanks, it's working out very well. We're good together.'

'Spare me any details, eh? But I know your dad would have been happy for you. He wanted you to find someone you could settle down with. He only ever wanted the best for you.'

Arthur took a swallow of his pint before he continued.

'You've heard about Matt Bryan, I suppose? Looks like another funeral coming up. I hope you'll be there?'

'If I can get time off,' Ted said awkwardly. 'It may not be that easy, now I've transferred. But my new boss is ok. If she can spare me, she will.'

'Just do us proud tomorrow, Ted. I know you can, and you will. And I'll make sure someone lets the boss know. He had high hopes for you. He was disappointed when you left. If you win one for the team tomorrow it will make his day.'

It was not so much an open competition the following day as a two-way duel between Ted and Inspector Caldwell. They might as well have been the only competitors in their classes since they left the others trailing so far behind on points.

As Arthur had predicted to Ted, she thrashed him soundly in the Sports Pistol class. Ted had his chance of revenge with a long-range rifle, though, with an outstanding score which put him way ahead of her.

She was gracious in defeat. As they stepped up to receive their prizes, she offered him a hand and said, 'Congratulations, Sergeant. That was some very impressive shooting.'

They were off duty; almost everyone was relaxed enough to be on first-name terms. Apparently not the Inspector. Ted decided to play it safe.

'Thank you, ma'am. You had me well beaten in the pistol class, though.'

'Perhaps we'll meet again one day and both see if we can improve on our positions today.'

As she moved away, Arthur came over, all smiles, to pat his protégé on the back and offer to buy him a drink.

'Bloody marvellous, Ted, you totally nailed it. Your dad would have been so proud. He always was, whether you won or lost. Are you staying over with the rest of us? There'll be a bit of a party tonight, going on into the wee small hours, no doubt.'

'I was going to, I'd booked a room. But I think I might just get off home.'

'Love's young dream, eh? Missing your young man?'

Ted grinned at him.

'There is that. But you know what these occasions get like.

And now I'm not drinking, it's a bit hard being round a bunch of people who are. I'm not sure how far I could trust myself just yet, until I get used to my new status.'

Arthur had got the drinks in and the two of them found a small table in a quiet corner.

'Ted, look, I wasn't going to say anything earlier on in the day. I didn't want to break your concentration. But I got a call this morning to say Matt Bryan died in hospital. As soon as I know when the funeral is, I'll let you know and I really hope you can be there for him.'

Driving home in the gathering darkness, fast, but keeping within the legal limit, Ted's analytical brain was wondering if he was subconsciously checking up on his new partner. It wasn't the first time they'd been apart but it was usually Trev who went away and he knew Ted would never cheat on him. Then he convinced himself that it was a romantic gesture, arriving home unexpectedly early, and that hopefully Trev would see it that way.

Ted had Kenny Rogers for a driving companion this time, singing along to some of his favourite country songs. When he came to the line, "We've got tonight, who needs tomorrow?" he wondered, as he often did, whether what he and Trev had was going to last.

He put his car away in the garage when he arrived back and let himself in quietly. He could hear the sound of the television on in the living room so went there first.

Trev was sprawled on the sofa with his long legs up on the foot rest, a glass of wine close to hand. Queen was planted on his chest, her head nuzzling the underside of his face, her purrs loud enough to be heard above the old black and white film which was being shown.

'Hey, you,' he said, tilting his head back as Ted bent over the back of the sofa to kiss him. 'You're home early. Are you checking up on me? If so, officer, I confess, I did sleep with someone last night.' He pointed to the little cat. 'This little monkey sneaked under the bedclothes with me, which was really nice because I was missing you.

'Did you win? Are you hungry? Do you want me to make you something?'

Ted sank down next to him, absent-mindedly scratching the cat behind the ears which increased the volume of her contented purring.

'I grabbed a sandwich on the way back, thanks. I was soundly thrashed in the pistol class by a woman inspector I've not seen before. But I beat her in the long-range rifle. I'm more of a sniper.'

Trev turned to him with a slow smile.

'Sleeping with a sniper? That sounds incredibly sexy, somehow.'

'I thought you were against the whole Firearms thing?'

'You should know by now that I am totally fickle. I think you should take me upstairs and tell me more about your weapons training.'

Ted laughed.

'You're impossible,' he said, but he put up no resistance when Trev switched off the TV and stood up, taking his hand.

Another cemetery. Another damp and chilly afternoon. Matt Bryan's funeral was also to be a cremation but this time there were hymns and readings. Ted was surprised. He'd never taken his former boss for a religious person. Perhaps it was more the choice of his wife, Jeanie, who was there in the front row with an older teenage boy Ted took to be their son.

He realised that he had known very little about the man he had served under for years. Bryan had kept himself to himself and, apart from a jar or two at the end of the shift on a successful day, there had been no socialising between him and the officers on his team.

Arthur was again going to say a few words. This time there

would be no wisecracks, no laughter. It was serious stuff, respectful.

As many of the team as possible were there, in full uniform, to pay their respects. Scott Hardwick was one of the white-gloved pall-bearers who carried the coffin from the hearse into the crematorium chapel.

It was a good turnout. Lots of Matt Bryan's serving colleagues as well as a few retired ones, displaying medal ribbons. He hadn't been the easiest boss to work for but he was well respected. They did him proud.

As they were filing out of the chapel after the service, when Ted stopped to shake Mrs Bryan's hand, offering the customary, 'Sorry for your loss,' he was surprised when she kept hold of his hand a moment longer.

'You're Ted, aren't you? Matt often spoke about you. He thought highly of you, you know. Did you win the trophy the other week? He said he thought you would.'

He wasn't quite sure what to say to that. The words were unexpected, so he just mumbled, 'I did, Mrs Bryan. If ever I can do anything ...'

'Thank you, that's very kind. You will join us now for a drink and a bite to eat, won't you? I know you're not on the team any more and Matt was disappointed about that. But it would mean a lot to him, I know, if you joined us. And thank you for coming.'

The next time Jeanie Bryan took flowers to the corner of the garden of remembrance which was her late husband's final resting place, she was surprised and touched to find a small engraved trophy, leaning up against the stone behind which was the urn containing his ashes.

"Full bore rifle. Long range. Winner: T. Darling"

Chapter Twelve

'Right, Clark, have you had any more luck talking to any of the girls? Only I haven't seen any statements from you.'

'I have tried, Sarge, honestly. But they just won't talk to me like they talked to you.'

The constable sitting next to PC Clark Kent gave him a hefty nudge in the ribs as he joked, 'I'm not surprised, Sarge. Have you heard Superman's idea of a chat-up line? It's bloody dire!'

There was general laughter from the shift officers but Ted cut across it.

'All right, everyone, let's not forget these are serious assaults on young women, some of them no more than girls, which rather takes the humour out of it a bit. Clark, I'll come out with you today and we'll go together to see if we can't make a bit more progress.

'We need people on the patch to know that we will always investigate crime and we're not into victim blaming. There are a lot of sections of society who don't yet believe us so won't always report crime to us. It's up to all of us to change that image.'

'Yeah, but Sarge, sometimes we daren't look into stuff otherwise we get accused of racism and stuff,' another constable pointed out.

'Which is why we need to show the public that we investigate everything equally with no bias towards or against any ethnic minority, profession or anything else. So we're going to show these girls the same consideration as we would anyone else.'

'Some of them are illegals though, Sarge, so won't they just wind up getting deported, whatever we do?'

'So does being an illegal immigrant make it all right for them to get beaten up? I don't think so. Also, we won't know their status until we investigate. What we're going to do is to investigate every crime that comes our way without prejudice then let the powers that be decide what happens next. That's the best way we're going to build any kind of relationship with the public.'

'We're police officers, in uniform, so we can't pretend to be anything else,' Ted explained to PC Kent as the young officer drove them towards the area where they were likely to find some of the street girls. Few of them would be out and about at that time of day, unless they were desperate to earn money for their next drink or drugs fix or were being hassled by pimps to earn more.

'But what we can do is to empathise with them, to let them see that we care about them as people, not just as a crime statistic.'

'We're always being told not to get too close though, Sarge. Not to get emotionally involved.'

'There's a difference between showing compassion and getting emotionally involved. Hopefully, I'll be able to show you how to manage the balance.'

They tracked some of the girls down to a greasy spoon in a back street, including one they'd spoken to before, the multi-coloured bruising on her face still showing beneath the heavy make-up. Ted remembered that her name was Ecaterina, though she'd told him she preferred to be called Cati.

'Would you mind if we joined you, ladies?' Ted asked them politely. 'We're just on a tea break. Clark, get me a cup of tea, please, and whatever you and everyone else would like.

He handed over a banknote which PC Kent took to the counter to get the drinks. When he came back, Ted and the girls were chatting amiably enough about nothing in particular. Kent handed the same note back to Ted.

'Guy behind the counter says it's on the house, Sarge, because we're helping the girls.'

'Well, please go back, thank him very kindly for the offer but tell him, politely, that's it's just too many forms to fill in to declare a gratuity. It's a good chance for you to assure him that we do the same for any victims of crime.'

Kent did as he was told. When he returned, he watched Ted avidly, to try to see what his secret was. Why he was so relaxed in the girls' company, and they in his, that the conversation was flowing. They would even answer the gentle questions he posed without any hesitation.

'Gratuity?' the one called Cati asked Ted. 'This means something for nothing, Mr Ted? So we can't give you anything, like a present, to show we are grateful to you.'

The way she was smiling at him left both officers in no doubt what kind of favours she was proposing. Kent went bright red, Ted just smiled politely.

'Nothing at all, ladies. We're just doing our jobs. Besides, you'd be wasting your time with me. But look, here's a card with my contact details. If ever I can do anything to help any of you, please just call me. And take care out there.'

As they walked back to the car, Ted turned to the young PC.

'You see? Just talk to them, like human beings. It's not hard. Be polite, listen to them, and they'll talk to you.'

Ted was again out with PC Kent, following up on a spate of burglaries, when a call came through asking for any units near to Devonshire Street at the junction with Lauderdale Crescent, where a serious ongoing assault had been reported. That was near where the previous assaults they'd been investigating had taken place, and close to where they'd talked to the girls in the café two days ago.

'Show us as responding, please. There may be a link to something we're already on. Has an ambulance been called?'

'Nothing immediately available but if you can give an update on arrival, they'll try to prioritise something for you if the situation warrants it.'

It was becoming more and more commonplace. The services were all under pressure. It didn't help that they were so often called out on false alarms and completely time-wasting exercises.

'Blues and twos, Sarge?' Kent asked hopefully, always after an excuse to play the boy racer.

'Just try not to run over anyone on the way, Clark, if ambulances are in short supply.'

As soon as they turned into the street they could see ahead that a handful of people were watching warily as a man appeared to be knocking seven bells out of a woman he was holding up against a wall. Ted could see instantly why no one was attempting to intervene. Although the attacker was using a fist, he had a knife in the other hand which he had apparently not yet brought into play.

Kent screeched the car to a halt near the scene and was just about to leap out.

'Risk assessment, Clark,' Ted reminded him. 'Don't go rushing in there and make yourself another victim. Spray and baton ready and don't try any heroics.'

He got out on the side nearest the pavement.

'Police! Stand still.'

He still had to make a conscious effort not to use his old Firearms warning.

A few of the onlookers had suddenly remembered urgent appointments elsewhere and were disappearing fast. One man stepped nearer to the police car saying, 'It was me who called you lot. I couldn't do anything to help because he's got a knife.

But I've got him on film.'

The attacker appeared only just to have noticed their arrival. He paused in raining blows to glance at them, weighing up what risk they posed him. He saw something in the way Ted was moving closer which alerted him to potential danger. He let go of the woman, turned and ran.

Kent moved to go after him but Ted stopped him with an order.

'Call back-up. Make sure they know he's armed. Watch which way he's heading and report it. Don't go after him, you'll only get knifed. Then get witness statements from everyone here. And make sure we get the video of the attacker for an ID.'

Putting his baton away, Ted moved quickly to the woman who had fallen on the floor and wasn't moving. Her face was a battered and bloody mess, and she was barely conscious but she was at least breathing. Ted put gloves on before attempting first aid, knowing the risks with an unknown victim.

'I'm a police officer. Can you tell me your name?'

One puffy eye tried its best to open. The other was swollen beyond making it even a possibility. Split and bloody lips tried to form words. Ted had to bend closer to hear what she was trying to say.

'Mr Ted ...'

It was Cati, the girl they'd spoken to previously. She'd bestowed the nickname on him the first time he'd spoken to her, after the earlier assault. This time her injuries looked far more serious.

'It's going to be all right, Cati,' he told her. 'You're going to be fine. I'm calling an ambulance now. They'll take you to hospital and you'll be fine.'

Clark Kent had made the calls as instructed. Now he moved nearer to where Ted was doing his best to make Cati comfortable and maintain her airway until an ambulance arrived. Kent was looking a bit green round the gills at the sight of her.

'Bloody hell, Sarge. Is this because she talked to us? Have we made things worse instead of better?'

'We can't know that yet. It may be unconnected. And how are we ever going to stop this sort of thing if we don't talk to the victims and try to do something about it?'

They escorted the ambulance to the Infirmary, then Ted followed the trolley being wheeled into the A&E department while PC Kent parked the vehicle. They were getting close to the end of their shift and Ted was acutely aware of it. He'd struggle to justify overtime on this but he was anxious to at least know if Cati was going to be all right before they clocked off for the night.

They were lucky in that she was seen fairly quickly and taken through to a cubicle for examination. It wasn't long before a registrar came out to find them with an update. Ted was able to give them her name, as she'd not been willing or able to tell them anything. She was still on the system from the last assault.

'You came in with this young woman, I understand, officer?'

'We were called to the scene of the assault so we came with the ambulance. Is she going to be all right?'

'She's had a fairly comprehensive going over this time so the concern is any internal injuries. We're arranging scans and further tests. The other problem, which manifested on her last brief visit here, is that she is drug dependant so we'll need to give her something to avoid severe withdrawal symptoms, which is about the last thing she needs in her current condition.

'There's nothing much more I can tell you at this stage. Are you Mr Ted? She's said that name a few times but very little else.'

'I've spoken to her a couple of times. It's a nickname she's given me. Look, I'll give you my contact details. Can you please get someone to let me know how she is, as soon as you

have some results back? And if you can, please let her know
that I'm willing to come and talk to her again any time she'd
like to speak to me.'

DCs Grieves and McGowan were at their desks once more
when Ted went up to the CID office the following morning.
Their DS, a man called McArdle, was also there.

As soon as Ted walked in the DS started singing,
'Everybody was kung fu fighting,' with actions, and loud
enough for him to hear, grinning at his two colleagues who
simply glared back at him. Ted ignored the jibe.

'Another assault on one of the girls yesterday. She's in the
Infirmary. In a bad way, but she will make it.'

'And you'd like us to send grapes? Or flowers, perhaps?'
McArdle asked flippantly. 'If it wasn't common knowledge
that you bat for the other team, I'd be worried about your
fascination for these girls, Ted.'

'She's indicated that she would talk,' Ted went on,
ignoring his flippancy. 'Name names. Clearly she needs to be
put in a safe place if she does. I thought I'd bring it to you
first.'

'Instead of running squealing to your new pal the DCI?'
Grieves asked him, clearly still smarting over the incident in
the gents.

'Look, it's up to you but in the spirit of cooperation, I'm
bringing it to you first. We've done the legwork. You're
welcome to take the credit for it. It's a big tick for you with
minimum effort. So do you want it or not? I'm arranging an
officer to stand guard over her while she's still in hospital, but I
do think we should consider a safe house for her as soon as
she's fit to be discharged.'

'We, now, is it?' McGowan asked. 'That's very matey.'

'We are supposed to be working on the same side, after all.
Someone needs to keep the DCI in the loop, too. Will you do it
or shall I?'

'Oh, I think we might just manage that all by ourselves, Sergeant. It's hardly crime of the year though, a prozzy getting knocked about. We can't go running to the DCI with every one of those which comes our way.'

Ted wasn't sure the three of them were taking this as seriously as he would have liked. He wanted them to get on and do something about it but he strongly suspected it would get pushed to the bottom of a pile or possibly even forgotten about for the time being.

The DS and McGowan seemed a bit casual in their approach to work in general, no more than that. But Ted realised the episode in the gents had made him an enemy out of Grieves. McGowan was just clowning around, but Grieves seemed to be looking for any excuse to make Ted's life difficult.

'Except that he did ask to be kept informed about any similar cases on our patch as it's part of an ongoing investigation he's setting up.'

'Oh, well in that case,' Grieves picked up his phone, without making a call, and mimed talking into it. 'Please, sir, that nasty Sergeant Darling is bullying us again because we won't let him play in the big boys' sandpit.'

The three of them were laughing now. Ted was working hard to keep his temper in check.

'Right, well, if you're not interested, I'll send a report through to the DCI and leave it at that.'

He turned to walk out, ignoring as he did so Grieves' high-pitched 'oooooh' addressed to his retreating form.

Back at his desk, Ted picked up his own phone.

'DCI Baker? Sorry to disturb you, sir, but we have another assault on one of the girls. Well, I should say another assault on one of the previous victims. This time we have mobile phone footage of the attacker. Would you like me to copy you in on everything as well as our own CID?'

Chapter Thirteen

'Right, Sergeant, today you're being poached from us by none other than DCI Baker,' Inspector Michelle Williams told Ted at the start of the morning briefing. 'He wants to see your street girl turned informer for himself, to see how credible a witness she'd make. And since you seem to have established something of a relationship with her ...'

She raised her voice slightly as there was a chuckle of amusement from the other officers present.

'Shut up, you mucky lot, I don't mean anything like that.

'As I was saying before the kiddies so rudely interrupted, you've established a rapport with her so he wants you to go with him. He'll be here in about half an hour, with a driver, and you can go with them to talk to her at the safe house. We'll try to manage without you.'

Ted was surprised. He thought that now he'd handed his notes over to the DCI, that was the end of his involvement with the case. He was secretly pleased to hear he would still have at least some involvement in what was clearly going to be a big operation. He was quite enjoying his new Uniform role but so far he'd not had anything big to get his teeth into compared to the cases he'd been involved with before, thanks to his specialist training.

'Just try not to get ideas above your station, mixing with those strange folk from CID. Especially them from DCI Baker's team.'

Ted was standing outside the station waiting when a black

Ford pulled up at the entrance. A plain clothes officer he didn't know was driving and the DCI was in the back seat. Baker leaned his bulk sideways to open a rear door for Ted who slid into the seat next to him.

'This is DC Robbie Hughes,' the DCI nodded towards the driver as he pulled smoothly away. 'And this is Sergeant Darling.'

Their driver did no more than lift his chin in acknowledgement, concentrating on his driving.

'Right, Operation Chantelle looks like a goer, as long as your girl ... what's she called, Ecaterina or something?'

It sounded strange coming from his lips, pronounced as it was with a broad Manchester accent and a long E at the beginning.

'She likes to be called Cati, sir.'

'Well, that's a bloody sight easier. As long as this Cati would make a credible witness, it looks like we can put an end to quite a big and a dirty operation. We've had our eye on a part of it for some time and she would just be the cherry on the cake, if she would talk and if CPS thinks she would stand up in court. She's not an illegal, you say, like some of the others?'

'No, sir, she came here legally to work in an old people's home but got in with the wrong crowd and they got her hooked on drugs.'

The DCI's face darkened.

'When I think of anything like that happening to my daughter ...' he rumbled. 'A good reason I want this lot off the street and behind bars so they can't do any more damage.'

The 'safe house' was in fact a shabby ground-floor flat in a far from salubrious road in Greater Manchester. Cati was now out of hospital, though still not fully recovered, and was being babysat by a female officer from Uniform, with an AFO on duty round the clock to protect her. The DCI was certainly doing his best to keep her safe.

Jim Baker told his DC to stay with the vehicle. He was

clearly not sure it would still have its wheels on if they left it outside unattended. Cati was sitting on a none too clean sofa, a big duvet piled over and around her, her knees drawn up to her chest in a protective posture. She had a mug of something hot which she was cradling in both her hands. Her eyes were wary as the DCI came in, seeming to almost fill the small room.

'Would you like a brew, sir?' the uniformed officer asked him.

'Aye, go on, why not. Coffee for me, strong as you like. Sergeant?'

'Tea, please, milk, two sugars.'

The DCI had already briefed Ted on the drive over that he would be the one to do most of the talking with Cati. He began by making the introduction.

'Cati, this is Detective Chief Inspector Baker. He's in charge of the operation to catch the people who did this to you. Would it be all right if we sat down a bit and talked to you?'

She was still looking suspiciously at the DCI.

'Is he good man, like you are, Mr Ted?'

'Yes, he is. And he has a daughter.'

She nodded her agreement. Jim Baker sank cautiously into a battered old armchair, the springs groaning in protest at his weight. It made the room look less crowded. Ted pulled a straight-backed dining chair out from under a table against the wall and positioned himself between Baker and Cati. He did most of the talking, going over the points they'd discussed on the drive over.

When he'd finished, Cati looked him directly in the eye as she asked, 'And will I be safe? If I do this, if I go to court and speak against these people, will they come after me? Kill me, maybe?'

Ted held her gaze as he replied, 'We will do everything in our power to protect you. You'll be put on a Witness Protection Programme, given a new identity, moved somewhere no one knows you. It will mean you won't be able to keep in contact with anyone you know from your time here.'

'Not even you, Mr Ted?'

Her smile was teasing.

'Especially not me. The most important thing will be your safety.'

Despite the earlier hot drink, the DCI told DC Hughes to stop at a takeaway café on the way back, to go and get them another one and not to hurry back. Once he'd got out of the car, Jim Baker turned to Ted.

'You're good with people. I've been asking around about you. Everyone says that, and I certainly witnessed it just now. I also hear that you have a bit of a tendency to be gobby with senior officers, though not enough to get yourself an official black mark. What do you have to say about that?'

'Sir, if someone tells me how to do my job when they're not qualified for the same role, I will always say something. It's a question of safety. Not just mine and my team but anyone around us. Only a more senior Firearms officer is qualified to tell me how to run that side of things. Apart from that, I can take orders.'

'Well, I bloody well hope so. Because I like what I've seen of you so far, so I'd like you in on Operation Chantelle. The final phase. When it starts to get interesting. You're SFO, I understand? Still up to date?'

Ted nodded and Baker continued, 'Right, well, I'll talk to your Chief Super about borrowing you. You'd go in out of uniform and carrying a handgun. Behind the first armed responders. We're going to have to go into places where there may well be other girls like Cati and you might be the best person in that role, especially armed. But not in full kit so you won't scare the devil out of them. Would you be up for that?'

Ted couldn't believe his ears. It sounded like exactly his sort of thing and he thought he'd left all that type of excitement behind him. The thought crossed his mind fleetingly that he'd have to square it with Trev if he was going to be carrying a firearm again in a potentially dangerous situation. But he couldn't wait to be doing the sort of work he was trained for once again.

'I'd be up for that, sir.'

'You look like a bloody Mossad agent but I suppose it will have to do.'

DCI Jim Baker scowled critically at Ted on the morning of the raid which would hopefully bring Operation Chantelle to a successful conclusion.

Ted was used to being in uniform on raids. He was not interested in clothes, despite Trev's best efforts at dragging him out shopping and trying to change his image. And he could hardly have asked Trev's advice on what to wear for this particular operation. He'd played down his own role and glossed over the fact that he would be armed once again. He wasn't shackled by any religious notions about omission being as big a sin as lying. He'd just decided that Trev would be happier not knowing what he was up to. He'd tell him more about it when it was all safely over.

Left to his own devices to dress himself, he'd opted for his black jeans, a dark polo shirt, his old tobacco-brown leather jacket and his Doc Martens' boots. They were nearly the same as his service boots and he knew he could move quietly and comfortably in them.

'It's my stealth cloaking device, sir,' Ted told him with a perfectly straight face. 'No one takes me for a cop at the best of times and certainly not dressed like this.'

He thought he saw the DCI's mouth twitch slightly at the corners in amusement but he decided not to push it. This was too big an operation to risk anything going wrong. For some reason Ted found himself anxious to make a good impression. It would be a good tick on his CV if nothing else if he was involved in some arrests on this case.

Ted hitched a ride with the Firearms officers heading for one of the houses being raided, one believed to be used as a brothel for some of the girls. The whole operation was being synchronised so that a number of properties would be hit at the same time.

None of Ted's former squad members were involved but he travelled with officers he knew. They were eyeing him strangely, wondering why he'd opted for his relatively mundane role in Uniform when he could have been doing this on a regular basis.

Then Ted was bursting through the front door behind the AFOs, his gun drawn. Joining in the shouted chorus of 'Armed police! Stand still!' Going from room to room to secure the premises, feeling the adrenaline once more coursing through his blood supply.

Some of the gang members were on the premises. They were overpowered and handcuffed with swift efficiency before any of them even had time to think of drawing the concealed weapons which were then taken from them. Clearly they'd had no clue of the impending raid.

A couple of the girls' clients, looking shifty and embarrassed, were rounded up and taken off to the nearest station to give statements. They appeared to be simply members of the public caught up in the net but they would need to be thoroughly checked.

Ted returned his weapon to its shoulder holster and went to talk to the girls. Some of them were completely out of it on drugs. The others seemed accepting of his calm manner and soft voice.

Once the property was empty and secured, it was back to the DCI's own station for the debrief. Everything had gone like clockwork, with all raids successful and passing off without incident.

When they'd finished up the formal stuff, Ted was surprised to find himself caught up in the general invitation for a pint at the nearest pub with the DCI and the rest of his team. He felt like neither fish nor fowl, a Uniform officer working in plain clothes with those who might not otherwise give him the time of day.

The DCI got the first round in, Ted asking for his now customary ginger beer with lime. When Jim Baker jerked his head at him to follow him to a quiet corner, Ted worried fleetingly if he'd done something wrong, although he couldn't think what.

'Good op today, Ted,' the DCI had switched to informal mode in the pub. Ted wouldn't risk doing the same with a senior officer he barely knew. 'Did you enjoy yourself?'

'I'm not sure enjoy is quite the word, sir, but it was a bit like old times.'

'And you left Firearms for personal reasons, they tell me?'

'Yes, sir. Setting up home with a new partner and he wasn't keen on me being an SFO.'

'Well, I don't profess to understand how you live your life and that's none of my business. If you come and work for me you'll quickly discover that I'm a bloody old dinosaur who can barely spell PC let alone be any kind of correct.'

Ted's drink went down the wrong way at the unexpected words which sent him into a paroxysm of coughing. The DCI thumped him on the back with bone-breaking efficiency.

'I like what I've seen and heard of you so far, Ted. I've been asked to head up a team, operating out of Stockport. They spent a bob or two on the recent refurb so they want their money's worth out of it.

'It will be a Serious Crime Unit, murders, serious assaults, that sort of thing. I've inherited a few bodies who aren't negotiable who may not all be up to the job and I've chosen a few others. The incumbent DI is not my choice but luckily I'm not stuck with him for long. He's coming up for retirement and he spends a fair bit of time on sick leave.

'I've hand-picked a decent DS, Jack Gregson, who's well

up to the task. But he's not fast track like you are and he's not done his exams yet. If you come in at DS level, I reckon you'd quickly be well up to taking over once the DI stumps off into the sunset to tend his allotment or whatever the bloody hell he plans to do.

'Anyway, I thought I'd sound you out on the idea first before going through the official channels. I need a people person because I'm not one. You've got proven leadership skills in Firearms and I've seen how good you were with the girls. That impressed me and I'm not easily impressed.

'So what do you say? Are you interested?'

'Sir, I'm flattered, but I've never worked in CID.'

'So what? You've got a bloody brain, haven't you? Graduate entry? You should flaming well have one. And you seem to be a bloody good copper, judging by your arrest record and your reputation. Are you interested or not? Or will you have to ask the boyfriend first?'

'Partner, sir. Trevor is my partner, not my boyfriend.'

There was just a slight hint of reproach in Ted's voice.

Jim Baker threw his head back and laughed loudly.

'Just like I heard. Gobby with senior officers. I stand corrected, Ted. Will you have to ask your partner or can we shake on it now and I'll get the ball rolling?'

Without hesitation, Ted put out his hand to take Baker's big paw and shake it. He hoped he was right in thinking that Trev would be pleased and proud to hear the news.

Chapter Fourteen

Nobody went into the station at Stockport without catching the watchful eye of Sgt Bill Baxter. Bill was no longer as mobile as he had once been. But as the injury which had slowed him down had also earned him a medal for bravery, it had not been a good PR move to sideline him. So the powers that be had made use of his assets and put him in the Charge office. From there, he also had a finger on the pulse of everything that was going on in the station.

There was nothing that went on in the whole of Stockport, never mind within the confines of the nick, that Bill didn't know about. He certainly knew about the anticipated arrival of a brand new DS to join the team, freshly plucked from Uniform, and he was keeping his eye out for him. He'd heard good things about Sergeant, now Detective Sergeant, Ted Darling. He guessed he would be early and he was. Bill also knew that the civilian who manned the front desk would be late, as usual, and she was. Bill took it upon himself to be waiting for the new arrival.

The person who came through the door with a Police ID tag round his neck didn't fit the image Bill had in his mind. For one thing, he was even shorter than he'd imagined. And he only looked like a bit of a lad. A cocky one at that. Or perhaps that was Bill getting older.

Trev had battled with Ted the night before about what he should wear for his first official day in plain clothes. Ted had flatly refused to wear a suit and tie, saying it made him look ridiculous. He'd finally conceded and agreed to a smart shirt with no tie and his decent chinos, though he couldn't be parted from his leather jacket.

Ted walked over to the reception desk, remembering as he did so that the last time he'd been in this station he'd been nine years old and barely tall enough to see over the old desk which had now been replaced, presumably as part of the recent refurbishment.

'DS Darling, joining CID here today,' he told the uniformed sergeant standing behind the desk, holding up his ID.

Bill gave him an old-fashioned look. He knew people. He could imagine how much of a struggle the new DS had been through in his career so far because of his name and his size, not to mention the fact that he was gay. Bill had been doing his homework on the new officer.

'And up until today you were a humble Uniform sergeant like me, although not as senior. So let's begin with the niceties first, shall we? Suppose you start with "Good morning, Sergeant" and we'll take it from there?'

Ted's apologetic grin made him look even younger, like a boy being pulled up by a teacher for a breach of the school rules.

'Sorry, Sarge, I'm a bit nervous. First day in CID and still finding my feet.'

'I'm Sgt Baxter. When you know me better, you can call me Bill. If you want to know anything about what goes on in this nick, ask me. If I don't know, nobody else will.'

'Can you start by telling me where my new office is, please? I've never been further than this desk and I don't want to go wandering around looking lost.'

'I'm under strict instructions from the Big Boss to get someone to come down and escort you. Perhaps he doesn't yet know you well enough to be sure you'd find your way on your own.'

The sergeant picked up the desk phone and called CID as instructed, to let them know the new DS was there. It made Ted feel even more like a pupil joining school part-way through term when everyone else knew where to go and what to do except him.

It was DC Robbie Hughes who came down to collect him. Again Ted got little more than a chin lift and an 'All right, Sarge?' before Hughes turned and led the way up the stairs. Clearly he was not impressed by the idea of a new DS with no previous experience in CID. Ted followed him through a door into the main CID office. There were two other, smaller offices partitioned off from the principal room. He guessed they would be for the DI and the DCI.

As if reading his mind, Hughes told him, 'DCI's office is over there. He'll be in before too long. The other is for the DI, but he's off sick again. And this is DS Gregson.'

A man had got up from his desk and was walking over, hand outstretched in greeting.

'Jack Gregson. Welcome to the team.'

Ted was relieved that the welcome appeared to be genuine. Gregson was the one he'd been apprehensive of meeting. Ted was, after all, coming in with no CID experience but because of his fast-track graduate entry, he could conceivably leapfrog over Gregson to become the new DI. Assuming he at least got through his first day without making a complete prat of himself.

'Ted Darling,' he told him, shaking his hand.

'DI's away so we can use his office for now. I thought you might like a rundown of ongoing cases before you jump in at the deep end.'

Ted rather wished he hadn't used the swimming reference. He was making some progress in the water, thanks to Trev's patient teaching, but he had a long way to go to lose the deep-seated terror of swimming he'd had since he was a small boy.

'We call them offices but there are bigger broom-

105

cupboards,' Gregson told him with a smile as he held the door open for Ted to go in first.

'Look, I'm sure it's no secret, but I haven't done this before so I apologise in advance if I ask stupid questions, until I get my head round it all,' Ted said as he pulled out a chair to sit down.

They were deep in conference when the door opened and the DCI came in, making the small office look even more like a cupboard. Ted half rose at the sight of his new boss, not knowing what the form was, but Baker waved him down.

'Thanks for bringing him up to speed, Jack. Ted, we're going to throw you in at the deep end right from the start. We've got a nasty piece of work in for a serious assault. Not his first offence, by a long chalk. Jack's going to interview him now, and you're going to observe over the monitor, take some notes. I think the victim could tell us more than she has done already. So once you've seen what matey boy has to say, I want you to go and talk to her. If she'll talk more to anyone, she will to you. Oh, and it's only fair to warn you, the attacker is her nephew. Her only family.'

'So is she likely to agree to testify against her own family, sir?'

'Highly doubtful, I would say,' the DCI admitted cheerfully. 'That's why we need a people person to give it a go. Mission Impossible on your first day. Show us what you're made of, Ted. Her nephew, Craig Betts, is a real piece of shit and he needs taking out of the equation. He gave his auntie a right thumping for her benefits to buy skunk with and there's a real danger he'll do more, and worse, again in the future if we don't put him away.'

'No pressure then, sir?'

'None at all. Just give it your best shot. And another part of what I want you to do is to assess the team members I've inherited and tell me if they can be made up to the standard I need for a unit like this. I'm going to start you off with DC

Maurice Brown. I see he's not even in yet, Jack. Any idea why?'

'More problems with the kiddies or the missus, I imagine, boss. I'll talk to him again.'

'Well, kick his bloody lardy arse while you're at it. He's lagging behind the others even when he is here. He's as much use as a chocolate teapot if he doesn't even bother to show.'

He turned to Ted to add, 'Now you can see why I want an impartial appraisal of him from a newcomer to the team.'

The missing Maurice Brown had clearly slunk in while the three of them were in the small office. When they came back out, there was a new face, working away at his desk, trying to look as if he'd been there for some time.

The DCI went straight to his own room as Jack Gregson took Ted over to introduce him.

'What's the excuse this time, Maurice? And the Big Boss noticed your absence today so it better be a good one.'

DC Brown was yawning widely and trying to disguise the fact.

'Sorry, Sarge, the twins have got a bug and they were grizzling all night. Barbara was knackered, she'd had them like that all day, so I stayed up with them, trying to settle them. Then I overslept.'

'It's getting to be a regular thing, you being late, Maurice. Get it sorted. This is DS Darling and he might not be quite such an easy touch as me.'

Brown stifled another yawn then said, 'Ted, is it?'

His accent was strong Geordie.

'It's DS Darling, and DS Gregson's right. I don't like unpunctuality. You're with me, talking to the assault victim, once DS Gregson has interviewed the suspect, so perhaps some strong coffee to wake yourself up before we go?'

'Why aye, Sarge,' Brown told him, with more than a hint of irony.

Ted knew he was going to have to assert himself early on

over a team who'd been doing this job for some time and who knew full well it was all new to him.

Maurice Brown drove them to their destination. He drove well enough, though his constant yawning was concerning. Ted was trying not to prejudge him but wondered if it was significant that his running commentary tour of the neighbourhood was based on the bars and pubs and where to find the best pint.

Their destination was a scruffy ground floor flat looking out over a patch of what might once have been grass but was now so trampled as to be little more than mud and fag ends.

Ted wondered again what possessed some people to saddle their children with names which would single them out for ridicule. The victim they were coming to interview was called Elizabeth Betts and Ted could imagine the difficulties presented by introducing herself as Betty Betts all her life, as that was what the paperwork indicated she called herself.

They heard sounds of slow footsteps in the hallway of the flat in response to Maurice's knock and a wary voice called out, 'Who is it?'

'It's the police, Miss Betts. DS Darling and DC Brown. Could we possibly have a word, please?' Ted asked politely.

They heard a chain rattle and the door opened only as far as its length allowed. The eye which peered suspiciously through the gap was bloodshot, the flesh all around it puffed up and multi-coloured. It must have hurt.

Ted held his ID up so she could see it and told her again, his voice quiet and calm, 'I'm DS Darling, Miss Betts, from Stockport CID. Would it be all right to come in and have a word with you, please?'

'If it's about our Craig, I've already told you lot all I'm going to tell you.'

'I'm new to Stockport. It's my first day, in fact. If it wouldn't be too much trouble, I wonder if you'd mind just going through your statement with me?'

Mumbling to herself, she fiddled with the chain to open the door and let them in, then led the way along a narrow, dark passage to a tiny kitchen at the end on the right. The glass panel to the back door, which opened on to a small garden, had been broken, a piece of chipboard roughly filling the hole.

Following their gaze, she told them, 'Our Craig did that, when I wouldn't open the front door. At least the local bobbies got it fixed for me, and got the chain put on the door. It won't keep him out though. Nothing will, when he needs to buy his stuff.'

'Shall I put the kettle on, Betty? We could talk over a cuppa,' Maurice suggested hopefully.

'You can put it on if you like, but I got nothing to make a brew with. Our Craig took the lot, and all me money. Nothing now while I get me next benefit.'

'I could just nip to the corner shop and get you the makings?' Maurice suggested, looking to Ted for his approval.

'Told you, I got no money.'

'I can stand you a cuppa tea, pet. I'll just put it on my expenses,' Maurice told her, with a wink in Ted's direction. 'Now, do you need milk, and sugar?'

Ted sat down at the kitchen table with the woman while Maurice went out to the shop. He was already seeing a different side to him than he'd expected to. It was encouraging.

Ted started talking to the woman, just making general conversation until Maurice got back and brewed up, making Betty's tea exactly the way she'd asked for. He put a splash of cold water in so she could drink it straight away, gently putting out a hand to steady the mug when her own hand was visibly trembling.

'Miss Betts, you do know that Craig is going to go on doing the same thing over and over unless you would help us to bring him to court.'

'Call me Betty. I can't do that. He's our George's lad. He's all the family I got left. Never had kids of my own.'

'He needs help, Betty. He needs taking in hand now, before this gets seriously out of control. Unless someone does something, it's only going to get worse.'

'By someone you mean me, right? Shop me own nephew? I couldn't live with myself.'

'And what if he hurts you worse next time, Betty?' Maurice put in. 'Or what if it's one of your neighbours? Maybe an older person, frail. He could end up killing someone.'

Betty herself was in her fifties, although with the injuries her nephew had inflicted, she looked older, vulnerable.

She was looking from one to the other, sipping her tea. They could almost hear the cogs in her mind working the problem over.

Ted carried on talking to her, his tone persuasive, not putting pressure on her, simply trying to convince her that she was doing the best thing for her own safety.

'Aye, go on then. Tell me what you want me to do. He needs help, the poor bugger.'

'And she went for it, just like that?' Jim Baker sounded surprised.

'She took a little bit of persuasion, sir. But once Maurice had made her a brew and I'd explained it was the only way to deal with him, she agreed. She's given us a full statement, which should hopefully encourage him to plead guilty and save her having to testify. But she has said she would, if it comes to that.'

The DCI looked from one to the other of them.

'Well, that's a bloody good result for your first day. A big tick on the books and another toerag dealt with. Well done, both of you. You'd best get off home now. And Maurice, get some bloody sleep and make sure you're on time tomorrow.'

As Ted was going down the stairs he saw that Sgt Baxter was coming out from the direction of the Charge room, putting his coat on and getting ready to knock off for the day. On a whim, he stopped to talk to him.

'I wondered if I could buy you a pint, Sarge? By way of apology for being a bit up myself first thing. I think there's a decent pub nearby, isn't there?'

'Have you ever known a nick that's not near a pub? If you're buying me a pint, you've earned the right to call me Bill. Welcome to Stockport, Ted. I have a feeling you're going to fit in here.'

Chapter Fifteen

'Hi, sorry I'm a bit later than I said,' Ted called out from the hallway as he hung up his jacket. He could hear that Trev was in the kitchen so he headed there to greet his partner with a kiss.

'How did your first day go? I made a treacle pudding. I know it's your favourite so I thought it could be either a celebration or comfort food, as necessary.'

'You spoil me. And definitely a celebration. It was good. I enjoyed it. And I helped crack a case, so that was a good start.'

Queen, the cat, hearing Ted's voice, came into the kitchen to rub round his legs, demanding attention. He picked her up, immediately rewarded by delighted purring.

'How's your new boss?'

'I wouldn't want to get on the wrong side of him. He reminds me of a big bear who's just woken up from hibernation so you have to be careful not to anger him. But I think I can work with him. I went for a drink with the charge room sergeant, Bill, after work, that's why I'm a bit late. By way of an apology. I went swaggering in a bit uppity so he pulled me up on it. He's a nice bloke. A bit lonely. Lost his wife young, lives on his own so he seemed pleased at the chance of a drink together.'

'I can't imagine you behaving like that.'

'I was feeling a bit nervous, trying to look confident.'

'I know that trick, all too well,' Trev told him, more serious now.

Both men had experienced bullying of various sorts when they were growing up. Ted had dealt with it through his martial arts. Trev had only taken up judo and karate when he was in his late teens. He coped when he was younger by developing the technique of looking completely unafraid and sure of himself.

'Speaking of such things,' Trev continued, 'I was going to suggest to Bernard that we think of starting up a self-defence group for children at the dojo. Teach them the basics, especially the looking confident so they're less of a target trick. What do you think?'

'I think it's a brilliant idea. My hours could get erratic now with my new role, but I'd be up for doing it whenever I could.'

Trev went back to checking his cooking then said, without looking at Ted, 'D'you think Queen is lonely? Would she like some company when we're out at work all day?'

Ted looked down at the cat in his arms, still purring, eyes half-closed.

'I don't think she's lonely. I don't think cats are pack animals, are they? Not like dogs, anyway.'

'You know that animal refuge near where I work? The bike developed a serious steering fault when I was going past there. It swerved uncontrollably off the road and I found myself wandering round inside looking at kittens.'

Ted smiled indulgently.

'If you're living with a copper, you'll have to come up with a better story than that if you want to be believed.'

'I just might have accidentally reserved two kittens. They're ours, subject to a home check, and we should waltz through that. Queen can tell them what responsible foster parents we are.'

'Seriously, though, if we've having a home check, we should do something about making the garden a bit safer, with the road so close and me growing lilies in pots. Queen's sensible enough but we might need to look at putting up some higher mesh to stop cats from straying near traffic. And I might not have as much free time as I did working shifts in Uniform.'

'I can help you.'

Ted smiled again. Trev's idea of helping with anything at all to do with DIY usually consisted of standing around looking decorative, passing him things and making endless cups of tea.

'All right, if you're set on kittens, I'd better go and start measuring up.'

Trev put his utensils down and crushed Ted in a hug.

'Thank you! I'll make sure you don't regret it.'

Three months later

'You look stunning and you smell amazing, but if you don't get a move on, we're going to be late,' Ted told his partner. 'And considering how much I've been jumping on the team about timekeeping, especially Maurice, I'll never live it down if I'm late for drinks at the boss's.'

'I want to look my best for you. I don't want to let you down. Will Maurice be there?'

'No, it's sergeants and above. Now can we please get going?'

'I just need to talk to the cats,' Trev told him, heading for the living room. 'Queen, you're in charge. And you pair of young hooligans,' he looked sternly at their two new young additions, Freddie and Mercury, 'the curtains are not your climbing frame, so please remember that.'

Ted finally succeeding in hustling his partner out of the house and into the car. He hated being late for anything, even a social event. He just hoped they didn't hit any traffic or roadworks anywhere on their way to Didsbury where Jim Baker lived. He was stressing at the prospect of being the last to arrive, but trying not to show it.

Christmas was approaching and Jim Baker had issued an invitation to some of his officers, with their partners, to drinks and a buffet at his home. Ted was looking forward to a chance to chat informally, get to know people better. The station had a newly promoted Uniform inspector, Kevin Turner, who would be there with his wife. He and Ted had spoken a few times for work purposes and seemed to get on well.

'There, you see, we're not late after all,' Trev told him as Ted hurried him up the drive to the front door, which the Big Boss himself answered when they rang.

'Sorry to be on the last minute, sir,' Ted apologised, proffering the bottle of good wine Trev had selected. Ted had never been a wine drinker.

'No worries at all, Ted, you're not the last and it's all very informal. So much so that it's Jim for this evening, off duty and in my own home. And this must be Trevor.'

Trev could charm the birds out of the trees. Ted knew his boss would be feeling uncomfortable, having admitted to being a dinosaur where same sex relationships were concerned. But as soon as Trev held out his hand to shake and said, 'I'm very pleased to meet you, Chief Inspector. Ted's told me a lot about you – all of it good,' the DCI visibly relaxed.

'Jim, please, to everyone for tonight. Now come and meet my wife, Margery.'

The woman he led them towards was slim, expensively dressed, and clearly not a natural blonde. Ted wondered if the flawless complexion with no trace of a wrinkle was entirely natural either. She barely gave Ted a second glance but homed in on Trev like a heat-seeking missile.

'Do let me show you the buffet, Trevor. I've had outside caterers in. I simply don't have the time for such things and they are very good.'

She had her arm around his waist as she led him away. Trev threw a pleading look over his shoulder at Ted and mouthed 'Help!' but his partner was busy talking to his Big Boss so was powerless to do anything.

'I'll introduce you to my daughter at some point, Ted. She's around here somewhere. Goodness knows where. And once we all start eating, shop talk is banned. But for now, tell me how you're settling in with us.'

Trev finally managed to escape and came back to find Ted, bearing plates of food for both of them. Ted excused himself to the DCI and the pair moved away to find a quiet corner, in the conservatory at the back of the property.

'Oh my god, Ted, that was seriously scary. I thought she was going to try to get into my pants right by the buffet table. She's a positive maneater and I didn't want your boss thinking it was me trying it on with her. Is she always like that?'

'I'd heard rumours, around the nick, but I thought that's all that they were. Was she really that bad?'

'I didn't know where to put myself.'

The elusive DI, Lennie Grimshaw, had put in an appearance with his wife and the two of them were helping themselves liberally to the buffet. Trev went off to get drinks as Kevin Turner sidled up to Ted.

'Look at him, the waste of space. Always miraculously better for anything that doesn't involve work. Sooner he retires and lets someone who's interested take over the post, the better. In the absence of anyone else, you'll have to do, Ted.'

They were already comfortable enough in each other's company to slip into banter.

'What's meant to be wrong with him? It certainly doesn't seem to have affected his appetite.'

'God knows. It comes and goes at his convenience. Seriously, Ted, trying to liaise with him is a waste of time. If we pooled resources a bit more, we could be making much more of a dent on the crime rate between us. Take all these young people going missing on our patch that we're always having to deal with.'

'But that's Uniform's remit, surely?'

'Five bloody minutes out of Uniform and you've already forgotten it's us lot who do all the work and you lot who take the credit. The trouble is, there's often more to it than a simple disappearance. Some of these kids end up hooked on drugs and robbing to support their habit, or on the game. If we worked together, there's a chance we could be preventing them from falling into serious crime and that would look good on our figures.'

Ted was looking round at those present.

'Is Bill not here tonight? I've seen Sgt Wheeler but not Bill.'

'He avoids stuff like this. Hates coming on his own. Just drinks too much, gets maudlin and it doesn't end well.'

The Big Boss loomed up on them at that moment.

'Now, lads, no shop talk while we're eating was the rule. Make sure you help yourself, there's plenty. I think the wife thought we were catering for the five thousand. Another drink? Kevin? Ted, there's some more of that dry ginger stuff if you want some.'

It wasn't quite what Ted liked to drink but at least his host had made an effort.

'I'm good, thank you.'

He dropped the sir but he didn't feel comfortable enough to call his boss by his first name yet, even in a social setting.

He could see Trev was over by the buffet, happily chatting to two women but having escaped from the clutches of the Big Boss's wife. The soft drinks were tending to go through Ted so he went to find the downstairs cloakroom. He was just about to go in when the boss's daughter, Rosalie, appeared at full tilt, looking dreadful. She pushed in front of him, burst through the door and sank to her knees, groaning.

Trev often used the phrase 'talking to god on the big white phone' especially after some of his more excessive nights out. It came immediately to Ted's mind as he saw the rebellious and clearly very drunken teenager hanging over the white porcelain toilet bowl bringing up her stomach contents while repeatedly muttering, 'oh god' and occasionally, 'I fucking hate my mother'.

Wordlessly, Ted stepped close enough to gently pull her long blonde hair out of the way, then ran one of the spotless white hand towels, piled in a basket next to the wash basin, under cool water. He handed it to her to wipe her face with.

'You probably don't, Rosie. It's the drink talking.'

He'd been introduced to her by the Big Boss earlier in the evening. As soon as Jim had called her Rosalie, she'd spat at him, eyes blazing, 'It's Rosie, Daddy. I keep telling you.'

'But she is such a bitch. She was all over your boyfriend, in front of my dad. It was obscene. How could you bear to watch her like that, pawing him? I'm surprised she didn't have her hand down his trousers.'

She had to pause in her ranting to do some more dry retching.

'Trev's my partner, not my boyfriend, and he can look after himself.'

He was looking at her critically now as he said, 'Tell me to mind my own business but I think you might do well to drink some water and take yourself off to bed.'

She was blinking up at him owlishly now, clearly still drunk.

'Are you trying to get me into bed, Sergeant? I don't think my father would approve.'

'I'm not, but you're quite safe with me in any case. Can you manage on your own or do you want me to help you? I promise there's absolutely no hidden agenda. I just think it might be better if you avoided your dad for the time being.'

She was about to reply but her stomach started heaving once more. There was nothing left to bring up but the effort left her weak and making low noises of pain. Ted took advantage of the pause to fire off a rapid text to Trev.

'Back soon. Drunken damsel in distress.'

Rosie rocked back on to her heels, scrubbing at her face with the damp towel, smearing her make-up everywhere so she looked like a grotesque clown. Ted held out a hand to her.

'Come on, let me help you. You'll feel much better after you've slept.'

She was taller than he was. That wasn't unusual. He let her drape a languid arm round his shoulders and he put a cautious hand around her waist to support her. He knew he was taking a hell of a risk. A drunken teenager could make all sorts of allegations about him if she was feeling malicious. He hoped he was doing the right thing.

He helped her upstairs to her room, took her shoes off for her but refused to allow her to remove anything else in his presence. He got a glass of water from the bathroom and made her drink some of it, then put a towel on the pillow next to her in case any of it came back. Then he pulled the duvet gently over her, put the light out and went downstairs.

Trev was waiting anxiously in the hall, looking out for him.

'What's going on? It can't have been Mrs Jim because she's still down here, stalking me. I'm sure I felt her try to grope my bum at one point so I've been standing with my back to the wall.'

'I just had to put Rosie to bed. She's pissed as a newt. And I need to go and tell the Big Boss, now, in case he gets hold of the wrong end of the stick. Then I think we can safely slope away.'

Ted went to find the DCI and drew him quietly aside.

'Sir, to put you in the picture, I've just helped Rosie upstairs. She's had rather a lot to drink. I put her under the covers, fully clothed, but you might want to keep an eye on her. And if it's all right with you, Trev and I will make a move now.'

Baker looked at him for a moment, hard, as Ted held his gaze.

'Thank you, Ted. That was very kind. I hope you've enjoyed yourselves despite that. Come on, I'll show you out, then I'll go and check on her.'

Just as he opened the front door, letting the feel of late

evening frost into the house, the sound of a car alarm going off split the air. Ted sprinted down the driveway and into the road, just in time to see a youth in a hoody with his hand through the broken window of a car belonging to one of the guests. There was another person close by on a moped. Neither was prepared for the speed with which Ted moved.

Jim Baker bellowed to his guests, who came streaming out of the house, just as Ted, with a few nifty martial arts moves, had the youth spread-eagled against the car he'd just broken into. The one on the moped sped away fast, but not before Ted had noted the number plate by the light of a nearby street lamp.

'Anyone got a pair of handcuffs on them?' he asked, keeping the youth in a secure arm lock.

The DCI gave a shout of laughter.

'Houseful of bloody policemen and not one of you has a pair of cuffs on you, you dozy buggers. Someone get on the blower and get some proper coppers here. Nice work, Ted.'

Chapter Sixteen

It was to be Ted and Trev's first Christmas together in their own place. Trev had been planning the menu for weeks. He loved cooking and was good at it.

Christmases past didn't hold particularly good memories for either of them. Ted's dad was an atheist, though he always tried to make an effort for his son, especially as he'd grown up without his mother for much of his life. Trev's father was a diplomat so his parents were often abroad for extended periods of time. Sometimes Trev would join them but the festivities would usually be official occasions with guests other than family. At other times he would be looked after by the housekeeper at their country home in Gloucestershire. On one occasion, he had been among the lonely few spending Christmas at their boarding school.

Ted knew he shouldn't have left it until Christmas Eve to tell Trev that he'd volunteered to be on call the following day. He'd been trying to pluck up the courage, knowing the news would not go down well and not wanting to spoil their time together.

'I just thought I should volunteer as I'm the newest team member and I don't have family.'

Trev looked hurt.

'Ted, that's an awful thing to say. I'm your family now. Me and the cats. At least I thought we were. I was really looking forward to us spending time together. A proper Christmas. I've never really had one.'

'I'm really sorry, I didn't mean it to sound like that. I should have told you sooner. It's just that mine isn't really a nine to five job. I might get lucky and not get called out all day.'

'So you can guarantee there's going to be no serious crime at all tomorrow?' Trev was still sounding put out. 'Honestly Ted, I was really looking forward to this.'

'I promise I will make it up to you. We can celebrate any day, it's not as if the actual date is special to either of us. And I've got New Year's day off, guaranteed, in exchange. I'll take you shopping. To the sales. In Cheshire. And I'll take you out to lunch.'

He was using everything in his arsenal to make it right. Ted hated shopping, especially at the expensive Cheshire outlet which Trev loved. But he would agree to anything to make up for the disappointment of a potentially spoiled Christmas Day.

'At least I wasn't home late this evening. We've got some time before we need to eat. Let me at least make a start at trying to make it up to you. I know I should have told you sooner and I'm sorry. I'll bring you breakfast in bed in the morning. Anything you like.'

'Anything?' Trev's expression was softening finally. 'How hungry are you? Because what I have in mind right now for starters might take a while.'

They managed to make it halfway through the morning of Christmas Day before Ted's phone interrupted them. True to his word, he'd got up early to see to the cats, leaving Trev to sleep on as he was never an early riser. Then he'd prepared breakfast on a tray with things he'd shopped for the day before on his way home. Freshly squeezed orange juice, *croissants*, *pain au chocolat*. He'd even added a few flowers, in a mug because he couldn't find anything more suitable to put them in.

They'd agreed to exchange only small gifts and to choose

anything bigger together. They'd enjoyed their leisurely breakfast in bed and had unwrapped their presents when Ted's phone rang on the bedside table. He made an apologetic face as he picked up the call. The duty inspector at the station, phoning to tell him there was a suspicious death near Bramhall.

Ted had just finished that call when there was another one immediately after. Sgt Bill Baxter.

'Morning Ted, Bill here. I heard you'd got a call out for this young lass at Bramhall. She was found by a dog walker. It's why I'll never have a dog. It's always dog walkers who find the bodies.'

Ted wasn't surprised that Bill was working on Christmas Day. It was one way to avoid the loneliness the season often meant for people on their own.

'Has the Big Boss been informed yet, Bill, do you know?'

'Next call after you. No earthly point calling the DI. He'd only take a sicky. Uniform are already on site, forensic lot are on their way. It's all quiet here on the Western Front so I've done some of the early calls. It gives me something to do until they bring me some guests to process.

'The duty inspector is tied up on something else now which sounds like a waste of time. I've informed the coroner's office and they'll send a pathologist. They have one on call, though the post-mortem may well have to wait until after the festivities. Do you want me to call any more of your team in?'

Ted hesitated. His first possible murder case. He didn't want to spoil anyone else's day if he could avoid it. But was he wise to try flying solo?

'It's not far from me. Why don't I go over now and have a look what's what, then I can decide who to call in? No sense in spoiling everyone's Christmas if I don't need to.'

Bill hesitated.

'Are you sure? You don't want to make a balls up of your first murder investigation, if it is one. Remember, the lone maverick detective is a thing of fiction. Big Jim would not be

best pleased if you go it alone on your first big case. And he'd
kick my arse for not stopping you.'

'You're right, Bill, thanks for the advice.'

'I'll phone Jack and get him to meet you there. He's got the
experience, and his wife and kids know better than to expect
him to be at home all day on Christmas Day. Besides, by this
time of day he might have had enough of family and be keen to
escape.'

'Thanks, Bill, I appreciate it.'

'You're abandoning me?' Trev asked him, as he ended the
second call.

'Sorry, I have to. Suspicious death. I've no idea when I'll
get back.'

'Well, if it's just me and the cats to pull crackers and watch
the Queen's speech, I may possibly get ever so slightly pissed.
So I'll be entirely at your mercy whenever you do finally get
home.'

Ted had seen dead bodies before in his job. Not only the one
he'd shot himself. He just wasn't quite sure what might be in
store for him if this was a murder case. He didn't want to make
a prat of himself by throwing up over a crime scene on his first
serious investigation, so he turned to an old friend. A
Fisherman's Friend.

One thing that Ted and his dad had done together when he
was a lad had been fishing trips to Roman Lakes. He never
remembered catching a thing, not even a tiddler, but he'd loved
the silent companionship of time spent with his dad. Joe had
always sucked the menthol sweets as they sat there on the
bank, often in the damp and the cold. He'd never let Ted have
one of the lozenges, but after he'd died, Ted had bought
himself a packet out of nostalgia and always put one in his
mouth for the gruesome bits of his job.

His destination was a footpath between fields close to
Bramhall. The scene was already taped off. A uniformed

officer with a clipboard was ensuring that only authorised personnel passed the barrier and were signed in first. Ted decided to play it cool and wait in his car until Jack Gregson arrived. He was worried he would stick out like a sore thumb wandering around a crime scene, not yet entirely knowing what he was meant to be doing.

His phone rang while he was waiting. It was the Big Boss.

'Morning, Ted. Welcome to life in CID. I hope it won't cause you problems at home, missing Christmas together, but that's how it goes in our job. Now, who have you got with you?'

'I've just arrived on scene, sir, and I'm waiting for Jack to join me. I thought the two of us should do an assessment first, to see who we need to bring in.'

'Good, excellent. I'm pleased to hear that. I was worried you might go blundering in on your own, trying to impress me. It impresses me much more that you're following correct procedure. Now, it's a waste of time me calling the DI, but if there's anything you're uncertain about, you call me immediately. Is that clear?'

'Yes, sir, clear.'

'You shouldn't need to. Jack Gregson knows what he's doing. He's been carrying Grimshaw for months now. But keep me posted.'

Gregson's car was just pulling up next to Ted's as the Big Boss rang off. Ted got out to greet him.

'Waiting for me, then, Ted? I thought you'd have gone in all guns blazing by now.'

'You're the third person who's said that, or something similar, to me this morning.'

Gregson laughed.

'Well, you know what a reputation you shooter types have. Right, down to business. Shoe covers and gloves on for starters. The Investigators will soon tell us if they need us in full monkey suits or not for this one. Shall we go?'

They signed themselves in then ducked under the tape the PC held up for them. Ahead they could see an incident tent had been set up to preserve the scene and the body. Jack Gregson headed straight for it, pausing in its entrance before setting foot inside.

'Morning, James, merry wotnots, and all that. This is Ted, our new DS. He's come from Firearms, originally. Ted, this is James, one of that strange band who are as happy carving up a body as a turkey on Christmas Day.'

'Welcome to the House of Fun, Ted. Firearms, eh? Well, I can confidently tell you that this young lady was not shot.'

Ted surreptitiously slid one of his menthol lozenges into his mouth as the pathologist waved them closer and he got his first close-up look at their potential murder victim.

'So what are we looking at then?' Jack Gregson asked.

'I'll know better once I get her back to our lair. Initial observations indicate that her head's been severely bashed about, probably by this large, blood-stained rock conveniently left for us.'

His tone was ironic as he spoke. Just another day's work to him.

'I can also tell you there are signs of sexual activity and again, initial indications would suggest that this was not with her consent.'

'What are you basing that on?' Ted asked him.

He was trying to look analytically at the body but his eyes kept being drawn to the damage done to what might once have been a pretty face.

'If you want all the ins and outs, literally, of what happened to this poor young lady, you should volunteer for the post-mortem. For now, I'm going on what looks like signs of restraint. Manual restraint, rather than her being tied up. But look here, on the wrists. Bruising. Her arms were clearly held hard.'

Jack Gregson shrugged.

'Some people like it rough, I hear, though that's not my thing.'

'Granted. But there's also bruising around her mouth. Or what's left of it. I can't tell you for sure yet but I'd say there's a chance that her attacker had his hand over her mouth to stop her screaming.'

Ted was intrigued, despite his initial revulsion at the sight. He was leaning closer, studying the body in detail. The young girl was small and slight, wrists skinny, although with some muscle to her legs. It would be relatively easy to overpower someone her size if her attacker was bigger and stronger, or if they simply knew the right techniques to employ.

'Both wrists are showing bruising, though. So if someone had one hand over her mouth, and was holding both her wrists, they must have been a lot bigger and stronger. Or there was more than one of them.'

James looked towards Gregson and smiled.

'Quite bright, this one, for a shooter,' he said. 'Especially one on his first possible murder.'

'How did you know it was my first one?'

'The way you're looking at her. Jack and I have seen plenty so we react differently. And the fact that you're sucking that cough sweet for all you're worth.'

Despite the seriousness of the situation, Ted couldn't hide a grin at being caught out.

'What can you tell us about the victim herself so far? Any ID we can go on?' Gregson asked.

'Not a lot. Short and slight, as you can see and I would say young, not more than mid-teens. Blonde hair, clearly, but I can't yet tell if that's natural. And I'm afraid I can't tell you an eye colour yet, for obvious reasons. No signs of any personal possessions here to ID her from.'

'When can you do the post-mortem for us?'

'Depends on when you can get us an ID. Find that today and I could do it tomorrow. I wouldn't normally be on duty for

Boxing Day but we've got a backlog of bodies and I know you'll need at least initial findings as soon as possible. It will need to be the Professor for this one, as there seems little doubt that it's a murder, and he's not back until tomorrow afternoon. But I can start the preliminaries and let you have those results to be getting on with.

'But as soon as I've done here, she's going into storage and I'm going home. If you need to get next of kin to ID her my assistant will get her ready for you, if you let him know. But if I don't at least put in an appearance with my family some time this afternoon, mine may be the next violent death you're investigating. Which one of you gentlemen will draw the short straw for the PM?'

'I'll take it, if you like,' Ted offered. 'I suppose I better start getting used to such things.'

'Ted, I'm liking you more and more with every day,' Gregson told him gratefully. 'Now, shall we leave James to get on and do some of his detective stuff while we go and do ours?'

'So what's first? Witness statements? Area search? Do we need more of our own team on this?'

Ted was happy to be guided by Jack. He was about to reply when Ted's phone rang.

'It's the Big Boss again, checking up,' Ted told him.

'All right, I'll organise Uniform to start searching for ID then I'll talk to the dog walker myself. You update Big Jim.'

'Sir,' Ted began as he picked up the call.

'Talk to me, Ted. What's the latest? Do you have any ID yet on the victim?'

'Not yet, sir, no. Jack's just organising a search for personal possessions. It looks like a definite murder though from her injuries, and a possible rape too.'

He filled him in on all the detail he had so far, and his discussion with the pathologist.

'Well for god's sake make sure the family are informed as

soon as humanly possible. I can't imagine what it must be like for someone whose daughter, sister, girlfriend, whatever, hasn't come home when they should have. Let alone on Christmas Day. As soon as you do know, get Uniform round there to break the news.'

'Sir, if you've no objection, I'd quite like to go with whoever does that.'

'You can safely leave it to Uniform, but tell me your reasoning.'

'Well, sir, with the statistically high likelihood of the killer being known to the victim, I just thought it might be useful if I could see for myself their reaction to the news. If you think that's all right, sir?'

'Not a bad idea, Ted. I brought you in because you're good with people so I'd better give you a chance to prove it. Keep me posted at all times, no matter how late. Get an extra body in to start things off while you're out. Who's on call?'

'DC Hughes, sir.'

'Right, leave Jack on site, you go back in and brief Hughes. With any luck, we might get an ID today then if they can crack on with the PM tomorrow that gives us a good head start.'

Robbie Hughes was already at his desk when Ted arrived at the office. He filled him in on what they had so far and asked him to start checking Missing Person for any likely matches, a young teenage girl, slim and not tall.

Ted was finding Hughes hard going. There was always an atmosphere between them, from Hughes' side. Jack Gregson had told Ted that Hughes was resentful of a DS coming in from outside when he'd clearly had designs on going for the post himself once he'd done his exams. It was always to be expected.

'What does the pathologist think so far?' Hughes asked him.

'Multiple head injuries and signs of a serious sexual assault.'

'A boyfriend, then,' Hughes said confidently. 'Bound to be. Tenner says it is.'

Ted found his attitude disturbing. He understood that people had different coping skills when dealing with violent crime, but he found the idea of gambling on it repellent.

'Not sure it's something to be betting on. We're talking about the life of a young girl here.'

'Oh, come on, Sarge, lighten up. We often have a flutter on the suspects. The DI doesn't mind. Well, he wouldn't. It's usually him who cleans up. He's not bad at guessing.'

'I'd prefer something a bit more than a guess to go on. And we don't yet know if she had a boyfriend.'

'We won't either, not until we know who she is.'

Almost on cue, Ted's phone rang. Jack Gregson.

'We've got a possible ID for you, Ted. Uniform found a youth group card in the name of Lily Barrow not far from the body. An address just outside Woodsmoor. Gives her age as sixteen. Worth sending someone round there to check it out. Maybe see if she's listed as missing anywhere?'

He was trying not to sound as if he was telling Ted his job while at the same time making sure that the newest team member was covering the right basics. Ted was grateful to him.

'I discussed with the Big Boss the idea of me going along with Uniform to break the news. I'd just like to get a feel for the family and their reaction.'

'Sounds like a plan. Keep me updated and I'll do the same on anything else we find here.'

Ted ended the call and noted the address he'd been given then looked across at Hughes.

'Right, possible ID. Lily Barrow, sixteen, from Woodsmoor. Can you run her name through MissPers and see if she's listed? I'll sort out someone from Uniform to go round and talk to the next of kin. I'll go with them.'

'That's one for the Woodentops, Sarge. You can trust them to manage that.'

There was a warning edge to Ted's voice, although he spoke quietly as he replied.

'Up until recently, I was amongst the ranks of the Woodentops myself, DC Hughes. It's how we all started out. I'd prefer to hear them referred to with a bit of respect, please, in my presence. And the same goes for talking about victims or possible suspects.'

Hughes's look was insolent but he said nothing, turning to his computer to do the searches as instructed. It didn't take him long. Ted had just arranged an officer from Uniform to go with him to the address he'd been given when Hughes turned to him to report no findings of Lily Barrow listed as missing. Her only criminal record was a caution for being drunk in a public place when she was fifteen.

'Thank you for that. I'll get over there now and see what we can find out.'

Hughes looked surprised at the thanks. It came naturally to Ted. His dad had brought him up to be polite and he almost always was.

Chapter Seventeen

A uniformed constable was waiting in an area car outside the station door for Ted when he got downstairs.

'PC Fleming, Sarge. Polly,' she told him, as she put the car in gear and pulled out of the car park. 'Is this a definite ID now? And what part do you want me to play? Hand-holder and tea-maker?'

Ted wasn't sure if she was teasing him so his response was guarded.

'I'm not one for gender stereotyping, PC Fleming.'

She smiled at him.

'That makes you a bit of a novelty among some other CID officers, then.'

'It's going to be a tricky one. We don't know for sure if our victim is Lily Barrow and the body won't be easy or pleasant to identify. We might need to arrange for some DNA samples to be collected from the house for cross-checking.'

'I could start by asking her mum, if that's who she lives with, what she was wearing when she saw her last?' Polly suggested.

It was helpful rather than a dig, although Ted realised he should have thought of that himself. He'd checked for any details they had of who else lived at the address they were heading for. The names which had come up were a Janice Barrow and a Ray Mann.

'Perhaps if you could start things off and see how we go?'

'Not a bad area this, Sarge. Do we know much about

them?' Polly asked, as she parked the car.

'We haven't found any criminal record, although Lily was cautioned for drinking when she was fifteen.'

PC Fleming straightened her hat as she got out of the car and prepared to follow Ted up the path of the small front garden, surprised that he instead stood aside to allow her to go first.

A woman answered the door, drying her hands on a tea towel.

'Mrs Barrow?' Polly asked, then continued, after the nod of confirmation, 'I'm PC Fleming, this is DS Darling. I wonder if we could come in and have a word, please?'

The woman looked uncertain for a moment. Then a man's voice called out from somewhere in the house, 'Who is it, love?'

'It's the police,' she called back, then stepped aside to let the two officers in. 'You'd better come in. Go straight through to the kitchen, Ray's in there.'

A man had appeared in the doorway of a room at the end of the hall.

'The police? We didn't nick the turkey, you know.'

His voice was light-hearted. Neither of them appeared too worried about a visit from police officers on Christmas Day.

Mrs Barrow was pulling out chairs for them, fussing around, inviting them to sit, clearly not sure what the correct procedure was. She sat down opposite them, next to Ray Mann who had resumed his seat. Ted noticed that Mann smelled strongly of some sort of minty fragrance, as if he'd recently got out of the shower.

'Is it about our Lily?' Mann asked them. 'Has she been drinking again?'

'Lily Barrow lives here then? She's your daughter, Mrs Barrow? And Mr Mann, what relation are you?' Polly asked.

'I live with her mam but we're not married, so I suppose you could call me her stepfather. Not a wicked one, though, we get on great.'

'Is she all right, our Lily?' the mother asked, starting to sound a bit concerned now.

'Do you know where Lily is at the moment, Mrs Barrow?' Polly asked her.

She looked at Mann before she answered, Ted noticed.

'Well, she's meant to be coming home later today. She was going to spend Christmas with us but you know what teenagers are like. She got invited to go and be with some of her mates yesterday so off she went. We haven't heard from her yet today but that's a bit like her, when she's with her friends. She's got a mobile phone, one of them pay as you go things, but she doesn't use it much at all. Certainly not to phone her mam, most of the time. Is she all right? Is she in some sort of trouble?'

'Can you tell me what she was wearing when she went out, Mrs Barrow?'

'I wasn't here when she went. I work as a cook in an old people's home and I was working late, getting all the Christmas food prepped and ready so I could have today off. Has something happened?'

Polly looked to Ted for guidance on how he wanted to play it next. He took over.

'Mrs Barrow, we've found a card with Lily's name and address on it, from a youth group.'

'Yes, that's this club thing she goes to with her mates. It's good for her, they're well supervised there. But where's our Lily?'

'I'm very sorry to have to tell you that the card was found near to the body of a young girl, approximately sixteen years old,' Ted told her, then hurried on, 'I must stress at this time that we have no formal identification, which is why it would be very helpful to know what Lily was wearing when you last saw her. Mr Mann, were you here went she went?'

The mother had gone ashen, the hand which went up to her

face trembling visibly. Wordlessly, Polly got up and went to put the kettle on. Mann was shaking his head in disbelief.

'Our Lily? No, it can't be. Not her.'

'You saw her when she went out, Mr Mann? Can you please tell us what she was wearing?'

'Eee, I don't know. I don't take much notice of clothes. Them ripped jeans they all seem to like, I think. Some sort of a top and like a bomber jacket thing. Like a Parka. Padded, sort of. But not our little Lil. Dear god, not her.'

'It's a mistake,' Mrs Barrow was saying. 'That's all. I'll ring her mobile now. She can tell you herself. That's all it will be. She dropped her card somewhere and some other poor lass is dead.'

She went to a nearby work surface to pick up a mobile phone and call a saved number. Then she shook her head, over and over, her face anguished.

'It's not working. There's nothing. Not even letting me leave a message. Oh, no, please tell me it's not my little Lily. Please.'

Gently, Polly guided her back to her seat then finished making tea, which she put in front of her. She offered one to Mann but he refused, grim-faced, teeth clenched.

'What happened to her? This lass that you found? It won't be our Lily. It can't be. But what happened to this other poor lass?'

'Mr Mann, it would be really helpful if you could try to remember anything about what Lily said or did before she went out yesterday. Anything at all which could be helpful to us,' Ted told him.

'She got a call from one of her mates, yesterday afternoon. Them from that club she goes to. She asked me would it be all right if she went off with them, to stay over for Christmas Day and come back this evening. I told her that her mam would be upset but she can be really persuasive, our Lil, so I said all right, as long as she came home today. She gave me a big hug and promised, so I let her go. Dear god, I let her go. If something's happened to her, it's all my fault.'

'Can you tell me what time she went out, Mr Mann?'

'I don't know, I didn't really notice. It was starting to come dark. Sometime after four o'clock, perhaps?'

'And did she get a lift or go out on foot?'

'No, she just went off on her own. She'd probably have got a bus into town to meet them. That's what she usually does.'

'Mrs Barrow, would it be possible for you to go with PC Fleming to have a look in Lily's room to see if you might be able to identify the exact clothes she was wearing when she left here? But could you please touch as little as possible? We might need to have a look in there later on.'

Lily's mother seemed pleased at the opportunity to prove to herself that whoever the body was, it wasn't her daughter. She was clearly still clinging on desperately to the faint hope of mistaken identity.

Ted stayed downstairs with Mann, watching him intently.

'How long have you been with Mrs Barrow, Mr Mann?' Ted asked him, almost as if he were making simple conversation.

'I, er, let's think. Just over five years now, I reckon.'

'And would you say you're close, as a family?'

'Yes, very. Lily was only little when her dad died and she was very close to him. I knew I could never fill his shoes, but I wanted her to know I would always be there for her.'

'And does she have a boyfriend at all? Or anyone she's close to?'

Mann snorted.

'Aye, she knocks around with a lad called Ashley. Ashley Barnes. Great useless long streak of piss he is too, but our Lil seems to like him.'

The two women were coming back downstairs now, PC Fleming walking behind the mother. She gave Ted a barely perceptible nod. He correctly interpreted it to mean that the mother had identified clothing the same as that found with their victim. It was looking almost certain that the dead girl was Lily Barrow.

As gently as he could, Ted explained this to the now distraught mother. Mann got up and put his arm around her, ineptly patting her back in a gesture of comfort. Ted told them that he would make arrangements for them to be taken to the mortuary as soon as possible so they could first look at the victim's clothing and then see the body. He fervently hoped that James's assistant could make it at least presentable before they did so. He and Polly would go separately to the mortuary. Ted wanted chance to talk to her on her own.

As they got back to the car, Ted turned to Polly.

'Can you tell me if you noticed anything about Lily's bedroom which struck you as odd, as significant in any way.'

'I did, Sarge. It was incredibly tidy, for one thing. And I know teenage girls can be obsessive about their privacy. I certainly was myself. But the bedroom door didn't just have a lock with a key on the inside. It had a bloody big bolt as well.'

Ted nodded to himself.

'I rather thought it might.'

'Have you got any suspects yet, Sarge?' she asked him conversationally, as they drove to the hospital where the body was being held.

Ted had phoned ahead to let them know the next of kin were coming in. Polly radioed in for someone to collect them and take them there.

'Bit too soon, until we get formal identification from the parents.'

'Family first? Isn't that usually the rule of where to look for suspects?'

'Statistically more likely than complete strangers but we could waste time chasing after someone because of preconceived ideas. We'd do better to wait for some evidence to go on.'

They arrived before the relatives. Ted went to find James's assistant to see if he was ready for them yet. They hadn't left him a lot of time to make the body presentable.

'We've done the best we can for them but it's not been easy,' he warned them. 'Just give me a shout when they arrive and they can see her more or less straight away. These things are never pleasant. There's no point in dragging out the anguish.'

Ray Mann had his arm round his partner, visibly supporting her with a strong grip. She looked drained of colour, apprehensive of the ordeal ahead. Even if the victim turned out not to be her own daughter, she was still going to have to view a young girl whose life had been violently snatched from her at a time of year when she should have been enjoying Christmas with loved ones.

Ted went to greet them, his voice quietly reassuring.

'We didn't find any personal effects with the deceased, Mrs Barrow,' Ted told her. 'No phone, or handbag or anything, just the clothing, which matches the description of what you told PC Fleming that Lily was probably wearing when she left the house. Would you like to see the clothing first, perhaps?'

The woman shook her head, tight-lipped.

'Let's just get this over with. It won't be our Lily, I'm sure it won't. But let me just have a quick look and then I can put you straight.'

'You've still not had any word from Lily?'

She shook her head.

'No, but that's Lil all over. When she's out having fun, she often forgets to call, then she's back home, all full of apology and promising never to do it again. But she always does.'

PC Fleming instinctively positioned herself next to the woman, on the other side from Mann, as they went into the room where the victim's body had been placed for them to view. As soon as Mrs Barrow saw the small, frail figure on the table, her hand flew up to her face in an attempt to stifle the anguished sob which burst from her.

'Oh, no, oh, no ...'

Now she was shaking her head violently from side to side, the other arm held out in front of her as if she wanted to block the sight from her eyes. Ted hated to have to press her but he knew he needed a definite answer. She could simply have been denying knowing the victim, although he knew she wasn't.

'Mrs Barrow, I'm very sorry, but can you please confirm for me. Is this your daughter, Lily Barrow?'

Mann was visibly angry now, tightening the arm which held the dead girl's mother up, preventing her from collapsing to the floor, which she looked likely to do at any moment.

'Of course it is, you stupid bastard. Can't you see from her mam? That's our Lil. That's our little girl. Why don't you get out there and find the bastard who's done this?'

The girl's mother was straining to get nearer to her daughter now.

'Can I hold her? Can I touch my little girl?'

The mortuary assistant, who had been hovering discreetly in the background, took a step forward.

'Of course you may, Mrs Barrow. Just hold her hand on this side and you can sit with her as long as you like. Please spend as much time with Lily as you would like to. This is your time with her.'

She moved hesitantly forward, putting out a trembling hand which lightly touched the still form under the white sheet.

Her voice was puzzled as she said, 'She's so cold ...'

'That's quite normal, Mrs Barrow,' the man said reassuringly. 'You can spend some time with her now, talk to her, if you'd like to.'

Mann was standing slightly behind her, leaving PC Fleming to be beside her, ready to offer support when it was needed. He seemed not to know what to do with himself. The lines of his face were set in what looked more like anger than any other emotion.

'Did she ...' Mrs Barrow tried to form a question but her voice broke.

She cleared her throat and tried again.

'Would she have suffered? Did someone do something to her? Before they killed her?'

The assistant looked to Ted, passing the buck on the difficult question.

'I'm afraid that Lily suffered a serious sexual assault before she was killed, Mrs Barrow. I'm very sorry.'

Mann's face contorted, darkening.

'That bastard lad she hung round with ...'

'We will be thoroughly investigating all the circumstances surrounding Lily's death,' Ted told them. 'With that in mind, as soon as we can, we would like to return to the house and carry out a thorough search, particularly of her bedroom. I'm afraid that means it would be best if you didn't return to the house until after we've carried out our examination. Is there somewhere you could stay for tonight? We can arrange a hotel room for you, if necessary.'

'You insensitive bastard,' Mann spat. 'Someone out there did this to our Lil. Coming and sniffing round our home isn't going to get you anywhere.'

As he spoke, he seemed to lose all semblance of self-control. Moving away from the girl's mother, he turned on the balls of his feet and swung a clumsy uppercut punch towards Ted.

It never connected. His target was simply no longer there. Ted neatly pivoted out of the way, putting out a considerate hand to steady Mann as he risked losing his balance and falling headlong on the tiled floor.

Ted kept hold of the man's arm, noting the strength of the muscle under his fingers, and deftly moved him further away, speaking quietly to him.

'Mr Mann, I understand your grief and I'm sorry for your loss. But seriously? This isn't the way to behave. Not here, not now. And certainly not in front of Lily's mother. She needs you now, and I need to be able to do my job, to catch her killer. Some aspects of it won't be to your liking but it's what has to be done.

'You spend as much time here as you need to, especially as Mrs Barrow needs to. We'll organise accommodation for you, if you need us to. Perhaps you can give me the keys to the house?'

'I'm not bloody doing that. Tell me when you want to go there and I'll meet you there. And we'll find a hotel for ourselves.'

'As you wish, Mr Mann. If you need to collect anything from the house, I'll arrange for the officer who brought you to accompany you inside. Please don't touch anything else.'

As he and Polly walked back to the car, she smiled at him as she said, 'Neat footwork, Sarge. I thought he was going to plant one on you for sure.'

'I wasn't going to stand still long enough to find out. Was that a natural reaction, do you think? Have you seen grieving relatives react like that before?'

'Grief does strange things to folks, and I have seen some sights, I can tell you. But there's something about Mann I don't really care for. He certainly seems to have taken against you in a big way, that's for sure.'

It was late by the time Ted got home, tired and more than a little hungry. He let himself in quietly and found Trev stretched out on the sofa, fast asleep, with the cats on top of him. One of the classic black and white film DVDs Ted had given him was playing quietly in the background and there was a glass and two empty wine bottles on the floor next to him.

Ted slid carefully down beside him. Trev only stirred when the cats did, Queen kneading his stomach with her claws out.

'Ow, Queen, you monster. Hey, you. How did today go? Did you catch the baddies?'

'Not yet. I'm sorry I'm so late.'

'Well, I can hardly complain, since it was me who pushed you into changing roles. Shall I get you something to eat?'

'Are you sober enough?' Ted asked doubtfully.

'Absolutely, officer. As a judge.'

Trev transferred the cats to Ted with exaggerated care then attempted to stand up. His legs weren't cooperating and he fell backwards in a giggling heap.

'Oops, I may have been exaggerating. Food's all ready though. And when you've finished you can drag me upstairs to have your wicked way with me.'

The meal was delicious but when Ted returned to the living room, Trev was sound asleep, snoring gently to himself.

Chapter Eighteen

James, the young pathologist, was certainly looking more cheerful than Ted felt at the prospect of an early morning inquest on a young female victim on Boxing Day.

Now that they had a name for their victim, he began with giving her details for the tape which would be running constantly for his findings as he went along. As he'd told Ted, he was only doing the preliminaries. A post-mortem on a murder victim needed to be done by a Home Office pathologist, in this case, Professor Gillingham. But James could at least give Ted something to be going on with, to get the enquiry started.

'I'm about to make the first incision, which is the part that some people find the most disturbing to watch,' James warned him. 'Ironic, really, as I'm afraid there is far more gruesome still to come. Will you be all right, do you think?'

Ted wasn't sure himself. He usually had a strong stomach but this was a whole new area for him. The clinical surroundings somehow made the pathologist's actions worse; a violation of the already damaged corpse in front of them.

'I'll just have to hope for the best. It's my first PM, too, so please excuse me in advance if I lose my breakfast. Well, I only had a cup of tea, just in case.'

'Here we go, then. Bite down on your cough sweet, think of England and all that. And remember, it's a perfectly human reaction to feel repelled by this. It's only odd types like us pathologists who are past such emotion. If anyone tells you otherwise, don't trust them.'

Ted managed better than he feared he might. At the end of the examination, he knew more about the victim than he had done before. James put her at about sixteen and put the time of death as approximately mid-evening on Christmas Eve. Although she was slightly built, James confirmed that she was fit, well toned. He suggested she may have done something like long-distance running, based on her musculature.

'We will, of course, be testing for any kind of trace of her attacker on her. Whoever raped her, and I'm almost certain from what I've seen that this was rape and not consensual, obligingly did it without a condom. We should get lucky with DNA from that source, if he's on record, but I'm afraid the results won't be speedy, not at this time of year.

'I'll email you my findings as soon as I possibly can. The preliminaries, at least, until the Professor approves the final version. He should be back later today. Various tests for drugs, alcohol, and so on will take a little longer. I'm inclined to hope she was drunk or drugged. At least that way she wouldn't have known much about what was happening to her.

'Poor lass, not a nice way to end up, and I'm sure it's just rare sentimentality on my part, but it always seems much worse when something like this happens at Christmas.'

Ted was surprised that he felt hungry when he left the hospital after the post-mortem. He found somewhere open and serving bacon rolls, even on Boxing Day, so got himself one and a hot drink which he demolished in the car before heading to the station to catch up with any developments.

He made a quick phone call on the way back in the car. He took a gamble and by-passed the DI, opting to speak directly to the DCI. He wanted to ensure he was doing the right thing in starting with a search at the girl's home, and to float the idea of a warrant, in case of any obstruction from Mann. He also wanted to ask about questioning the boyfriend and who would be doing that.

'You still have doubts over this Mann character, then? Don't forget that grief can make people behave in some strange ways, often completely out of character.'

'I appreciate that, sir, it's just that he lost it as soon as I mentioned searching the house. It could have been a coincidence, of course.'

'Right, well, you take charge of the house search. Just try not to get yourself thumped in the process. You did right to get them out of the house and tell them to stay out. I'll send Jack out to find the boyfriend. As least we can trust him not to rough him up like Hughes might. He can start interviewing him, and you can go through the tapes of what was said with Jack later on. Then we'll have a bit of a catch-up at the end of the day.'

'And the DI, sir? I haven't updated him yet. I thought I'd speak to you first as you'd told me to keep you informed at all stages.'

'You leave the DI to me. It's time I took more of an overview on what's been going on here. Get yourself back here now so you can liaise with Uniform for some bodies to help with the search, and get on to the crime scene lot. There may be nothing to find at the house but let's rule out the obvious before we go any further.'

Ted made sure he was at the house before the time he'd told Mann and Mrs Barrow that the search was taking place. He'd taken the precaution of having the doors sealed as a scene of crime to avoid anyone tampering with any evidence. He hoped Mann wasn't going to make a scene. It was distasteful for all of them but it was simply routine. The DCI was poised to sort out a warrant the minute it was needed.

Mann was immediately angry and defensive, as soon as he arrived but Mrs Barrow silenced him with a hand on his arm.

'Just let them do their job, Ray. We've got nothing to hide. We just want to see the monster who's done this to our Lily behind bars, where he belongs.'

Then she turned to Ted.

'Go ahead, love, you do whatever's necessary to find who killed our Lily.'

'Thank you, Mrs Barrow. We'll try not to inconvenience you for too long, and I really am very sorry for your loss.'

Ted headed first to the girl's bedroom with some of the Forensics team. They might as well start with trying to find out all they could about their victim from how she lived her life. Her mother had told them which room it was. Mann was still looking disgruntled by their presence in the house.

One of the investigators opened the door to the room and pushed it back so they could get a look inside without immediately going in.

'Well, my teenage daughter always keeps her bedroom door locked from the inside when she's in there and from the outside when she goes out,' the investigator observed to Ted. 'So this one obviously wasn't as paranoid about her privacy as some.'

'When I was here with PC Fleming, she noticed that there was a big bolt on the inside of the door,' Ted told her. 'So that would seem to indicate she didn't want anyone going in there when she was inside it.'

'The bed's been stripped,' the investigator observed. 'That's a bit odd, surely? Didn't she just go out with friends on Christmas Eve? Surely she didn't strip her bed before she went? I know my teenthing certainly wouldn't have thought of doing that, without a very good reason.'

'I don't have children and I don't know all that much about teenagers really, so any help you can give me would be greatly appreciated. Sorry, I don't know your name.'

'Isabel,' she told him.

'Ted.'

'Well, Ted, the next thing that strikes me is I wish that my daughter kept her room as tidy as this one. Was this how it was when you first saw it, or have the parents been tidying up for some reason? Why are there no clothes strewn all over everywhere? How old was the victim?'

'Sixteen,' Ted told her. 'And no, the officer who came upstairs with the mother to look at what clothing the girl might have been wearing said it was obsessively tidy. And the parents haven't been back in, without supervision, since they ID'd the body.'

'Strange, but possibly not significant. Right, I'd best get to work and see if I can find anything to help you.'

The room revealed very little. It was neat and tidy everywhere; even the laundry basket was empty. The only significant finding was an empty vodka bottle, underneath the bed in the far corner where it was easily overlooked.

'Perhaps this is the reason she had that bolt on the door?' Isabel suggested. 'If she was in here getting hammered, she wouldn't want the parents to know, I imagine.'

'She had been cautioned for a public order offence involving drink, when she was fifteen.'

'Well, I'm not telling you how to do your job, Ted, but it might be worth finding out what was going on in her life to make her hit the bottle like that. It may be something and nothing. We all know there's a worrying trend towards a heavy drinking culture in young people.

'A lot of it is to do with peer pressure, of course. But sometimes there are underlying issues which lead them to heavy drinking. Trying to blot out stuff going on in their lives which they can't deal with. Sixteen can be a pretty miserable age. All that teenage angst.'

'I really appreciate all your help, Isabel. It's no secret that this is my first murder case and I honestly know nothing about teenage girls.'

'What, nothing?' she ask him teasingly, then light dawned on her face. 'Oh, sorry, Ted, that was a bit tactless. Teenage boys, then, perhaps?'

Ted grinned at her. It made him look like a teenager himself.

'Much more my sort of thing.'

Ted arranged for the laptop found in the girl's bedroom to be tagged and taken back to the station. It was possible that it could reveal a lot about her from her emails and internet history. He also asked Mrs Barrow about the stripped bed but she looked at him blankly.

'I noticed that when I went up with the police lady yesterday but I didn't do it and I can't think why Lily would have. Not at Christmas, not when she was going off out to be with her friends.'

'I did it,' Mann muttered. 'I thought I was being helpful. I was putting some of my shirts on to wash and you're always going on about making it economical with a full load, so I had a look in our Lil's room to see what needed to go on. I thought I'd take the sheets and what was in the basket.'

Ted didn't miss the look the woman gave him. It was clearly unusual for him to do anything like that. He logged it away in his mind with other unanswered questions.

'Where are they now, Mr Mann?' he asked.

'Still in the bloody washer, for all I know. Funnily enough, once we got the news about a lass's body being found, the last thing on my mind was sorting out the bloody laundry, I was that worried about our Lily.'

'We'll take all Lily's things with us for testing,' Ted told them.

Mrs Barrow looked puzzled.

'I don't understand. Does that mean you think that something happened to Lily here? In our house? Was she not killed where she was found?'

'It really is just routine,' Ted reassured her, neatly evading the question.

He tried to think of something plausible to say which sounded like a reasonable explanation.

'There may be no need, but it's better to take everything now so we don't have to come and disturb you again. We're also going to need to take a DNA sample from you, Mr Mann. Again it's routine. You mentioned that you hugged Lily just before she went out so clearly we'll need to be able to eliminate you from our enquiries.'

Mann's face darkened and he looked to be on the point of exploding.

'Just let them do their job, love. Please,' Mrs Barrow implored him 'Anything that will help them catch whoever did this to our Lily. Please, Ray.'

The look of open loathing Mann was sending Ted's way was disturbing. He may be overreacting, imagining things that weren't really there. He was probably going to look foolish, ordering a load of freshly-laundered bedding and underwear to be seized and taken for one thing, but he was prepared to take that risk. There was something about Ray Mann that he didn't like.

Ted and Jack went for a pint together at the end of the day. For the time being, progress on the enquiry was slow, other than writing up notes and waiting for forensic evidence from the site and from the body. They hadn't yet tracked down the boyfriend.

Ted sent off a quick text to tell Trev he'd be slightly late. Trev had been to lunch with his boss, Geoff, and his wife. Ted had been invited but had had to cry off, with the murder case to deal with. It meant he had a valid excuse for an after work drink without feeling guilty. There was still plenty of food at home, the leftovers from Christmas dinner, so there would be no problem over what to eat. He suspected Trev might not need to eat much anyway, after a big lunch, although he always had a voracious appetite.

Knowing how much his partner liked a drink, Ted had insisted he get a taxi to and from his boss's house, and had left cash out to pay for it. There was not only the risk of an accident. Ted didn't think it would go down all that well at his new station if his partner was booked for drink-driving.

The nearby pub which the station's officers favoured was called The Grapes, handily close by. The landlord, Dave, was getting to know Ted, the newcomer, by now.

'Pint for you, Jack? And one of your ginger beers, Ted? I could make you a proper Gunner if you like? It is Christmas, after all.'

'I don't even know what it is,' Ted told him.

'Similar to what you usually drink, ginger beer and lime, but with some ginger ale and Angostura bitters.'

'I'll give it a go, but can you leave the Angostura out, please?'

'Are you as religiously tee-total as that, Ted?' Jack Gregson asked him. 'Have you always been a non-drinker?'

'Not by a long chalk,' Ted grinned. 'I was known to put away the odd snakebite or four. My dad was an alcoholic, though. I decided I'd better stop when it killed him, in case it ran in the family.'

The two men took their drinks over to find an empty table. Ted, always an SFO by training, positioned himself so he could see the whole of the bar, especially the door. As he sat down, he self-consciously tugged down the hem of his black jeans, realising he was wearing the Willie Nelson socks Trev had bought him as a joke Christmas present.

The gesture was not lost on Jack, though. He grinned and hitched up one leg of his own trousers, revealing bright shocking pink socks covered in sparkly Christmas trees.

'You think those are bad? This was the wife's idea of a joke. But she said if I dared to wear them at work all day I'd get to unwrap her stocking when I got home, so it was worth giving it a go.'

They spent a companionable half-hour in each other's company, talking shop some of the time, the rest of it just making conversation, getting to know one another better.

When he got home, Ted put his car away and let himself into the house. He followed the sound of the television and found his partner on the settee watching the same film he'd slept through the day before. He was, as usual, buried under cats.

Ted kissed him and sat down next to him.

'Hard day? Any closer to a result yet?'

'Not yet, but we're working on it. Did you have a nice lunch? And who's this?'

He was looking pointedly at a fourth purring feline, curled up and seemingly quite at home amongst the other three.

'This?' Trev asked innocently, stroking the small bundle of long grey fur. 'You noticed, then?'

'Of course I noticed. I'm a policeman. What was it, another catastrophic steering failure going past the cats' home?'

'This is Brian. He's been hanging around work for a while now, all thin and hungry. You don't mind, do you?'

'Well, as nobody else seems to, it would be churlish of me if I did. Especially at Christmas.'

He reached over and gently picked up the new addition.

'Hello, Brian. Welcome to your new home. And now we've got Queen, Freddie, Mercury and Brian, I suppose that only leaves us with John and Roger to get next.'

Chapter Nineteen

It was back to work as normal for the team the day after Boxing Day, with everyone in now there was no Bank Holiday pay to worry about for the budget. Now they had an ID for their victim, they could start the enquiry in earnest and they needed all hands on deck.

Ted wasn't surprised to see the DCI turn up for morning briefing. But he was more than a little surprised to see the DI, Lennie Grimshaw, had left his sickbed to attend. Jack Gregson saw Ted's expression and sidled over to murmur in his ear.

'A nice sexy murder case, with lots of Brownie points up for grabs? You can bet your last pay cheque our Lennie would drag himself off his deathbed to get his name stuck on that as SIO. Watch him, though. He goes off hunches. His are good, a lot of the time; he has a good nose. But he doesn't bother to back anything up with mere formalities like evidence. That's left to me and the footsoldiers to chase up, so we've lost more than one case because of him.'

Grimshaw was looking daggers at the two of them by now.

'If the two sergeants could stop gossiping like fishwives for a moment, we can perhaps get on. DS Darling, I hear you went to see the family at the house then went with them to the mortuary when they identified the body, although I'm not sure I understand why you needed to do both.'

Jim Baker was standing a little way behind the DI, his arms crossed over his barrel chest. His voice was a low rumble as he put in, 'That was sanctioned by me, DI Grimshaw. I thought

DS Darling might be able to give us a valuable insight into the family circumstances from the start, then we don't waste time rushing off on wild goose chases. Let's hear what he has to say.'

'Advantage Big Jim,' Jack Gregson said under his breath to Ted. 'Lennie to serve. New balls, please, for the next balls-up.'

Ted bent his head in a show of looking at his notes to hide a smile. He liked Gregson, loved his sense of humour and he was certainly invaluable with his insider knowledge. He put on his serious face then delivered his observations on Lily Barrow's home circumstances.

He tried to keep it factual, but he added, 'I just wondered about Mann, the stepfather. He was very quick to tell me how he'd hugged Lily the last time he saw her. And then there was the question of the big bolt on the inside of her bedroom door.'

DC Robbie Hughes made a scornful noise.

'I'm guessing you don't have kids then, Sarge? And certainly not stepchildren? I hug my stepdaughter most days. Does that make me a kiddy-fiddler or a killer? And my son is so obsessive about keeping his bedroom private he'd install land mines if he could get away with it.'

'I was just flagging it up as possibly worth a mention,' Ted replied, keeping his tone neutral. 'It may be perfectly innocent. But it could, of course, also be him alibiing himself for any of his DNA being found on the body.'

'All right, you two, play nicely,' Grimshaw cut in. 'Tell us about the boyfriend, Ted. It'll be him. The stepfather's too obvious.'

'My money's already on the boyfriend, boss, you'll get no argument from me,' Hughes said virtuously.

'Behave, the bloody pair of you,' the DCI cut in, his voice angry. 'A young lass is dead, don't any of you forget. Those of us who have children, especially daughters, know better than most how bloody insensitive it sounds for you to be gambling over this.'

There was a mutter of 'Sorry, sir,' from the DI and DC Hughes but Ted noticed that they rang particularly hollow.

'The stepfather gave me the boyfriend's name, Ashley Barnes, and his address, in Hazel Grove,' Ted continued. 'He's eighteen, a student. We've run checks on him and he's come up squeaky clean. No record for anything, not even any cautions or interviews recorded.'

'Let's haul him in and interview him. Robbie, you talk to him. If he knows anything, you'll get it out of him, if anyone can.'

Ted didn't like the tone with which he said that, nor the wolfish grin of anticipation which appeared on Hughes' face.

'Sir, shouldn't we at least start with some basic enquiries, to see if the boyfriend has an alibi, before we bring him in? I'd also like to dig a little deeper into Ray Mann's background. There's something about him and his reactions to all of this which doesn't sit quite right with me.'

'And you're basing this on your vast experience of ... remind me how many murder cases you've worked on so far, DS Darling?' the DI asked him sarcastically.

Before Ted could answer, the DCI straightened up and took a step forward, pointing a thick finger straight at him.

'What he said,' he rumbled decisively. 'The DS is absolutely right. There's no bloody point bringing anyone in until we're a bit more sure of ourselves. Then we do it properly, by the book. We start with the evidence and work from there. And that means we may have to wait for some DNA results, which won't be quick. Not at this time of year. We do not guess at a suspect then try to make the evidence fit them. We've been down that road before on other cases, it's cost us, and we're not going there again.

'DS Darling was quite right to start with the house search. That's just basic procedure. We've got the DNA sample now from the step-dad so he can be ruled out – or in. We're going to get DNA samples from any and all males she's likely to have had contact with. We're going to look for means, motive, opportunity. You know. Proper bloody police work.

'And if I hear any more talk of betting going on to do with an ongoing case, then I'm going to rip up the rule book and kick arses so hard you won't know what's hit you. Everybody clear on that?'

This time the collective mumble of, 'Sir,' sounded much more convincing.

'Right, get on with it. Let me know the minute we get any update at all, particularly from the PM or the DNA samples. But I don't imagine either is going to be quick, Ted?'

'James promised we should hopefully get the full PM results some time today, once the Professor is back and has gone over everything. He's also trying to hurry through the analysis on the semen sample from the body but again, it's not going to be immediate. Preliminary findings suggest death from multiple head wounds from a blunt instrument, probably the large stone found near the body, and evidence of rape with manual restraint.'

The DCI turned on his heel to head back to his office, saying over his shoulder as he did so, 'DS Darling. A word.'

Jack Gregson made a sympathetic face at Ted as he followed the DCI, wondering why he'd been singled out. He thought he'd followed correct procedure to date and been as thorough as he could, but maybe he'd slipped up somewhere.

'Shut the door,' Baker said as he sat down at his desk. Ted wasn't sure what he should do so he stood there like a spare part.

'Good for you, having the balls to challenge the DI like that. Between you and me, Lennie is a complete arsehole, although I shouldn't say it. I suspect you've already worked that out for yourself, though. He's on his way out, probably sooner than he realises, if he doesn't get his act together. This case is his last big chance to make a name for himself, so watch your back. He's after the glory and he won't care how many faces he tramples on to get it.

'Right, pull up a chair and tell me what you think about the rest of the team, while we've got a bit of a lull waiting for test results. If you're planning on staying with us – and I hope you are – I want to know which ones you'd want to keep and which you think we should be moving on. Like I said, I've inherited some of them and they wouldn't have been my first choice, so I'm interested in your opinions on them.

'There's some coffee in the machine there. Help yourself, and pour me one, will you?'

One swallow of the foul, thick, black brew from the glass jug was enough to tell Ted it was not something he should be drinking, even early on. Not unless he wanted his heart to be racing and fluttering in his chest for the rest of the day. He made a token show of sipping it, then put it to one side, glad of the excuse to talk about the team members rather than force himself to drink it.

'You were right about Jack Gregson, sir. He's first rate. An excellent DS, really knows his stuff. He's been a great help to me, and very tactful with my lack of experience. It can't be easy for him having to babysit me and knowing I'm on fast-track, but he's been brilliant about it.'

Baker nodded his agreement, taking big swallows of his coffee. Ted had no idea how he could stomach it.

'Robbie Hughes has a bit of attitude. He clearly resents me being here. I suspect he's also someone who likes to take short cuts. And from what the DI said just now, I wonder about his interview technique, sir.'

'Spot on, Ted. We have to keep an eye on him. More than one suspect he's been alone with has had an unfortunate fall and gained a black eye or something. We've never caught him out, but I wouldn't trust him further than I could throw him. Go on.'

'Maurice Brown, sir. I get the feeling he's a bit of a skiver...'

'With a capital S.'

'And maybe a plodder. But he was brilliant with Betty Betts. So kind to her. It was a different side to him. I can imagine he's a fantastic dad to his twins.'

'But does that necessarily make him a good copper? Especially as you've already seen how that side of him affects his time-keeping. Does it earn him a place on the team?'

'I think so, sir. Maybe some more supervision, a tighter rein, can sort out his negative side. But no amount of training can give someone that kind of human quality. I imagine he'd be good with any type of victim.'

'You've not heard his nickname, then?'

When Ted shook his head, Big Jim went on, 'They call him Daddy Hen because he's so good with all the little chicks. He's a lazy bastard and you're right, he's a Class A skiver. But he's got a quality that's hard to find. He's a genuinely kind man, would do anything for anyone who needed his help. Good, Ted, you're summing them up much as I would. Who else?'

'DC O'Connell, sir. Rob. He's young, he's new, so far he's quiet, but he shows a lot of promise, I think. Intelligent, thorough.'

The DCI was nodding again in agreement.

'Can I say something, sir?'

'That's the general idea.'

'You might not like it, though.'

'Try me. I'm not likely to try kicking your arse. I've seen your CV. I know about all the black belts and the shooting trophies.'

'Well, sir, there's the question of gender and ethnicity imbalance in the team.'

'God help me, you're not going to go all PC on me now, are you, Ted? Just as I was getting to like you and agree with what you were saying.'

'It has to be said, sir. And I'd be surprised if I was the first to mention it. The team is entirely IC1 males at the moment.'

'That's because I pick coppers on their ability to do their job, not for whether they're white or black or any other colour, and not just for their gender. I don't do positive discrimination.'

'But if you were thinking of bringing in anyone new, sir, could I at least suggest you consider bearing that point in mind?'

Jim Baker was looking at him over the rim of his coffee mug as he drained the last of the contents. Then he set the mug back on his desk.

'You've got some bottle, I'll give you that. You're right, of course. It has been mentioned. The team isn't yours yet, but play your cards right, especially with this case, and there's a chance it could be, one day. Then we can discuss how we can make it more inclusive.

'Anyway, I've taken you on, haven't I? I'm not hypocritical enough to pretend I'm entirely comfortable with the way you live your life. But you're the first qu ... openly gay officer I've ever had on my team. So that's a start.'

'Gay, sir. It's only right to say "openly" if you'd call yourself openly straight.'

'Go on, get back to work, you cheeky bugger, before I regret my decision,' Baker told him, but Ted noticed the slight grin with which he said it.

Chapter Twenty

Ted ran into Kevin Turner on the car park as they both headed into work at the start of the day.

'You've got my officers worried, Ted,' he told him.

'Why's that?'

'All this please and thank you stuff, from CID to the humble Woodentops. It's almost as if you think they're human beings. They think you're an imposter.'

'Well, with my own recent experience with a couple of clowns at Longsight, I'm trying to stay polite.'

The briefing room, when the team started filing in, was beginning to look like a serious crime enquiry was under way. The Big Boss was leaning against a desk in the background but he looked poised to intervene the minute there was anything he didn't like and wanted done differently.

DI Grimshaw was conducting the briefing. Ted was surprised at the change in him. He looked animated, eager. He could clearly smell the chance of a good result. Ted remembered the warnings about him being the one to grab any glory which was going. He didn't care. As far as he was concerned, the job was about getting justice for Lily Barrow and her family.

'First off, we need the boyfriend bringing in. Jack couldn't find him yesterday, so Robbie, that's one for you.'

'Not couldn't find him, boss,' Jack Gregson told him. 'He wasn't there. The neighbour told me he and his mam and dad had gone over to spend Christmas with the nan, in Holmfirth.

L. M. KRIER

They do it every year. They're due back today.'

The DCI spoke up.

'I want DS Gregson on the boyfriend. And I want DS Darling with him.'

'Two DS's to haul in one suspect, boss? Is that really the best use of manpower, with respect?' the DI asked him.

The look Jim Baker gave him told all present what he thought about his 'with respect'.

'DS Darling would be the first to admit he lacks a bit of experience in murder enquiries. Look on this as a training exercise. DS Gregson has the experience and the proven record. Therefore I'd like him to be the one to show DS Darling the ropes on this.

'And for the record, we are not "hauling in a suspect". We are interviewing someone with known connections to the victim with a view to deciding whether or not to bring him in for interview under caution.'

Lennie Grimshaw wasn't used to having his chain jerked in public and he didn't look best pleased about it. He wanted to go out in a blaze of glory, with a nice big fat tick on the crime statistics in his name.

'Whatever you say, sir. You're the boss.'

Jim Baker was too professional to take it any further during a briefing, but from the expression on his face, the matter was a long way from over between the two of them.

'In the meantime,' the DI continued, 'we need to be looking into Lily's circle of contacts. We need to find out everything we can about her, the people she hung round with. Trace her last known movements. Get some door-to-door done, see if anyone saw her leave her home on Christmas Eve. Was she on her own? Where was she heading?

'Check cameras, including traffic cams, to see if she went off somewhere in a vehicle. We need to fill in the blanks between her leaving the house at … What time did the stepfather say she went out, DS Darling?'

160

'Some time after four, as it was starting to turn dark, sir. He said she went out on foot, probably with the intention of catching a bus into town.'

'Right, so, we check the buses near her house, see if anyone saw her. We've got the photo from the parents, let's get that circulated. Posters, if we need to. "Did you see this girl?" That sort of thing. Press conference, yet, boss?' Grimshaw asked the DCI.

'Let's just see what legwork can produce first, keep that in reserve if we can't get anywhere.'

'What about the stepfather, sir? Are we looking into him?' Ted asked.

'What is it with you and the stepfather?' Grimshaw asked him, making light of it. 'You seem to have him convicted already on the strength of him saying he'd hugged the lass. We'll look into anyone connected to her, of course, that's just routine.'

'And would it be all right if I looked into that caution the girl received, sir? The one for drinking? Just in case she gave any reason at the time for behaving like that.'

Grimshaw gave a theatrical sigh and looked up towards the ceiling, shaking his head.

'Teenagers get drunk, Sergeant. Quite often. Maybe you never did but it's really not all that unusual. You must surely have come across it in your Uniform days? There isn't always a particular reason for it.'

'I appreciate that, sir. But sometimes people drink because they're deeply troubled. It won't take up much time if I talk to Inspector Turner to see if anything was recorded on her file at the time.'

'If it makes you feel happy. But just remember, this is a serious crime investigation. We're not bloody social workers.

'Right, all of you, you know what needs doing. Get cracking. Let's see if you can't have something positive to report by the end of the day.'

As the briefing broke up, Jack Gregson moved closer to Ted and spoke quietly.

'I'm with you, Ted. We need to look into all aspects of this. It worries me that Lennie's doing his usual trick of blithely going after the person he thinks is guilty. We're taking an awful lot of what Mann told you as gospel without checking it out.'

'I'm glad it's not just me who thinks that. Mann might be innocent, but the DI seems to be accepting his word for it that the girl went out by herself on Christmas Eve and that's the last time he saw her. Shouldn't we be getting some corroboration of that?'

Gregson chuckled.

'Careful, Ted, you're starting to sound like a proper detective. Of course we should. Look, there's no point us rushing round to see the boyfriend. Let's give them enough time to get back from Holmfirth and at least unpack their bags. If the lad actually comes back from there, that immediately makes me think he might well be innocent. Why would he come back here if he'd killed his girlfriend?

'You go off and talk to Kevin Turner, see if there are any notes about that drinking offence, then we'll try a visit to Hazel Grove late morning.'

Ted tapped at Kevin Turner's door and waited for a response before going in.

'I wondered if you had a minute, sir?'

'Sir? Don't be bloody daft, just because we're in the station. You only need that in public, and only then if you're showing off. Plonk yourself and tell me what us humble minions in Uniform can do for you high-flyers from upstairs in the gods. And you forgot to say please.'

Ted explained what it was he was interested in and his reasoning.

'I may be going off in completely the wrong direction, but I just want to explore all angles.'

'If you're going the opposite way to Lennie then you're probably right. He's had some good results but it's mostly been guesswork. He's lost a few, too. More than a few.'

'Why's he still in post, then?' Ted asked him.

'Oh, come on, Ted, don't be naive. Friends in high places? Funny handshakes? It all goes on, you know. Talking of high places, how's the Big Boss bearing up, with the latest news?'

Ted gave him a querying look.

'I don't follow you.'

'This place is a gossip mill. I'm surprised you've not heard. It seems his missus is now shagging an executive officer. She's gone right through the ranks and now she's after bigger trophies.'

'I try to stay out of gossip,' Ted told him, with a mild hint of reproach. 'There's been enough rumours flying round about me. Most of them untrue. So I don't listen.'

'Well, I'm with you as a rule, but it's an open secret, what she's like. I can't have been the only one who noticed she had her hands all over your Trev at the boss's drinks do. I suppose it was only a matter of time before she set her sights on the top brass. I feel sorry for Big Jim. He's a nice bloke, a proper family man and she's just a maneater, for some reason.

'Leave this with me. I'll see if there are any notes on your young lass that might help you. Terrible thing. I can't imagine what it must be like for the parents. Happy to help if I can.'

Jack Gregson drove the service vehicle the short distance to the house in Hazel Grove where their information told them that Lily Barrow's boyfriend, Ashley Barnes, lived. There was no sign of a parked vehicle at the property, unless it was already in the garage, so there was no way of knowing if anyone was at home.

Jack and Ted went to the front door and rang the bell. It was an old-fashioned, rather cheesy, chiming tune, but it led to the door being opened. A tall, lanky youth stood in the doorway, looking at them through thick glasses which gave him a studious air.

'Ashley Barnes?' Gregson asked him. 'DS Gregson, DS Darling, Stockport police. Could we have a word with you, please?'

They were holding up their IDs and Ted noticed the youth had to lean closer to see them.

'What's it about?'

His voice was curious rather than suspicious.

'Can we come in please, rather than talk on the doorstep? It's none too warm out here.'

'Yes, sorry, of course. Come into the kitchen. We've just got back from my nan's. My parents have gone straight back out shopping. Mum was worried we didn't have enough food in but honestly, we've eaten so much there over Christmas we could do with a day off from food.'

He led the way into a bright, clean kitchen and indicated the pine chairs around a scrubbed table. If he had any knowledge of or involvement in Lily Barrow's death, he was certainly a cool customer. He didn't sit down. He stood leaning up against a work surface looking at them.

'Do you know Lily Barrow, Ashley?' Jack Gregson asked him.

'Yes, she's a friend of mine. Is she all right? I've been trying to contact her over Christmas but I've not had a reply to texts or calls.'

'Is she your girlfriend?'

'No, not in the sense you probably mean. She's a friend who is also a girl. Is she all right?'

The two men exchanged a look.

'Ashley,' Gregson began. 'I'm sorry but we're here because we're investigating Lily's death. She was found dead on Christmas morning.'

Ashley Barnes swallowed loudly. Then he did it again. It wasn't enough. He whirled round, shoved his face into the kitchen sink and started heaving and groaning.

Wordlessly, Ted went to him, ran him a glass of water and passed him some kitchen roll from the holder nearby.

'Are you all right now, Ashley?'

'It's the shock. I never expected … What happened to her?'

'Sit down for a moment. Shall I make you a drink of something hot?'

'No. Thanks, no, I'll be fine. Just give me a minute.'

He was looking up at Ted now, myopic eyes blurred by tears which looked genuine enough to him.

'How did she …? Was it some sort of an accident?'

'Not an accident, Ashley,' Ted told him quietly. 'We think she was murdered.'

Now the youth was staring at him in undisguised horror.

'Murder? But why would anyone … Was it him?'

'Who?' Ted asked him. He saw shutters go down on the youth's face but pressed on, 'It would really help us with our enquiries if you shared any suspicions you have. Anything at all.'

'No, nothing, forget it. I don't know anything. I've been away at my nan's. I haven't seen Lily since I went.'

'Can anyone verify that?' Gregson asked him.

'All of my family. Most of nan's neighbours. And all of the congregation for Midnight Mass at Holy Trinity. My nan's very well known in the community. People were popping in and out all the time so lots of people saw me right from when we arrived, on Christmas Eve, until we left this morning. When did it happen?'

Jack Gregson ignored his question and carried on with more of his own.

'How did you travel over?'

'With my parents. My dad drove.'

'Did you use the car on your own at any time?'

'I don't drive.'

'Don't or can't?'

'Both. I don't because I can't. My eyesight isn't good enough. I can't see well enough to even try driving, let alone read a number plate to pass a test. I need surgery to correct my vision but they want to wait a bit before they do it, until I'm a bit older.'

Ted took over the questioning.

'Ashley, who did you mean when you asked "was it him"? You clearly had someone in mind. Who was that? Did Lily confide in you about something?'

'She was my friend. Sometimes she told me stuff, in confidence.'

'How did you meet her?'

'She threw up on my shoes in a pub.'

'Did she often get drunk?'

'Quite often, yes. She had a lot going on. She drank to forget.'

'Were you sleeping with her, Ashley?' Jack Gregson asked him.

'No. We were friends. It wasn't like that. She didn't want to sleep with anyone.'

Ted hitched his chair a little closer to the kitchen table and leaned on his arms, looking closely into Ashley Barnes' face.

'And did that have something to do with the reason she had a solid bolt on the inside of her bedroom door, Ashley?'

Barnes blinked rapidly. Several times in succession. Ted pressed on.

'Ashley, we're not interviewing you as a suspect. You're someone with information which could be vital to our enquiries. Anything at all you could tell us might be helpful. At some point we may need you to come to the station to give a statement on the record, but we just need some help now. What can you tell us?'

The youth gave a resigned sigh.

'Lily drank a lot and kept her bedroom door bolted from

the inside because she told me her stepfather was raping her. Regularly.'

'Lennie's not going to like this,' Jack Gregson chuckled as he drove them back to the station. 'He's got his money firmly on the boyfriend. We can check Barnes's alibis out easily enough, but what did you think of his credibility, Ted?'

'I found him very credible. I also think that the DI saying the stepfather was too obvious is a perfect application for Occam's razor.'

'Now you've lost me there. I'm not as smart as you graduate entry types. Explain.'

'One application is "other things being equal, simpler explanations are generally better than more complex ones". And the simplest is that Mann had the means and the opportunity to sexually assault Lily. He was also the last person to see her alive, as far as we know at the moment.

'It's easy to dismiss him as too obvious. But sometimes the most obvious explanation is the correct one. If you hear galloping hooves and you're not on the plains of Africa, it's more likely to be horses than zebra, as someone wiser than me once said.'

'So now all we need is some solid forensic evidence to connect Mann to Lily for more than just a hug. No wonder he stripped the bed. Even if he didn't kill her in the house, if he made a habit of sleeping with her, he wouldn't want us finding any traces on the sheets.

'We'll need to get the Professor on the case. James will have done a good job but it's Hard G who'll need to sign off on this one if we want to get a solid murder conviction.'

'Hard G?' Ted queried.

Gregson laughed.

'You've not yet had the privilege of meeting our Home Office pathologist. Professor Roger Gillingham. With a Hard G, as he always tells everyone. And that's not the only hard thing about him. He has a terrible reputation with the women. He's like the male equivalent of the Big Boss's wife. Yet he's a brilliant forensic pathologist. Reputedly the best in the country. If anyone can help us get Ray Mann, Hard G will be the one.'

Chapter Twenty-one

'That's just hearsay though,' DI Lennie Grimshaw scoffed when Ted and Jack reported back on their visit to Ashley Barnes.

'We're liaising with the West Yorkshire force in Holmfirth to see if they can check out his alibi for us, but it looks likely to be pretty solid. Lily was killed on Christmas Eve, according to the preliminary PM report. It's hard to see how Ashley could have slipped away from a family gathering to drive his dad's car, when he can't drive, to get back here, kill Lily, then drive back there for the rest of the Christmas celebrations, boss.'

'Hearsay again, Jack. How do you know his eyesight's as bad as he says?'

'We'll check his medical records, of course, but he certainly has never been issued with a licence,' Gregson told him patiently.

DC Rob O'Connell was new to the team. Ted hadn't heard him say much, although whatever he did add was always worthwhile, and he was a hard worker. He spoke up now.

'Sir, I've made a start on traffic camera footage. We've got a sighting of a car registered to Ray Mann on Bramhall Lane South, near to the junction of Midland Road, heading towards Bramhall just after 19.00 hours on Christmas Eve. Single male occupant.'

Grimshaw was quiet for a moment. He'd been so sure it wasn't the stepfather. Then he reverted to one of his old tricks.

Deflect the embarrassment from himself by instant scapegoating.

'Did you not ask him for his movements when you spoke to him, DS Darling?'

'Not yet, sir, no. That's why I asked if he would be interviewed.'

'Right, well, I'd be happier with a bit more to go on than a traffic camera sighting and a lot of rumour. Let's start chasing up Forensics and see what they've got for us. And someone get on to the Professor to see when we can get the definitive PM report. Still if he's got anything more since the preliminary findings or if not, when he will have. Keep me posted.'

With that, he disappeared off back to his office and shut the door firmly behind him. Rob O'Connell had clearly been about to say something else so he looked to Gregson, his DS. Jack and Ted went over to hear what he had to say.

'Good work, Rob. Let's get the images enhanced and see if that gives us anything more to go on,' Gregson told him.

'Sarge, there's more. The DI just didn't give me enough time to say so.'

Rob was scrolling through images as he spoke. He froze the screen on a particular one.

'Here. You can't make much out, but there on the pavement, in front of Mann's car. There's someone hurrying along on foot.'

Both Ted and Jack were peering closely at the screen.

'You think that might be Lily? And Mann might be chasing after her in the car?'

'No way of being sure at the moment, Sarge, but I'll see if getting it enhanced makes any difference. But surely it will leave Mann with some explaining to do, at the very least?'

Ted looked to Jack Gregson as he asked, 'So what now? Do we bring Mann in, or wait until we have a better hand?'

Jack moved back to his own desk, jerking his head for Ted to follow him.

'Let's just get a bit more to hit him with. Much as I hate to agree with Lennie, it is mostly hearsay at the moment. If we just have one concrete fact to slap him with, I'd be happier. I'll sort out some more house-to-house, see if anyone spotted either the girl leaving on foot or Mann taking his car out on Christmas Eve.

'Because you're new, and I'm kind, I'll talk to the Professor, rather than leaving that to you.'

'Is he as bad as that?' Ted asked curiously.

Jack put on a plummy accent as he replied, 'Oh, my dear boy, yes.' Then he reverted to his own Stockport accent as he continued, 'Totally up himself. Independently stinking rich. Thinks we're all stupid plebs without a braincell to our names. Bloody good at his job, though. The best there is. If there's anything at all anywhere on Lily's body that links Mann in the way we're looking for, he'll have found it, even if James missed it.

'You chase up Forensics, see if you can get some early results for us. If you treat them right, they can be surprisingly helpful. Who was in charge?'

'Isabel.'

'Oh, she's great. Turn on the charm and she'll do all she can to help.'

'It might not work,' Ted grinned. 'She already knows I'm gay.'

'Even better. She might enjoy the challenge.'

'Hello, Ted, I was just about to call you,' Isabel told him when Ted got through to her. 'I wanted to know your secret. You must be the jammiest officer in the force. If I saw anything like this happen in one of those TV crime dramas I sometimes watch, I would be laughing my arse off at how far-fetched it was.'

'I don't follow you.'

'You know you were apologising for sending us a bag of

clean washing? Well, your Mr Mann was clearly not used to doing the laundry. He'd put it in the machine, put washing powder in, set the programme and everything. Only he'd then forgotten to switch it on.'

'You're kidding!'

She laughed.

'I told you it was far-fetched. The even better news is that we've been able to identify semen stains on the sheets, which I believe are the ones from the victim's bed. Now, contrary to what you will see on those TV shows, we can't get an immediate DNA match but we're pushing that through as fast as we possibly can because I know you're up against it on this one.

'And look, I don't want to try telling you how to do your job, but may I make a suggestion?'

'I'd be really grateful. I make no secret of the fact that I'm new to this and I want to get it right.'

'Well, we recovered the sheets from the washing machine, not the bed. So we have no evidence to show that they came from the victim's bed. Mann will simply claim they were from his own bed and he'd been having sex there with his missus. All perfectly normal and hard to disprove.

'But if you could get us the mattress from the girl's bed for testing, there's a possibility that we might be able to recover enough from that to show semen stains there and get a match to those. We can also probably match fibres from the sheet and the mattress. Now that would make it much harder for him to explain away any plausible circumstances in which he would be ejaculating in his stepdaughter's bed.'

'Isabel, that is amazingly helpful. Thanks so much. I really appreciate it. I don't suppose I could buy you a drink some time, by way of a thank you?'

'Why, Ted, are you asking me out?' she asked teasingly.

As Ted started to put her right, she laughed again.

'Don't worry, I know it wasn't meant like that. And yes,

I'll happily have a drink with you, one to celebrate when you put this piece of filth away, with the help of the evidence.'

Jack was just finishing up his conversation with the senior forensic pathologist as Ted looked across to him. He was speaking politely but his accompanying hand gestures told a different story altogether.

'Thank you, Professor, that's really helpful, I appreciate it. And of course, the sooner you can get us those results, the better for us.

'Yes, of course, I quite appreciate that, and I know you'll do your best. Thank you, sir.'

He put the phone down and grinned at Ted as he said, 'Wanker.'

Then, noting the expression on Ted's face, he said, 'All right, you're grinning, so I'm guessing it's good news? Mine is, too, but you go first.'

'The laundry never got washed. Mann forgot to turn the machine on. And there are semen stains on the sheets. They're just waiting on a cross-match from Mann's DNA.'

'Excellent. And potentially good news from the smarmy Prof, too. Because of the sexual assault, it's routine to check for things like alien pubic hairs. And they've got one. Once again, they're waiting on DNA cross-matching. But it looks like we're suddenly making a degree of progress.

'Next time it will be your turn to speak to him, though. I can't stomach it all that often. Play your cards right and he might even invite you to one of his swanky dinner parties at the big house up on The Edge.'

'Alderley Edge?'

Gregson nodded.

'Where all the serious money is. I told you, he's loaded.'

Ted made a face.

'Not my thing at all but it would be right up Trev's street. Different backgrounds. His father has a knighthood. Mine was a miner.'

Switching back to work mode, Ted mentioned Isabel's suggestion about getting hold of the mattress. Gregson nodded.

'Now in theory, we should take this to the DI. That would be the correct chain of command. But it might involve him doing some work, such as getting warrants if necessary. So I suggest we go straight to the Big Boss. We can use the excuse that he was already on standby to sort warrants from the last search. We might not need one, of course, if they've not yet gone back to the house.

'As long as Lennie can grab the glory at the end, he won't much care how the result arrives. And we can fill him in at the end of the day, when we've got things sorted. He's probably asleep in his office anyway. It wouldn't be the first time.'

DCI Jim Baker left the two of them standing in front of his desk while he heard what they had to say. Jack Gregson did most of the talking, leaving Ted to add his bit at the end.

'Why haven't you taken this to the DI?' was the first thing the DCI asked them.

'Because you were already on standby to sort warrants, sir,' Gregson replied glibly.

'Bollocks. You know correct procedure by now, DS Gregson. But the main thing is we get this bastard, if it is him. Just remember, in future, the DI's not retired yet. You go through the proper channels until he has. Clear?'

Both Ted and Jack went back to the house with the Forensics team to collect anything else they thought might be of use to them. Their run of good luck was still holding. The couple were back at the house but Mann was out. It was Mrs Barrow who opened the door to them. As they expected, she put up no objection to them taking anything they wanted to.

'If it will help to find out what happened to Lily you can strip the house bare,' she told them. 'Have you got anything to go on yet? Do you have any idea who did it?'

They'd agreed between them that Ted would speak to

whoever was at the house, leaving Jack free to oversee the seizure of further items. Ted skilfully steered Mrs Barrow towards the kitchen and offered to put the kettle on for her.

'It's too early to say for sure, Mrs Barrow, but we will keep you in the picture with any new developments. I wondered if I could ask you a few questions, while I'm here?'

'Anything. I mean it. Anything at all. I know nothing's going to bring our Lil back, but I won't rest until whoever did this to her is behind bars where they should be. I just wish to god they still hung people for things like this.'

'Were you close to Lily, Mrs Barrow? Would she confide in you if there were things going on in her life?'

'Well, she always did. She was devastated when her dad got killed in a road accident. We both were, of course. We were very close after that. Then I met Ray, and Lily was coming up to her teens and you know what they can be like at that age. She didn't talk to me quite the same as when she was younger, but I think that's normal.'

'And did she get on with Ray? It can't have been easy for him, coming in to fill her father's shoes. Were they close?'

'Oh yes. She was Ray's little princess. He used to spoil her rotten. Always buying her things. Whatever she wanted. And they'd always cuddle up on the settee together watching telly. Not so much lately, of course. She's got too old for that stuff.'

She paused to wipe tears from her eyes.

'You will find whoever it was, won't you?'

'We're doing our very best, Mrs Barrow, and we will continue to do so. I can promise you that.'

'You look tired. Hard day?' Trev asked him as Ted got home from work.

Trev was in the kitchen, laying the table. He'd clearly showered when he got home. He smelled of the spicy shower gel he preferred. It made Ted think again of Mann's apparent obsession with cleanliness. He imagined he now knew the reason for it.

'I thought telling the parents their daughter had been murdered would be the hardest part. It turns out it gets harder. It's looking more than likely I'll have to tell the mother it's the bloke she brought into the home who's the killer.'

Trev put the cutlery down to give him a hug.

'Oh, crap. Are you all right? You're not regretting your switch to CID? It's got to be better than shooting people, though?'

Ted smiled at him.

'I didn't do it all the time, you know. I'll get used to this kind of stuff, I imagine. It's just another part of the job.'

'And you're definitely going to get time off at New Year? They won't suddenly pull everyone in to finish the case off or something like that?'

'No danger of that. With the budgetary restraints the way they are, they'd try to get away with no one at all on duty for a Bank Holiday if they could. I'm surprised they've not got us working from home already to cut costs. So you will have my undivided attention all day long, to do whatever you want to do.'

'Shopping!' Trev exclaimed, with evident delight. 'Until we drop.'

Inwardly groaning, Ted replied, 'Fine. If that's what you want to do, we'll do it. It's your day. I promised, because I seriously screwed up for Christmas.'

This time Trev's hug nearly knocked him off his feet.

'I do love you, Mr Policeman. I know you would do it for me and I know you'd hate every minute of it. So let's compromise. A long leisurely lie-in – well, not too leisurely, clearly – then some shopping, then lunch. Then after that, we could go and do something you'd enjoy more. Take clothes to change into and go hill walking, maybe?'

'I just want us to be all right. Our relationship. It's not easy, being saddled with a copper. Jack's marriage isn't brilliant and it sounds like Big Jim's is in serious trouble. I try not to listen to station gossip but apparently his wife's now sleeping with an executive officer and just about everyone seems to know, so I imagine Jim does too. Must be very hard for him.'

'The bitch. I thought I was the only one. Seriously, though, that must be so difficult for him. Usually, in the circumstances, I imagine he could go round and punch the other bloke's lights out. But that must be very hard if it's someone who outranks him.

'I hope you know that, even if I do drive you mad with my shopaholism, I would never cheat on you. Never.'

Chapter Twenty-two

Lennie Grimshaw was clearly in his element. There was the prospect of a fairly straightforward enquiry with an easy enough conviction at the end of it. Just what he'd been hoping for as his swansong.

He looked more animated for the morning briefing the next day than Ted had ever seen him before. The DCI was once again in attendance, a looming presence in the background, ready to dive in when he considered it necessary.

It wasn't yet a big team. The DI, Ted and Jack, then the three DCs, Robbie Hughes, Rob O'Connell and Maurice Brown. They were all in, eager to crack on now it looked as if they had a strong suspect in their sights. Ted had noticed that even Maurice Brown seemed to be making more of an effort to get in on time.

'First priority today is to bring Ray Mann in and see what he has to say for himself,' Grimshaw began.

Ted couldn't stop himself. He knew it wasn't going to go down well but he took the chance.

'Sir, shouldn't we just wait on the results of the DNA testing? That way we've got something solid to put to him. He'll have difficulty denying scientific evidence, surely? He's not likely just to throw in the towel and confess unless he knows we have something irrefutable, is he?'

Grimshaw's look was scornful.

'As the DCI reminded us, DS Darling, this is your first murder enquiry and you're still on a learning curve. So you perhaps aren't familiar with how we work. There's no harm in bringing him in for a chat. We've got everything we need from the house. It's not as if he's going to start destroying evidence if we talk to him. We've already got it all.'

Ted was surprised when Maurice Brown joined in. Even more so when he heard what he had to say. It seemed as if he was aligning himself with Ted against his own boss.

'You think it might be him now, eh, boss? I thought you were dead set against him and putting your money on the boyfriend?'

'I never said that I'd ruled him out,' Grimshaw retorted defensively. 'And we still can't write off the boyfriend until his alibi and his medical records have been checked out. But for now, we can concentrate on Mann. We'll haul ...' he looked towards the DCI then corrected himself, 'we'll bring him in and Robbie and me will listen to what he has to say for himself.'

'Before I say my two penn'orth, I'll just remind everyone present that this isn't my first murder enquiry. Far from it,' the DCI put in. 'Perhaps with DS Darling being newer, he's more acutely aware of correct procedure and perhaps that's a useful reminder to all of us. And I agree with him on this one. We'd be wasting time and resources bringing Mann in too soon. We've nothing like enough to hold him on for long. CPS would laugh at us if I asked to charge him on what we have got so far.

'This is how it's going to be. You're all going to spend today, and as long as it takes after today, pulling together every single bit of evidence or potential evidence we can find to put Mann firmly in that young lass's bed, or having had any kind of intimate contact with her.

'That includes getting out there and talking to anyone who knew her. Anyone she might have confided in. Maybe people at this club she belonged to. Perhaps even someone from her school, or college or wherever she was. Jack, Ted, liaise with Uniform for extra bodies to help cover it.

'If we show our hand too soon a good lawyer will simply tell him to say the girl was alive when she left the house after having had sex with him by mutual consent, and we have bugger all at the moment to take it further than that.

'So we need to build a solid case against him. We need more camera footage of him, after that shot we've got now. We need proof that when she left the house, he followed her. We need sightings, if we can. We need to put him at the murder scene. We're a mile off being there yet. So let's get some bloody basic police work done, before there's any more talk of bringing him in.'

The DCI turned to go. He paused at his office door to say, 'DI Grimshaw, a word in my office, now, if you'd be so kind.'

'Naughty boy, Lennie, six of the best from the headmaster for you, my lad,' Jack Gregson said quietly in Ted's ear, making him grin, in spite of himself.

'Close the door please, Lennie.'

The DI looked around hopefully for a chair.'

'I can't stand for long, boss. Not with this back condition.'

'No, no, of course not. Look, here's the spare chair,' the DCI passed it to him from his side of the desk where it had been pushed under a corner. 'Take a seat then, by all means. Make yourself comfortable.'

Grimshaw was wary now, trying to detect any note of sarcasm in the DCI's voice.

'Actually, it's your health I wanted to talk to you about, DI Grimshaw. It's becoming a matter of some concern to me. As it no doubt is to you.'

'Well, yes, boss, that's absolutely right. I feel sometimes I'm letting the team down when I can't always do all the shifts I'm on the rota for. It's one of those conditions that comes and goes, and I can't always predict when.'

'Yes, indeed. That must be very difficult for you. That's why the Chief Super and I have been talking about what to do to help you. To see if we can't make life a bit easier for you, in the short time before you retire. That's why we both think a nice cushy desk job back in Uniform might be the perfect way to see out your time with us.'

Grimshaw's face drained of colour.

'I'd rather soldier on, boss ...'

'Yes, I'm sure you would, Lennie, and that's very commendable of you. But it's just not really working out at the moment, is it? Our hours are not predictable, because of the nature of the work. I'm trying to build a strong team here, with someone with good leadership skills to take it forward. Unfortunately, your health is getting in the way of that being you. So the Chief Super and I are offering you a way of taking it a bit easier while you work your ticket.'

'Is this an ultimatum, sir? If it is, I'll need to talk to my Federation rep before I respond.'

'Of course you will. The Chief Super and I both anticipated that. Take as much time as you need to reach a decision. Talk to whoever you need to.

'Of course, another way round it would be ...' he made a show of looking at notes on his desk, then looked back at Grimshaw.

'You're less than a couple of months off your pension now. You must have quite a bit of accumulated annual leave, and I'm sure we could work something out about a bit more sick leave to cover any gaps. That way you could just ride off into the sunset, say at the end of this week?'

Grimshaw's face was darkening now in anger. He was being stitched up like a kipper and he knew it. He needed a way to cling on by his fingernails to do his thirty years to qualify for the pension he'd had his sights on for years now. The deal the Big Boss was offering him looked like his only hope of getting his hands on it with his dignity intact.

'I'll let you know as soon as I've decided, sir.'

As he left the office, closing the door none too quietly behind him, Big Jim licked his index finger and chalked himself up a point in the air. He didn't often play politics or mind games. It didn't mean he wasn't good at it when he did.

The DI disappeared off for the rest of the day after his interview with the DCI. He told Jack Gregson to get on with overseeing what was needed for the day.

Ted was in his element. He'd always been a stickler for paperwork and spending desk time with the team would help him see who was up to the mark on the routine side of the job.

It was clear that DC Hughes was not pleased at the prospect of routine evidence gathering when he'd hoped to be interviewing a prime suspect. He did a lot of grumbling, some of it under his breath. He volunteered to go out door-to-door. He clearly wanted to be the one who brought home the biggest lead.

To his surprise, Ted found that Maurice Brown, although slow, was a methodical worker who didn't miss much. He was particularly good at picking up links and gaps between the various information that was being collated.

'Sarge?' Brown said, looking from Ted to Gregson and back. 'This is getting confusing, with two of you. But whoever, we need to check out what time Mrs Barrow got home from work on Christmas Eve. We need to know how long Mann was on his own with Lily. And as soon as we start asking her, he's going to get suspicious. Do you want me to phone the home where she works and ask them her movements? I can do it as just routine enquiries. It shouldn't set too many alarm bells off. They must have heard by now.'

'Good one, Maurice,' Gregson told him. 'You sort that. We'll have a catch-up at the end of the day, see where we're up to. But the objective needs to be to have enough on Mann before we bring him in to be sure we can rattle his cage before we start interviewing him.

'His brief is bound to advise him to say nowt on first interview, but if we can supply them with an impressive file, sooner or later, he's going to have to start talking.'

Nobody was surprised when the DI didn't appear at the end of the day. The DCI came out of his office and it was clear from his manner that for the time being, at least, he was running this case. He looked from Jack to Ted. They'd decided between them that Ted should present the day's findings. It was a good chance for him to show what he could do.

'DC O'Connell's been liaising with Holmfirth, sir, checking Ashley Barnes' alibi. It's tight. His nan is well known, in a good way. One of the officers goes to the same church, and he saw Ashley there with his family. They asked around for us and there are lots of reliable sightings of them there, and at the house earlier. And several neighbours confirmed that his eyesight is very poor.

'Forensics have been going flat out for us. We've just this minute had confirmation that the semen stains on the sheets match Ray Mann's DNA, so we've got him in Lily's bed at some point.'

'The dirty bastard,' the DCI growled. 'Let's see him talk his way out of that.'

'DC Brown's been speaking to the home where Mrs Barrow works. She didn't leave there until gone eleven on Christmas Eve, by the time she'd prepared all the food. So that appears to leave Mann, possibly alone with Lily and with no alibi for the whole of the afternoon and evening, from when Mrs Barrow left for work at midday to when she got home.

'So far we haven't got any other sightings of Ray Mann's car but we are still checking cameras everywhere. Even with the images enhanced, we can't ID who was driving the car, nor who the figure on the pavement is. It could be Lily, it might not. There's just a chance that if we show it to him, it will rattle him. And when we do talk to him, we need to ask him for his explanation of where he was going in his car, then check out his story.

'That's as far as we've got today, sir.'

The DCI looked round at them all.

'Well, I'd say that's a bloody good start. And a reasonable point at which to call it quits for today. Tomorrow, we'll have Mann in. DS Darling, you'll be interviewing him. You, me and DS Gregson will get our heads together first thing in the morning to decide on the line of questioning.

'DC O'Connell, you can go with someone from Uniform to pick our guest up and bring him in. I want it doing right. No rough stuff, no intimidation.'

He saw DC Hughes' expression at this news and turned to him.

'You missed out on the chance, DC Hughes. You backed the wrong horse. You and the DI dismissed him too easily. What you can do tomorrow, all day, if necessary, is to find something, anything, which links Mann to the crime scene itself. Go over all the crime scene findings again, see if anything's been overlooked which places him there. And don't look like that. Just get it done, then we can nail the bastard.

'Right, everyone, off home to your nearest and dearest. It's getting late. Bright-eyed and bushy-tailed in the morning. Good work, all of you.'

Ted was just about to phone Trev to see what they were doing about an evening meal when his mobile rang. Trev calling him. It was later than he'd intended to be leaving, but while they were on a roll, they'd kept going.

Trev had told him he'd be going for a drink straight from work with some of his mates from the karate club. There was no club over the holiday period but they'd decided to have a drink together on the evening when they would usually have met up.

'Hey, you, are you still at work?'

'Just leaving now. Did you want me to pick up a take-away?'

'I wondered if you could pick me up? I may just accidentally have got slightly too pissed to ride the bike home, officer. If it's not too much trouble.'

'It's no trouble. I'm on my way. Will the bike be all right?'

'Keith's letting me put it in the back yard. I'll wait for you outside.'

Keith was the landlord of the pub near to the karate club.

'I'll come in and get you. It's chilly to be standing around outside.'

Trev was waiting on the pavement outside the pub when Ted pulled his Renault up near to the kerb. He leaned over to give the passenger door a bit of a shove from the inside. It could be temperamental. Ted wasn't interested in cars. He used a service vehicle when he needed something reliable, keeping the Renault for personal travel. Trev was constantly telling him he should get something newer but he was reluctant.

Trev slid into the passenger seat and fumbled for his seat belt. He smelled of wine and seemed to be in a good mood.

As soon as Ted put the car in gear and pulled away, he heard a noise.

'What was that?'

'That?' Trev asked innocently, fumbling with the zip on his motorbike leathers.

Ted heard the same noise again. The unmistakable meow of a small kitten.

'Another one?' he asked.

'This is Roger,' Trev told him, his hand gently stroking the small furry head which kept trying to butt its way out from inside his jacket. 'I met a man in the pub who said he had some kittens and he was going to drown them in a bucket. I was being public-spirited and preventing a murder, officer. And I did only take one. Wait until you see him, Ted, he's gorgeous. He must be half Siamese. Chocolate point, with stunning blue eyes.'

'He probably wouldn't have drowned them. I reckon he knew a soft touch when he saw one.'

'But he might have. And he really is too adorable. I couldn't take the risk.'

'Hello, Roger,' Ted smiled indulgently. 'Welcome to your new family.'

Chapter Twenty-three

'Mr Mann, you know now, from the disclosures made to you and your solicitor, that the sheets which were taken from the washing machine at your house had not, in fact, been through a wash cycle. Forensic testing has shown us that semen stains detected on those sheets match your DNA.'

Mann was maintaining a stubborn silence. Ted was interviewing him under caution, which gave him the right to say nothing.

'When those sheets were taken, Mr Mann, you told me that they were the sheets from Lily's bed which you had decided to wash to make up a full load. What do you have to say about the forensic findings on those sheets?'

'You misunderstood. They were the ones off my bed. Me and the missus have sex. So what?'

'But Mrs Barrow was present at the time you told me they were the sheets from Lily's bed. She didn't contradict you. Surely she would have done if you had, in fact, decided to strip the bed you shared with her? Because you would then, presumably, have had to replace them with clean sheets, and I imagine she would have noticed.'

Mann turned to look at his solicitor. She bent close to him so her words would not be overheard. Ted immediately leaned back in his seat so as not to appear to be impinging on their discussion.

'I'm saying nothing.'

'That is, of course, your right, as I'm sure your solicitor has just told you. But you must realise, Mr Mann, that the implications of these findings are serious. We can, of course, carry out further tests to see if the sheets match fibres on the mattress from Lily's bed or from your own. But this might be the ideal opportunity for you to offer a plausible explanation.'

'He's good, isn't he, sir?' DS Jack Gregson commented to the DCI as the two of them watched the interview on the monitor.

'A different technique entirely to the DI, but I think he's going to be effective,' Baker agreed. 'I'm not refilling the DI post until Lennie has officially retired. But if I do, and if I was considering putting Ted into the role, would that bother you, Jack?'

'Not in the least, boss,' Gregson assured him. 'He's got the exams, he walks the walk and talks the talk. You must have noticed the team's improving already. Even Maurice is getting in on time. And this gambling on the cases isn't being mentioned any more. I should have jumped on that long ago, but it was hard when the DI was doing it too.'

'What about Robbie Hughes? He doesn't seem to be Ted's biggest fan.'

'Hughes is a dick, boss. Excuse me for saying so. He's had it cushy with Lennie for too long. They're very pally. He's not enjoying being expected to play by the book.'

'Well, he can either learn to play nice or go and find another sandpit if he doesn't like the way things are shaping up here.'

The two men turned their attention back to the progress of the interview.

'Mr Mann, allow me to remind you of the words of the caution: "it may harm your defence if you do not mention when questioned something which you later rely on in court." If you can offer a valid explanation for your semen being found on Lily's bedclothes, now might be a good time for you to mention it.'

Again, the solicitor turned her head to murmur to her client. Ted wondered if he imagined something of an expression of distaste on her face. It couldn't have been a body odour issue. Mann once again smelled strongly of toiletries.

'All right, I'll tell you. Me and Lily were sleeping together. It didn't start until she was sixteen and it was with her consent. Obviously her mam didn't know. We were going to tell her. We were in love; we wanted to be together.'

'I see,' Ted said, his tone neutral. 'So you slept together some time on Christmas Eve?'

'As soon as her mam had left for work. It was like that with the two of us. Couldn't wait to be alone together. Couldn't keep our hands off one another. But she was alive and well – very well – the last time I saw her, going off to spend time with her mates.'

'So you admit to sleeping with your partner's daughter. Yet you clearly weren't using a condom. Was that not rather risky? Or were you planning to have a child together?'

'No, er, no, nothing like that. We were careful. Lil checked her dates. When it was risky, I ... you know.'

'You used the withdrawal method?'

Mann nodded.

'Moving on, Mr Mann. You will also have seen, from disclosure, that your car was captured on a traffic camera, driving in the direction of Bramhall later in the day on Christmas Eve. After the time you say you had consensual sex with Lily Barrow. Where were you going, Mr Mann?'

'The offy,' Mann said promptly. 'I decided we didn't have enough drink in to have a good time over Christmas, so I thought I'd go and get a bottle of Tia Maria for Janice. Bit of a treat for her.'

'And before you went out, you stripped Lily's bed, to remove incriminating evidence of sex which your partner might otherwise have noticed?'

Mann nodded again.

'Is that something you regularly did? Presumably if you'd been having unprotected sex with Lily for a few months now, in her bed, the same risk would have arisen before? Unless she perhaps brought boyfriends home with her and had sex with them, so Mrs Barrow wouldn't have thought anything of it?'

'No, she never. There was just me. I told you. We were in love. Lil saw to that side of things. With her mam working long hours sometimes, she did her own washing to help out a bit.'

'So which off licence did you go to, Mr Mann? The camera shows you heading up towards Bramhall, yet surely there are nearer ones to your home? And what about the supermarkets? What made you head for Bramhall?'

'There's one up there I like. It has good offers on sometimes.'

'They'd know you there, then, if you go regularly? They may well remember you going in on Christmas Eve?'

'No, I, er, in the end, I didn't go in. I realised when I got nearly there that I'd forgotten my wallet.'

'That's annoying. Still, perhaps not surprising, in the circumstances. You clearly had a lot on your mind. So you have no alibi for the time between this traffic camera capture and Mrs Barrow returning home some time after eleven o'clock?'

'Is my client being interviewed as a suspect or a witness, Sergeant?' the solicitor asked him. 'If as a witness, surely he doesn't need an alibi?'

'I apologise, ma'am, that was a slip of the tongue,' Ted said smoothly. 'I should have said corroboration rather than alibi. We're just establishing the whereabouts of anyone close to the victim as part of routine enquiries.'

'Nice recovery, Ted,' the DCI muttered to himself from the next room.

'Allow me to rephrase that question, Mr Mann. Can anyone confirm your account of how you passed your time on Christmas Eve between you having sex with Lily Barrow and the arrival home of her mother later the same evening?'

'I never saw no one. I was just going out to buy some drink for Jan. I forgot my wallet, so I went back home.'

'And then when you found your wallet at home, you presumably went out again to get the drink? And Mrs Barrow would have enjoyed some of it. Perhaps a nightcap, when she got home from work? So she'll remember that thoughtful little gesture on your part? And wherever you bought it from might well have CCTV images of you in the shop. Off licences often have cameras, because of the high risk of theft, of course.'

Mann looked confused for a moment.

'No, I ... in the end, when I got back home and checked in the cupboards, there was still plenty in, so I didn't bother going back out again. You know what the shops get like, on a Christmas Eve. I thought I'd save myself the hassle, after all.'

'Probably very wise. Now, Mr Mann, if I could just ask you to take a look at this photo. This is an enhancement of the one which you've already had sight of. From the same camera which captured your vehicle in Bramhall Lane. It shows a figure on the pavement, near to your car when it was caught on camera. Who is that figure, Mr Mann?'

'Oh, please, Sergeant,' the solicitor cut in. 'That could be anyone. It's impossible to tell from this shot.'

'It is indeed. But, of course, Mr Mann was there, in person. So it might have been clearer to him. Did you happen to notice that pedestrian, Mr Mann, and could you tell us who it was, please?'

'I've no idea. I didn't notice anyone. I was just concentrateng on my driving.'

'So, in summary, is it right to say that you never saw Lily again after you'd had sex with her, some time in the early afternoon on Christmas Eve, several hours before her death?'

'That's right. I already told you. I've admitted to sleeping with her. You may think that's morally wrong, but there was nothing illegal in it. She was over the age of consent, and she certainly did consent. We've fancied one another for ages but we waited until she was sixteen. I know the law.'

'It's not my place to question your morals, Mr Mann. I'm just here to gather information in relation to a criminal case. That will be all for now. Thank you for your time. We may well wish to question you further at some point.'

Ted went in search of the DCI when he left the interview room. He was still with Jack Gregson.

'Sorry I couldn't get more out of him, sir ...' he began.

'Sorry? Behave yourself. That was bloody good work. We've got him admitting to sleeping with the young lass. If we ever get to the stage of putting him in court, that's not going to endear him to any jury, especially not one with parents in it. I know Mann's not related to the girl so it's not legally incest or anything, but morally? A bloke in his forties sleeping with his girlfriend's teenage daughter behind her back? That's about as low as it gets, in my book.

'You did a good job in there, Ted. Very professional. I like how you kept control of yourself. I have to confess I might have found it hard. Especially having a teenage lass of my own, not much older than young Lily.

'Right, so, let's keep on gathering the evidence. Slowly but surely. We'll have another get together at the end of the day to see where we're up to and if any more new evidence has come to light. Based on that, we'll decide when to talk to Mann again.'

'Sir, at some point, are we going to have to tell Mrs Barrow what we know so far?'

'Tricky. A bit of a minefield. We'll have to tread very carefully.'

Ted's mobile phone was ringing as he went back upstairs to his desk.

'Ted? Isabel here. Can you keep your DC Hughes on a lead, please? We've not yet quite finished at the scene and it's not helping my Investigators having him there harassing them. We really are doing all we can for you. If we go any faster, we risk making mistakes, which doesn't help any of us.

'You'll probably have seen the same email as me by now, from the Professor? Confirming that the pubic hair found on Lily's body matches Mann's DNA. Does that nail him for you?'

'Unfortunately not. I've just been interviewing him and he's played his get out of jail free card. He's admitted having sex with Lily but says it was consensual. They were in love, apparently.'

'Excuse me while I throw up. A common law stepfather in his forties sleeping with his partner's sixteen-year-old daughter? I do hate to judge but that sounds pretty revolting to me.'

'Sorry about Hughes. I'll have a word with him. He's just keen to get hold of our killer.'

'We all are, Ted, believe me. We're on the same side, but we can't work any faster than we are doing.'

Maurice Brown was later than anyone else returning to the office to report on his findings. Ted hoped he hadn't been up to his old skiving tricks, especially not on a case as important as this one. They were just about to begin when they heard his heavy tread on the stairs and he came in, slightly out of breath.

'Sorry, boss. Took me a bit longer than I thought,' he said apologetically, heading for his desk.

'You're here now, so let's get on. For those who don't yet know, Mann has admitted sleeping with the girl but says it was consensual.'

'Dirty bastard,' Hughes muttered angrily.

'So the evidence of the sheets doesn't help us all that much at this stage. What we need is some hard evidence placing him at the crime scene. Otherwise Mann is just going to stick to his story that she was alive and well when she left the house after they'd slept together.'

'Sir, can I say something?' Maurice Brown asked the DCI.

'If it will advance us, Maurice, the floor is all yours.'

'Well, boss, I was thinking about those stained sheets. Unprotected sex. Young lasses these days are pretty clued up on sex stuff, it seems to me. If it was supposed to be consensual between her and the step-dad, and they weren't using any protection, unless she was on the pill, she might be in need of the morning after pill.

'Anyway, long story short, I tracked down a Youth Worker, the sort who sees youngsters in that sort of situation. She didn't want to breach any confidentiality, of course. But she'd seen on the local news that Lily had been found dead, so she agreed to talk to me a bit, though not on the record at this point.

'She'd seen Lily a few times, given her access to the morning after pill. She'd also advised her, on more than one occasion, to go to the police. That's because she first saw her over a year ago. In other words, when Lily was under sixteen.'

'So as long as we can prove that, we've got him on statutory rape, if nothing else,' Jim Baker growled. 'We need to get a warrant to search their records. I'm presuming they keep records?'

'Yes, boss, they do, I checked. And I did mention that we might need access to them.'

'That's bloody good work, Maurice. Anyone got anything to top that?'

'Not top it, sir, but corroborate it, maybe,' Rob O'Connell put in. 'Through the youth group, I tracked down a girl Lily was friendly with. Becky. She wasn't keen to talk to me at first but she did finally say Lily had told her much the same thing. That Ray Mann had been raping her for some time now.'

'Why did the lass never approach anyone officially? Why didn't she come and report it to the police?' the DCI asked.

Maurice and Rob exchanged glances. It was Maurice who spoke.

'Rob was probably told the same thing I was, boss. She didn't think anyone would believe her, or take her allegations seriously. She thought it would be her word against Mann's and that her mam might even side with him against her. It's a public confidence thing, sir.'

Chapter Twenty-four

'First of all, Mr Mann, ma'am, I apologise for the late disclosure of this document. It's only recently been received from the computer forensics team,' Ted began.

'Do please call me Ms Castle, Sergeant. I dislike ma'am intensely,' Ray Mann's solicitor told him.

Ted flashed her his most charming smile as he responded, 'Excuse me, Ms Castle. You will, of course, be given time to discuss the contents of this document with your client before we go much further. What I would like to do now is simply to read the first entry from it and ask Mr Mann for his reaction to its contents.

'For the tape, the item in question is a printed transcript taken from the computer belonging to the victim, Lily Barrow. It's the contents of a folder found on that computer and entitled "Mann-handled". Mann being spelled with two N's. Like your name, Mr Mann.'

'I strongly object to this theatrical performance. I request time with my client before we go any further.'

'Just indulge me for one moment, Ms Castle. Please.'

Ted put copies of the document on the table in front of both Mann and the solicitor, then picked up his own copy.

'As I said, I'm just going to read the first entry from this document for the benefit of the tape. The document takes the form of a diary, a journal. Different entries, each with a different date. You'll see that the first entry is dated more than two years ago. Which would mean that at the time of writing it,

Lily Barrow was just fourteen. The date on which it was created has been confirmed by the computer forensics team. It's not simply a document which was made retrospectively.

'I'll read it now: "Today I was in my room, trying to do some studying, but mostly looking out the window and listening to some music with me earphones on. I saw mam go out and off up the road to go to work. She works as a cook. It was half term so I was off school.

"Even if I'd heard anything I wouldn't of thought anything was wierd about Ray coming upstairs. But he come into my room without knocking and he knows I hate that. He makes a joke, says he pays the morgige so it's his room really, but usually he's ok and he respects my personal space.

"He come over to the desk were I was sat and asked me what I was doing sat up here on my own. I said I was studying. He said I was a good girl to be doing that in half term. Then he put his hand on me shoulder. I don't like touchy feely stuff so I shook it off. He put it back again. Then he bent down and tried to kiss me neck."

Mann's face had drained of colour and his hands were shaking as he held the top sheet of the pile in front of him. His solicitor cut in, her tone angry.

'I really must protest before you go any further, Sergeant. I need to speak to my client.'

'It's only a short entry, Ms Castle. Please just bear with me a moment,' Ted told her, then continuing reading in the same measured tone.

"I told him to do one, that I didn't let no one kiss me like that except me mam, not since me dad died. He just laughed and carried on, pawing at me. I tried to shove him off, but he's dead strong. He does wait lifting and stuff. I jumped up to try an get away. He put his arm round me and pulled me against him. I could feel he had a hard-on. I wanted to be sick. He started kissing me on the mouth, sticking his tongue down me throat. I was struggling as hard as I could but I couldn't stop him. He was too strong.

"Then he shoved me down on the bed and fell on top of me. He had one hand over me mouth, nearly smuthering me, and the other was just tearing at me clothes. He pulled me top up, stuck his hand up my bra and on me tits. He was rubbing himself against me all the time. Making like a moning noise."

'This has gone far enough, Sergeant,' the solicitor snapped sharply. 'This is highly inappropriate and I shall be making my feelings known at the highest possible level.'

'As is, of course, your right, Ms Castle,' Ted told her smoothly. 'But for now I'm happy for you to consult with your client. Please take all the time you need. There will be someone outside the door who can inform me when you're ready for the interview to continue. Interview suspended.'

With that, Ted switched off the tape, picked up his own files and left the room, heading straight to find the DCI. He and Jack Gregson had once more been watching Ted in action.

'Was that all right, sir?' Ted asked him anxiously. 'I read as far as I thought I dared go, with the solicitor pressing for a break to consult.'

'Bloody masterful, Ted. You're not a card player, are you? I'd hate to sit across from you for a poker hand. Right, we'll regroup now over a coffee in my office, to discuss how this interview should go from here on. It will be interesting to see what yarn Mann decides to try spinning on this one. I can't begin to think how he's going to talk his way out of it.'

'I'll just grab a cup of tea, sir, if that's all right? I'm not much of a coffee drinker.'

Jack Gregson laughed as Jim Baker lumbered off to his office and he went with Ted to get something else to drink.

'Can't stomach the Big Boss's evil brew then? Not surprised. I've no idea how he can drink the stuff. I wonder if he ever sleeps, drinking as much of it as he does, as strong as it is. Mind you, with a missus like his, maybe he needs something that strong.

'Bloody good job in there, Ted, anyway. What a piece of shit he is, eh? Looks like we may have him on the back foot now, though.'

It had been a late one the evening before. Ted had fired off an apologetic email to Trev to say the Big Boss wanted to go over things with him, in light of the computer findings which they'd received just as they were thinking of knocking off for the day. Jack Gregson had joined them, in case he had to take over from Ted for any reason. They'd ordered in a Chinese takeaway and settled themselves down for a long session.

'It's a shame you're up against Ms Castle for this, Ted. It's a bit like sending a toddler into the paddling pool and finding there's a shark swimming round in there. No offence intended.'

'None at all taken, sir. I'm rubbish at swimming.'

'Are you sure you feel confident? It's a big ask, but from what I've seen of your work so far, I think you can do this. As long as you know there's no shame in pulling out if you feel you'd rather.

'Right, so, Ms Castle is no doubt going to claim this is all hearsay and not admissible.'

'To which I argue that it would have been admissible if Lily was still alive, so should still be considered, in the interests of justice.'

'Good. Make sure you can slap her with chapter and verse from the Act, because she'll know it inside out and back to front.'

'Sir.'

'Read the first entry of that diary thing to Mann, if Ms Castle doesn't stop you, and let's see what his reaction is. She'll no doubt be screaming for a break as soon as you start, but keep going for as long as you dare. Then when you resume, let Mann give his explanation, if he decides to say anything at all.

'It's at this point you need to disclose that Lily emailed the document to this girl Becky whatever her name is, and also to Ashley Barnes. With one of those "if anything happens to me" type messages. Which clearly shows she intended it to be used as evidence, should it become necessary.

'What we three need to do now, in effect, is to second guess what Mann's story is going to be, so we're ready to refute it, whatever it is.'

'Hard to see what he could say to refute this, boss,' Jack' replied.

'The only thing I can suggest is he might say it was all just teenage fantasy on her part,' Ted put in. 'He'll claim there was a mutual attraction there early on. He might admit to the occasional kiss but he didn't take it any further because he was being the responsible adult. So Lily took to acting out her fantasies on paper, but it was entirely the product of a teenage girl's imagination. Perhaps. That's the best I can come up with, boss.'

'It's a pretty good best, Ted. So what's the pre-emptive action?'

'I've already told Rob O'Connell to go back to see this girl Becky. Becky Adler. And to take a female officer from Uniform with him. See if it'll make her feel more comfortable to talk about it with a woman present.

'Forensics show the email and attachment as having been sent to her. We need to check she got them, if she still has them, and if she considered doing anything about what Lily told her. Same with Ashley Barnes. I've put Rob on to talking to him as well, after Becky.

'As far as second-guessing what her creative writing skills were like, I know it's still the school holidays, but we need to find a way of getting to talk to whoever taught Lily at school. I've put Robbie on to that tomorrow, for as long as it takes.

'I also want Maurice to go back and talk to that Youth Worker again, this time armed with Lily's diary. There's a strong possibility that she may well agree to talk to us more, on the record, if she knows that what she tells us is corroborated by Lily's own testimony. I think Maurice is ideal. It's so obvious he cares passionately about the young victim, if she'll talk to anyone, it will be him.'

Jim Baker nodded his satisfaction.

'I'd go along with all of that, Ted. Well done. Let's try to get ahead of this slimy bastard, deal with anything he might come up with before he even says it. Jack, see if you can put a bit of gentle pressure on Forensics for any more findings from the crime scene. A positive finding there could give us the last nail in his coffin. Otherwise we'll be trying to make a case that as his is the only DNA we've found on Lily's body, then it's likely he was the last, if not the only one to have had sex with her before she died. Then no doubt Ms bloody Castle will come back at us with the old "absence of evidence is not evidence of absence" line.'

'At some point, boss, one of us needs to talk to Mrs Barrow, surely? Get a feel for what, if anything, she knew.'

'I can't believe any parent would knowingly let that type of thing go on with their daughter,' Jack said, shaking his head. 'She talked about them cuddling up together to watch telly so perhaps she's naive enough to think that's as far as it ever went.'

'If anyone ever did anything like that to my Rosie, I'd cut their dick off and happily go down for it,' the DCI rumbled menacingly.

'Now, anyone want the last of the prawn crackers?'

It was no surprise to anyone, when the solicitor and her client reappeared and declared themselves ready for the interview to continue, that it was a tight-lipped Mann who answered only 'no comment' to anything further which Ted put to him.

'That's fine, Mr Mann, that's your right. There are just another couple of points I need to inform you of. Again, my apologies to you both for late disclosure. Once again it's something we've only recently had.

'I appreciate, Ms Castle, that you will be advising your client that this document from Lily's computer is arguably hearsay.'

As she went to interrupt him, he held up a hand, still speaking politely.

'If you would please allow me to finish, Ms Castle. I was about to say that it will be a matter for the CPS initially and later for the court to decide on its admissibility. For now, we're treating it as a significant piece of evidence.

'We're following up certain leads in connection with it, and we will, of course, be making disclosure as and when new information comes in. I will just say at this stage that we believe Lily passed this information on in electronic format to at least two people, and that she discussed the contents with at least one other in person.'

He could see immediately that this disclosure had rattled Mann. It had clearly never occurred to him that Lily would tell anyone. Perhaps he'd managed to convince himself that there was nothing wrong in what he'd been doing.

'That's all for now, Mr Mann. You will be informed of when we need to interview you again. Thank you for attending. Interview terminated.'

'It can be a bit stop and go in this job, Ted, you'll get used to it,' the DCI told him when he came out of the interview room for the second time. 'It's all stop now but then all of a sudden, it'll start rolling along like a runaway steam train. You'll see.

'Let's see what the rest of the day brings us, and then we can look at getting him in again. We're still a long way off having enough for me even to call CPS about charging him, but we're definitely going in the right direction. Good job, for now.'

It was close of play by the time all of the team got back from their assignments. They reported various degrees of success and clearly had a lot to feed back to the full team. The DCI took a balanced view.

'All right, everyone. We've let the prime suspect go home for now. It looks like we're going to have plenty more ammunition to throw at him tomorrow. But whatever you have to report, I don't think we're risking losing anything if we call it a day now.

'Let's bring morning briefing forward half an hour then you can all feed back on your findings. I'll make some calls, bring in anyone who may have anything to contribute. After which we can decide on where to go from there. So go on then, before I change my mind. Get off home to your other halves and don't be late in the morning. That means everyone. You too, Maurice.'

'Sir.'

Ted wasn't going to say no. He'd been up for hours after he got home the night before, swotting up on the laws involving hearsay evidence, knowing that was going to cause potential problems.

He sent a text ahead to let Trev know he was on his way and found him in the kitchen, preparing supper. Ted made an exaggerated show of counting the number of cats prowling round, rubbing up against his legs.

Trev noticed and laughed.

'Still only five, officer.'

Trev had been right about Roger, the newest feline acquisition. He was a stunning-looking cat, with the self-assurance and arrogance of one who was aware of his own good looks.

'What time did you finally get to bed last night?' Trev asked him. 'Sorry I was asleep. You should have woken me.'

'I'm not sure. Getting on for three, maybe? It would have taken a bomb to wake you. You were well away. And talking in your sleep.'

'Really? What was I saying?'

'I don't know. It was in foreign.'

'I'm not asleep now. And this needs to simmer for half an hour or so. If you're not too tired?'

'I was tired, when I came in. Suddenly I'm not any more.'

Chapter Twenty-five

The morning briefing had more attendees than usual. Inspector Turner and Sgt Wheeler from Uniform, together with some of their officers, were present. Isabel, the Forensics Coordinator was also there to present her team's findings to date. Anyone who might have some input had been summoned by the Big Boss.

There was an air of anticipation about those in the incident room. The case against Mann was slowly building. Each of them was able to supply another brick in the mounting wall of evidence and they were eager to bring him to justice.

The DCI was running things, as Senior Investigating Officer. Jack Gregson was positioned by the white board which had all the available data so far, ready to input anything new which came up during the course of the meeting.

'So far, from what I've seen of him, and based on what DS Darling and I have discussed, I don't think Mann is likely to crack and confess any time soon. So it's up to us to build such a strong case against him that we stand a good chance of getting a conviction, even with a not guilty plea.

'Now, in the absence of him even attempting to alibi himself convincingly, we would seem to have means and opportunity for him to have been the killer. What's looking a bit uncertain at the moment is motive. That and the fact that we can't definitively place him at the crime scene.'

Two hands were lifted to attract his attention at almost the same time. Isabel, the Forensics Coordinator, and DC Hughes.

'Isabel, please. Ladies first.'

The DCI scowled round at all present as he added, 'And before anyone starts with all the feminist equality stuff, I'm old-fashioned. A dinosaur. I try not to give offence, but that's the way I was brought up. All right?'

'Fine by me,' Isabel smiled, 'especially as I think you might well be rather pleased with what I've got for you. Again, apologies for the delay, but you know what it's like at this time of year, with people off on leave.

'We now have a bit more balance of probability evidence for Mann's presence at the crime scene. We found a small semen stain on the ground by Lily's body. We rushed it through as a priority and it's now been matched to Mann's DNA. You can, no doubt, all imagine how Mann's team will argue that it was leakage from the earlier sexual encounter with the victim, which he has admitted to. It's not my field of expertise, but fortunately, I know someone who does specialise in such things, so I'm consulting him on his views. With his help, we may be able to rule that out as a possibility'

'Excellent. So now we come back even more so to the motive. Mann admits sleeping with the girl at home before she went out. But for some reason, he went after her, raped her again, this time apparently violently, then bashed her with a rock. Any theories?'

'Sir, I may possibly have a likely explanation.'

There was no mistaking the self-satisfied smirk on DC Hughes's face. He was after the glory.

'Even though her school is closed for the holidays, I tracked down first the headmaster, then Lily's form teacher. She told me Lily wasn't at all into creative writing. Anything she produced was on the dull side, although factually accurate. Her best subjects were geography, food technology and running. She was a member of a cross-country running club. Pretty good at it, too.

'And, this is maybe the clincher, she was planning to sign

up for the Navy to go and train as a chef as soon as she could. She was going to be leaving home, soon, probably going to get postings abroad in the future. Taking herself as far away from home as possible.

'So what if she told Mann that? What if when he was raping her in the afternoon, or when she left to go out, she told him she wasn't going to be around for very much longer. Maybe that's why he went after her and totally lost it.'

'Sir, just playing devil's advocate here for a minute, that bolt on the bedroom door is a problem for us, surely, with the rape allegation?' Ted began. 'I'm talking about the recent one, not when she was under the age of consent.'

The DCI nodded for him to continue.

'Well, sir, that was a substantial bolt. And when I saw it there was no evidence that it had been recently forced or damaged. In other words, the defence is surely going to raise the fact that Lily must have voluntarily let Mann into her room to have sex the day she was killed. She could simply just have kept him bolted out if she didn't want him to touch her.'

'It's not our job to find ways of clearing him, Sarge. We're here to nail the bastard,' DC Hughes sneered.

'Is the incorrect answer, DC Hughes,' the DCI told him. 'And kindly watch your language in a full briefing. Especially with ladies present. Which I probably shouldn't say, but I make no excuse.

'DS Darling is absolutely right. We should be looking at both sides of the argument, not just giving one side. I need to present CPS with a case that passes the threshold, that looks like it has a good chance of success, with limited risk of a future finding of an unsafe conviction. So is there a simple explanation why Lily opened her door to him, knowing what he was like?'

'Sir, sorry if this sounds flippant. It's not meant to. But unless she kept the vodka bottle in there for peeing in, she'd have had to open the door at some point to go to the loo. Her mother was out on a long shift, she might have been bursting after a few hours,' PC Polly Fleming suggested.

'Just supposing she knew Mann was downstairs, and he was making noise to let her keep thinking that. She sneaks out of her room to go to the bathroom and while she's in there, Mann creeps quietly up the stairs and is waiting for her when she comes out of there.'

There was a hush in the room while they all considered the implication of that.

'The dirty ...' the DCI stopped himself in time. It was one thing him swearing in front of Ted and Jack, perhaps even his full team. But when there were others present he wouldn't allow it from anyone, not even himself.

'This is probably stating the blindingly bloody obvious, but we haven't had Mann's clothing for the day of the offence. His shirts that were with the unwashed load had no traces of blood or anything similar on them. Is there a reason for not having the others?' Isabel asked.

'At the time, he wasn't a suspect,' the DCI told her. 'He also provided a DNA sample without a murmur, so there was no immediate suspicion of him. I suppose they'll have been washed by now.'

'They might not, sir,' Ted put in. 'We know Mann stripped Lily's bed and put the bedding and all her clothes from the laundry basket in the machine with some of his shirts to make up a full load, which he then forgot to switch on. Supposing he disposed of the clothes he was wearing when he killed her in some other way? Put them in the bin or something? Is it worth a search of the area near his home? They may well have had considerable bloodstaining on them.'

'He surely wouldn't have been stupid enough to put them in his own dustbin?' the DCI sounded dubious.

'Probably not, sir,' Ted agreed. 'Maybe he took them somewhere else? Are there any communal bins nearby? Any builder's skips, perhaps? One thing I've noticed about him is he seems to spend a lot of time showering. He always smells strongly of some kind of shower gel. He may just be clean by nature but he may desperately be trying to rid himself of any lingering traces of Lily. Not just physically but psychologically.'

'Can we get back in that house and do a much more in depth search?' Isabel asked. 'There is just a possibility, if his first thought had been to get himself into the shower and scrubbed clean, a bit of a Lady Macbeth moment, that he may have dropped his clothes on the bathroom floor. In which case, we could well find traces of Lily's blood and other bodily fluids there, which would be almost impossible for him to explain away.'

'Right, good, this is more like it. Let's get him back in here with his lawyer later today. Ted, you keep on with him, see what else you can get out of him. Let's use our twenty-four hours to hold on to him and meanwhile, Isabel, we need a ruddy miracle from you and your team, please.

'We also need to get the wife out of the way to talk to her while the house is being searched, but I don't want her brought in here while Mann is in the building. Maurice, you go with PC Fleming to pick her up and take her to another station, borrow one of their rooms and have a nice long talk with her. See what, if anything, she knew.

'Anything else, anyone?'

'Sir, probably something and nothing,' Sgt Wheeler put in. 'We had a call on Christmas Eve. Someone complaining of a car parked on the pavement so they couldn't get past with a wheelchair without going on the road.'

'Was it followed up?'

'Sir, seriously? With the staffing levels we have at the best of times, let alone on Christmas Eve? We also had a call about someone throwing chips out of a car window. We didn't follow that one up, either. I just raised the parked car because it was near the footpath where Lily's body was found. It was a dark-coloured car, possibly a Ford but the caller wasn't sure. And Mann does drive a black Ford, doesn't he, although they're hardly rare. No registration number taken, though, and no model given.'

'Get someone back to that eye witness and get more from them. Anything they noticed. A sticker of some sort in the back window, perhaps. We need to be able to place Mann's car there.

'Any sightings of Lily anywhere else? What about on the buses going up to Bramhall?'

'Sir, that footpath is a short cut towards Becky Adler's house, so it looks as if that might have been where Lily was heading,' Rob O'Connell put in. 'And I wondered if, because she was a runner, she might just have run there. Becky told me Lily hadn't phoned or texted her to say she was on her way but that was typical of her. She didn't use her phone much and she'd often just turn up there on the doorstep.'

'Had she phoned Lily to ask her out for Christmas? We haven't found Lily's phone yet. What about records from the network provider? Let's chase that up.'

'Sir, no, Becky didn't call, she had her own plans. She wasn't expecting them to meet up. But she said Lily often came round on spec and she'd sometimes stay over. Becky's parents didn't mind. She also confirmed that Lily would frequently run there, as a training exercise.'

'That's the bit that's bothering me, sir,' Jack Gregson said. 'If Lily was a runner, and a good one, and if Mann left his car at the end of that footpath to go after her, how did he manage to catch her? And from the position where the body was found, he caught her over quite a short distance.'

Ted again spoke up.

'That could be a physique thing, sir. Cross country runners are often small and skinny. I've done a bit myself. If you look at the top sprinters, though, it's all about power, strength. We know, from what we've seen of him, that Mann is powerfully built, muscular. Lily mentioned in her diary that he does weightlifting and that would certainly fit with my impression of his build when I had hold of him at the mortuary. I could see him easily overhauling her on a short distance.'

'Makes sense to me. Right, anyone got anything else at this stage?'

'Just to remind you that even if we find blood or whatever on the bathroom floor, we can't realistically get you any results within your twenty-four hours. Nothing like that. It sadly doesn't work like that outside bad crime fiction,' Isabel reminded the DCI then, seeing his expression, she went on, 'But we will of course perform our usual miracles, with an added dollop of the impossible.'

'But you can tell us if you find blood traces or not?'

'That we can. Just not immediately whose blood it is.'

'Can whoever does the bathroom search please just check if he's a wet or dry shaver? I'm getting to know our Mr Mann a bit now. I'd put money on his excuse for any blood stains being the old "cut himself shaving" ploy,' Ted asked her.

'Sir, I went back to see that sex worker ...'

Despite the serious situation, a ripple of amusement interrupted DC Maurice Brown's input.

The DCI sighed and shook his head.

'Sexual Health Worker, Maurice, you plonker. A sex worker is something else entirely.'

'Aye, right, sorry, sir. Well, this Maxine, the one who had dealings with Lily. We compared notes and dates from Lily's diary with times she'd been to see her, and what she'd said. A lot of it matches. She needs to check with her bosses but she'd be more than happy to give us all her notes, if they okay it.'

'Why did she never think of reporting this to the police? Perhaps going with Lily to make an official complaint?'

'She did, sir. Maxine, I mean. Not to this station, but she did go to the police and she did tell them her concerns about Lily and gave them copies of what she'd been told.'

For the second time, the room went quiet. Then Jim Baker started to rumble, like a volcano perilously close to erupting.

'Right, this one won't be our enquiry but I want chapter and verse from you, Maurice, on everything this woman told you. Which station she went to, who she spoke to, what details she gave them, and did she ever chase it up.

'It looks to me like a strong possibility that some lazy or inept copper, or possibly even a bent one, has sat on his hands over this. And that means that his lack of action may have directly contributed to the death of this young lass. We're going after Mann until we nail him, if he's guilty, but I also want whichever officer has let this slip through the net hung out to dry.

'And I want those clothes found. Make sure the forensics team turn the place inside out and Inspector Turner, can you get some of your Uniforms on to searching bins in the area? Bins, skips, anything they can think of. With luck, there may not have been a collection in the area since Christmas Eve so let's crack on with it, see what we can find.'

The briefing was breaking up. Jim Baker nodded to Ted and Jack to stay behind.

'No pressure, Ted, but clearly we need something a bit more than we've got now before I can persuade CPS to let us charge him. We might be able to go ahead on the sex with a child under the age of consent for now, but we want him on that murder.

'Bloody good point about the razor, too. Second-guessing him is our best way forward now. That and getting lucky enough to find those missing clothes. At least he can't have burnt them. If he'd lit a bonfire anywhere on Christmas Eve, some nosy neighbour would have reported him. Jack, I want you to get out there and supervise the Uniform search for them. That's still our best hope.

'Before you go, just give Maurice a prod to get all his notes sorted about what this Maxine woman told him. I need it asap to put to CPS. Sex worker, eh? Good old Maurice. You can always rely on him to put his foot in it. Still, she was happy to talk to him and that's the main thing. And he's definitely going to be the best one to talk to the mother, to find out what, if anything, she knew or guessed.

'In the meantime, I'm going to be looking into who this was reported to and why no action was taken. And god help them if I find out it was just brushed to one side. We could have put a stop to this before it got this far if some lazy bastard somewhere had taken the action they should have done.'

Chapter Twenty-six

'Thank you, Constable,' Ted told the uniformed PC who had come into the interview room to pass on a message to him in a low voice before leaving.

'Mr Mann, I've just been informed that the Forensic Investigators have found traces of blood on the bathroom floor at your house. I wondered if you had any explanation of how they got there.'

Mann looked unconcerned and shrugged.

'I must have cut myself shaving.'

'But don't you use an electric razor? The team report that there is one in your bathroom.'

'That's just for a quick tidy up, before I go out somewhere. If I want a really close shave, I use a disposable razor.'

'I see. And where do you put the disposable razors, after you've used them?'

'Really, Sergeant? Mr Mann is being patient and cooperative. Is it essential to quiz him about his shaving routine?'

'I'm just trying to be thorough, Ms Castle. We want to make absolutely sure that we get the person responsible for Lily's rape and death, and that we don't waste valuable time going off in the wrong direction.'

'Well, this is a waste of time. Our Lil wasn't killed at the house.'

The solicitor made a gesture to silence her client as soon as he started to speak but she was too late. He'd said it, and Ted had heard him.

'Was she not, Mr Mann? We're still trying to establish all the facts surrounding her death. Including where it took place.'

Mann started to bluster.

'Well, you told me she'd been killed where she was found. Up Bramhall way.'

'I don't believe I did, Mr Mann. I think I told you where she'd been found but nothing more than that. I apologise if there was any misunderstanding. Now, back to the disposal of the razors you use.'

Mann made an effort to recover his stride.

'I'd have chucked them in the pedal bin thing in the bathroom, then it would get emptied into the dustbin.'

'And yet our investigators haven't found any such disposable razor in either place.'

'Well, the bloody bins will have been emptied by now, of course,' Mann retorted.

'Yet the blood is relatively recent, according to the team. And the bins haven't, in fact, been emptied since a few days before Christmas. But let's move on from that. When you cut yourself shaving, do you not just grab a bit of toilet paper and stick it over the nick to stop the blood going everywhere? I know that's what I do.'

The solicitor put in impatiently, 'Fascinating though it is for you to be comparing shaving habits, is it really getting us anywhere, Sergeant?'

Ted pointedly ignored her and continued doggedly on.

'You see, there was rather more blood found than the team would normally associate with a shaving nick. There had been an attempt to clean it up, but they have the means to detect the smallest trace. Can you offer any explanation?'

'I don't know. Perhaps something happened to the missus. Or to Lily? Women's things, maybe? Period stuff? I don't know. Could be something like that.'

'I see. Well, we have officers talking to Mrs Barrow now

so as you say, no doubt she can throw some light on it for us.'

Mann's eyes narrowed at this news. Ted pressed on.

'Mr Mann, do you happen to remember what you were wearing on Christmas Eve?'

'No, I don't. Do you?' Mann snapped, his patience clearly starting to wear thin.

'It's purely a matter of routine, sir, but we would like to examine those clothes. Perhaps they were among the items you put in the washing machine? The load you failed to start?'

'No, they were ...'

Once again the solicitor made a gesture to silence him, at the same time that Mann himself realised he'd almost walked into a trap.

'You remember sufficiently well to be sure they were not among the clothes you put in the washing machine on Christmas Eve?'

Before any of them could say anything further, the door to the interview room opened and the DCI walked in.

'For the tape, Detective Chief Inspector Baker has just entered the room,' Ted said, wondering if he'd done something wrong which necessitated the Big Boss coming in to pick up the pieces.

The DCI pulled out the seat next to Ted and lowered his big frame on to it. He nodded to Ms Castle, obviously knowing her by sight.

'Mr Mann, as DS Darling has just said, I'm DCI Baker, the Senior Investigating Officer in this case. I have to tell you, Mr Mann, that the search team at your house has found some blood-stained clothing in a bin bag, partially buried in a skip outside a property three streets away from yours. These clothes are the same size as ones found at your house and the same make as some of them.

'In addition, I've just been informed by the officer who's speaking to Mrs Barrow, that they look like clothes which you own, according to her. Is there anything you'd like to tell me now about these items?'

A momentary panic flashed over the man's face. He blustered to hide it.

'You had no right showing stuff like that to Janice. She's been through enough already.'

'We needed to get the clothes identified, Mr Mann, prior to sending them off for testing to see if the blood on them is a match for Lily's.'

Mann seemed to recover his stride.

'Nothing to do with me, mate. I'm not responsible for what someone else chucks in their skip.'

'You don't have to say anything at all at this stage, Mr Mann,' the solicitor told him.

'Further tests will, of course, also reveal the DNA of the person who wore the shirt. In view of this latest finding, I believe that we are now past the threshold of evidence required to consider you as a prime suspect for the murder of Lily Barrow. I've spoken to the CPS and they agree with me.

'Raymond Mann, I am now arresting you in connection with the murder of Lily Barrow, and on a further charge of engaging in sexual activity with a child under the age of sixteen. I'll just remind you that you are still under caution. You'll be taken to be charged and held here pending further investigations. You will, of course, be allowed to consult with your solicitor.'

'This is ridiculous. I didn't ...'

'Don't say anything further,' his solicitor interrupted him sharply.

The same PC in uniform had followed the DCI into the room. He took Mann to the charge room, the solicitor trotting in their wake.

'Have we got him, sir? Enough to make it stick?' Ted asked the Big Boss when they had left the room.

'Too early to say for sure, Ted, but CPS are happy with me charging him. This is where the hard work really starts. Most of all, we need forensics to pull out all the stops and get us a miracle. We need full analysis of those clothes we've just found, and we need that done in bloody record time.

'With that in mind, we'll all adjourn to The Grapes when we knock off, and I'll ask Isabel to join us. See if you can work your charms on her to give us high priority on this one.'

'I'll be a bit late tonight. We're all going for a drink after work,' Ted told Trev when he found a quiet moment to make the call.

'That sounds good. Does that mean you caught the baddy?'

'Well, we've charged someone, but we still have a long way to go to make a watertight case against him. This is just an early celebration. And I'm in charge of chatting up the Forensic Coordinator to make sure our results get pushed through as fast as humanly possible, and definitely before anyone else's.'

'I hate him already. Is he better looking than me?'

Ted chuckled.

'You're quite safe. He's a she. Goodness knows how Big Jim thinks I'll be able to charm her. And no one is better looking than you.'

It was Trev's turn to laugh.

'You say all the right things. And of course you can charm her. You can be very charming and very persuasive when you try. I should know.'

'I won't stay any longer than absolutely essential.'

'It's fine. Don't worry. Go and mingle with your new workmates and be devastatingly charming to this poor lady from Forensics. Now there's some progress, does that mean we can definitely spend New Year's Day together?'

'I told you. That's guaranteed, because I volunteered for Christmas Day.'

'Sssh, don't tempt fate. What if there's another serious crime and they pull everyone in?'

'Seriously, they won't. Just don't tell the criminal fraternity that there won't be anyone in the office at all that day, just on call at the end of the phone.'

'I'll see you later. I'll keep something warm for you. And some food, too.'

Ted hoped he wasn't blushing when he went back to rejoin the team and head over to The Grapes with them.

He was surprised to see that Maurice was looking morose, sitting on his own, nursing a half-pint. He went to join him, before he spoke to Isabel.

'What's up, Maurice? I know we've a long way still to go, but this is a good result so far.'

Maurice moved his raincoat so Ted could find room on the bench seat next to him.

'It was talking to Lily's mam this afternoon, Ted. Having to show her those blood-stained clothes and watching the look on her face when she realised that it was the bloke she's been living with who'd killed her daughter.'

He slipped naturally into informality now they were finished for the day and out of the office.

'I mean, she's lost everything. Her little girl, her bloke, and her home. He owns it, so whatever happens to him, she can't go on living there, and I doubt if she'd want to. I just couldn't imagine losing my two. I love the bones of them.'

He paused to pull out a handkerchief with which he wiped his eyes then blew his nose.

'Ignore me, Ted, I'm a soppy sod when it comes to anything to do with kids. And I know we're not talking shop here, or not supposed to, but I'd bet everything I own that poor woman knew nothing about what was going on. Which is going to make it even harder for her. I wonder what's going to become of her?

'The one consolation is if we do succeed in getting him put away, a nonce like that is going to get a very bad time inside. Especially when it gets out that she was effectively his own stepdaughter.'

Ted wondered the same thing about Mrs Barrow as he took his Gunner and went over to find Isabel. His brief exchange with Maurice had confirmed the opinion he'd already formed of him. He may well be a skiver and a plodder but he genuinely cared about people. To Ted, that was an important quality.

Isabel was just finishing her drink when Ted joined her and offered her another.

'That was good timing, Ted. Yes please, I'll take a dry white wine with you. Although I should warn you, if you're plying me with alcohol in order to obtain special favours, you're wasting your time. We are honestly going as fast as we can.'

'I know you are and we appreciate it. I think we're all just a bit on edge, wanting to get this wrapped up.'

'Cheers,' he added as he came back and handed her the wine he'd just bought for her.

'All the best. I've enjoyed working with you, but this will be our last case together.'

'Was I as bad as that?' Ted joked.

'No, not at all, I'm just transferring to another area. My mother's had a stroke. Dad's finding it very hard to manage everything on his own. The kids and I are moving up there so I can help him out a bit when I'm not working.'

Ted stayed discreetly quiet. She noticed and smiled her appreciation.

'No, there's no other half I need to consult before making the decision. Thank you for not asking. He headed for the hills long ago, and good riddance to him.

'I know already who my replacement coordinator is going to be and I think you're going to get on with him. I hear on the grapevine that you like cats.'

'We have five, at the moment. Or we had when I left for work this morning. My partner's the real cat fanatic. He could well have smuggled another one or two in by the time I get home tonight.'

'Well, Doug is potty about them. I don't know much about them, not my thing, but I do know he takes them to shows and such like. Not sure what they are. Short Coats? Does that sound right? Something like that.'

'British Shorthairs, probably. Thanks for the tip. I'll be sure to ask after them when we meet.'

'It sounds strange but he's the semen stain expert. Weird though it sounds, and I dread to think why, but he's made that his speciality.'

Ted laughed.

'I'll probably stick to conversations about cats, until I get to know him better.'

There was a television high up on the wall behind the bar, showing the early evening local news. A cheer went up from the team as they recognised their own Chief Super doing a piece to camera outside the station to announce that a forty-three-year-old man had been changed in connection with the murder of Lily Barrow. One or two less than complimentary comments about him were made in a low enough tone that hopefully the DCI didn't hear them.

Big Jim came across to talk to Ted with his half-full glass in his hand as Isabel finished her drink and left.

'You've done good work on this case, Ted. Very impressive. You know that the real donkey work starts now and I'm counting on you to make sure the whole team get all their notes together speedily. I know you're good at paperwork, so I'm putting you in charge of it to make sure it's all in order. Jack's a good sergeant, a good team leader, but he'd be the first to admit he's not the hottest on the paperwork side. He'll be glad enough to hand it over to you, let him get on with running the rest of the legwork.'

'Yes, sir. Sir, I was wanting to talk to you about an initiative that I think we should consider, arising out of this current case,' Ted began enthusiastically.

'Ted, behave yourself. We've finished for the day. We're off duty. Work will wait. Whatever your brainwave is, and I'm sure it will be a good one, it will keep until tomorrow. Now why don't you get off home to that young man of yours? I enjoyed the brief chat I had with him at our Christmas drinks do. You'll have to bring him again. He's clearly very intelligent, well educated and travelled. He seems very nice.'

The Big Boss was suddenly stumbling over his words, clearly uncomfortable.

'Not that I'm ... I mean, he was nice to talk to ...'

Ted smiled patiently.

'It's fine, sir. He said much the same about you. That you seemed very nice.'

Big Jim grinned ruefully.

'I do try, Ted, I honestly do, but some things are a bit beyond my comprehension and I'd be the first to admit it. You seem very happy together, at least. Perhaps your relationship will fare a bit better than the average copper's marriage. We don't make very good marriage material, especially in our line of work.'

There was a note of bitterness in the DCI's voice, Ted noticed. If the rumours about his wife were even half true, he didn't envy him his home life and was inwardly grateful yet again for his own. He still could hardly believe his luck that he and Trev were so good together.

On a whim, on his way home, Ted stopped and bought a single red rose wrapped in cellophane. Trev was a classic film buff, especially early black and whites. Ted's taste was much simpler. For reasons he couldn't really explain even to himself, Mel Brooks' controversial comedy film *Blazing Saddles* remained one of his favourites. There were times when its juvenile humour was just what he needed at the end of a hard shift.

He'd introduced Trev to it, and the scene with the sheriff presenting the showgirl with a 'wed wose' as she'd lispingly called it, had become a special joke between them. He wanted something to show Trev how much he appreciated his support, without which his work would have been that much harder.

It had the desired effect.

'Can you leave me the car tomorrow and go in on the bike? Only I need to take John to the vet at some point. He's riddled with worms, for sure, but I just want to check his skinniness is no more than that.'

'John?' Ted queried, looking round the kitchen where their five cats were prowling round in search of food and attention.

Trev put his finger to his lips then pointed to a chair pushed under the table. Ted bent down to look and saw a small kitten curled up in a tight ball, apparently sleeping peacefully.

'Meet John Deacon. Our latest band member.'

'Hello, John. Welcome to your new home.'

Chapter Twenty-seven

'Come in, Ted. Take a seat. Have some coffee.'

It was more an instruction than an invitation. The Big Boss had already plonked it on the far side of his desk in front of Ted. It looked like a cup of hot molasses. Ted wondered fleetingly if it was some sort of initiation test, to determine pecking order in the team.

Trev had bought Ted some expensive organic green tea as a Christmas stocking filler. Ted had initially been sceptical but Trev had told him teasingly that it was totally zen and would help rebalance his chakras. He was slowly acquiring a taste for it, liberally laced with honey. It was certainly easier on the palate than the ordeal facing him now.

'I wanted to give you a chance to talk about this idea of yours, while we've got a bit of a lull waiting for the rest of the forensic evidence on Mann. Have they finished with the house yet?'

'Yes, sir. Mann is living there alone now and it's a condition of his bail that he remains there.'

'And what about Lily's mother?'

'She's gone to stay with a sister in St Helens, sir. I imagine she'll break off all contact with Mann. Even if he's cleared of killing Lily, he's still admitted to sleeping with her. Even if it did only happen once she was sixteen, which is looking more unlikely the further we dig, it's still a hell of a thing for Mrs Barrow to come to terms with.'

'Right, well, first I wanted to fill you in on what's

happening with the team. I've already talked to Jack and he's on board with the whole thing.

'I'm impressed with your work so far. The paperwork's good, as I knew it would be, and I liked your interview technique with Mann. Like I said to you early on, with Lennie only weeks away from his official finish date, the DI's slot is coming vacant.

'The slight problem is that you've got the exams but not the CID experience and Jack has the experience but not the exams. I couldn't possibly make you up to DI yet, not even in an acting role. I've talked at length to the powers that be and this is what we're proposing. Jack steps up as Acting DI with immediate effect, as we know Lennie isn't coming back. You work closely with him and, providing you don't make a total balls-up of anything over the next six months or so, the DI's role is yours at the end of that. How does that sound to you?'

'It sounds incredible, sir. Thank you,' Ted responded, trying not to choke on his coffee.

'Well, for god's sake don't start getting soppy on me. It's not a bloody Oscars speech. We also need to expand the team. I've been asking around at Command meetings and I've put the word out on Force Orders that we're recruiting. I've got provision for two more DCs. Two because, as I'm sure you're aware, I have a feeling Hughes won't want to stay with us for long. He's too much Lennie's man, and his methods don't fit with the new ethos here.

'And just to prove I do listen, I've let it be known that we welcome applications from anyone. I absolutely refuse point blank to go down the positive discrimination road. I want good coppers. Outstanding ones. I don't want them just because they tick some box or another for gender or race or disability or anything else. But if we find some good ones who just happen not to be IC1 male, that's all the better for us. And it's only right that you and Jack should have some input on who we appoint as you've got to work more closely with them than anyone else, and get the results we need out of them.'

He downed a good half of his coffee in one swallow. As well as a cast-iron stomach, he must have had a throat of asbestos as it was still too hot for Ted to do more than take the odd sip at.

'So now tell me about this idea.'

'Well, sir,' Ted began, glad of a valid excuse to ignore his drink for a bit longer. 'I know Lily hadn't been reported as missing before her body was found. But with what had been going on with her, and with the reports from the Sexual Health Worker, it occurred to me that with someone like her, if we'd known earlier what was happening to her, we might have been able to keep her safe.'

The DI got up to serve himself more coffee. He lifted the jug towards Ted in a gesture of invitation, but Ted shook his head.

'On that subject, the PC who took the initial report and didn't instigate any action on it has been traced and put on notice of disciplinary action. He'll probably just get a slapped wrist and retraining but it's a mistake he'll never make again, hopefully.'

'I wondered if it was worth going through the files of any missing young people on our patch and doing a bit of digging, to see if we might be able to find out what made them disappear in the first place.'

'It's a nice idea, but there's bugger all budget for preventative policing at the moment. And this team is supposed to be for Serious Crime. You know, the murders, rapes, abductions, serious assaults, that sort of thing. There are already designated units for missing persons.'

'I appreciate that, sir. But if ever we do get a lull, it's possibly something Maurice could do. He'd be good at that, it's right up his street. And it might make less work for us in the long run. If we can find young people and get them to a place of safety, that will be one less murder or rape or whatever on our patch for us to deal with.

'Trev and I have set up a self-defence club for youngsters at the dojo where we train. The schools they attend tell us it's already having a dramatic effect on bullying rates. Give a kid a bit of self-assurance and they become much less of a target. That's why I think if we look into the cases a bit more and try to address why youngsters have decided to go on the run, we may be able to bring more of them home safe. That's surely worth a try, sir?'

'Now you're wanting to talk us out of the crimes we've been set up to investigate?' the DCI asked him, but he was smiling as he said it. 'It sounds like an idea that's worth exploring. I know you're good at putting proposals on paper, so work one up on this for me. But not at the expense of the Mann case. I want that piece of work off the patch first of all.

'Good work, Ted.'

As Ted stood up to leave, the Big Boss told him, 'Don't forget to finish your coffee before you get back to work.'

'Where's your report on your interview with Mrs Barrow, Maurice?' Ted asked him. 'Come on, I should have had that by now. I shouldn't need to be chasing you for paperwork all the time.'

'Sorry, Sarge, just finishing it up now. Give me ten minutes.'

'I'll give you five, and that's being generous. Once you've done that I want to talk to you about something else I want you working on whenever you have a moment. And that doesn't mean it's an excuse to drop everything else and sit at your desk pushing files round, looking busy.'

Ted had already got DC Brown's measure. He saw the good qualities in him but he also knew that without constant supervision, he would always opt for the easiest option and least work. He turned to go back to his own desk then paused to add, 'And Maurice? Purple sparkly nail varnish? You know the Regs say pale pink or transparent only.'

Maurice returned his grin sheepishly.

'Aye, sorry, Sarge. The twins wanted to play princesses and I got roped in. Then I couldn't find any of that stuff to take it off with. I'll get some on the way home and get it sorted.'

'See that you do, before the Big Boss notices. Now get a move on with that report.'

It took him longer than five minutes. But when Maurice brought his report across to Ted's desk, it was well presented. Ted told him to pull up a chair while they talked. He started by explaining his idea for tackling some of the missing persons files pro-actively.

Maurice nodded enthusiastically.

'Bloody good idea, Ted.'

'We're at work now, DC Brown, not in the pub,' Ted reminded him.

'Right you are, Sarge,' he responded cheerfully.

'What I need you to do for me is go through the MissPers files for our patch and see what you can pick up from them. Any hint anywhere of a possible reason why these young people left in the first place. If you can pinpoint that, even in one or two cases, we might be able to get somewhere.

'And Maurice, remember this isn't a skiver's charter. I want a proper job done on it, and some results to show for whatever time you spend on it. Once you've got something, if you find any leads, you and I will take a drive round and see if we can do something with them.'

'Right you are, Sarge, whatever you say.'

New Year's Day

'That was very nice. All of it.'

Trev stretched languidly, one lazy hand brushing *croissant* crumbs from the crumpled sheets. John, the young kitten, went to investigate if they might be edible and of feline interest. The vet had confirmed he was carrying a heavy worm burden but although that had now been dealt with, he still seemed to have a voracious appetite.

'You're sure we won't be interrupted today? We can definitely do shopping, and lunch, and perhaps some more shopping after lunch?'

'I told you. This is officially my day off. Do not disturb. And it's my Christmas present to you. Whatever you want to do, whatever you want me to buy you, that's fine. It's my way of saying thank you for everything you do for me. I know it's not easy being with a copper and I do appreciate you.'

'That's so sweet. Now, if I'm about to inflict extreme pain and suffering on your credit card, we'd better start economising. So we should start by sharing the water for a shower.'

'We might not get out until lunchtime if we do,' Ted warned him, but followed him meekly to the bathroom.

It was late morning before they got to the retail outlet. The car park was almost full already. It was Trev's idea of heaven, Ted's idea of hell. But he'd promised.

'While it's later than we planned, do you want to have lunch first then shop afterwards?'

Trev draped an arm around his shoulders as they walked towards the entrance. They could see straight away that it was crowded with people, avariciously eager to find bargains in the sales.

'It's heaving in here. Why don't we shop now then pick up a picnic and go and find somewhere quieter?'

'But this is your treat. You prefer fine dining. A decent restaurant. I'm more the bag of chips at a picnic table sort. A proper pleb.'

Trev stopped, ignoring the throng of people trying to push their way through. He turned to face his partner, put both his arms around him and pulled him close, ignoring the tuts of annoyance.

'The thing I love about you most of all is how selfless you are. In everything. You're always thinking of me, making sure I'm happy and getting whatever I want. I know you hate this, which is why I appreciate you doing it. So let's compromise. Take me shopping first and spoil me horribly. Then we'll pick up an outrageously expensive gourmet picnic from a deli and go somewhere quieter to eat it and do some walking.

'We could whiz down over the border into North Wales, find a hill or two. Moel Famau perhaps? That's not far, and it's good for blowing away the cobwebs.'

'It'll be heaving as much as this place,' Ted warned him. 'You know how popular it is for families on a Bank Holiday.'

Trev gave him one of his most mischievous grins.

'Then we'll just have to behave so outrageously that all the old grannies and the families with kiddies will flee back to the safety of their homes and leave it to us.

'Now come on, open your wallet, blow away the moths and get ready to spoil me rotten. I absolutely must have new jeans. And a new shirt or three. And whatever else takes my fancy.'

Ted was back at work the next day in time for morning briefing. He could feel the heightened buzz in the team which he knew could only mean good news on the Mann case.

He'd enjoyed his day off, even though it had been an expensive one. Trev must have tried on almost every pair of jeans of his size in the shop before settling for the first pair he'd seen, plus a second pair in a different colour. Which naturally meant two expensive designer shirts, one to work with each shade, and a cashmere sweater which would work with either. Ted didn't mind. He considered it a small price to pay to see his partner happy.

They'd been the only couple mad enough to be using the picnic tables where they'd stopped to have their lunch. The cold weather had also kept the number of fellow walkers on Moel Famau down to a few hardy souls. It meant they'd both spent part of the day doing something they loved. It also meant Ted had arrived back at work feeling clear-headed and ready for action.

'Developments?' Ted asked Jack, just as the DCI came in to address the team.

'Oh, yes. Possibly the final straw to break the camel's back.'

'Right, everyone, for those who've not yet heard. I just got the results this morning. Forensics really did pull out all the stops for us. The bloodstained clothing. The blood matches Lily Barrow and they have the evidence to show that the clothes were worn by Ray Mann. So unless he's going to come up with the story that someone else had access to his wardrobe and wore his things to murder Lily without leaving their own traces, I would say we have him where we want him.

'We need to interview him again today, in the presence of his solicitor, put these latest findings to him and see what he has to say for himself. Ted, you carry on interviewing him. You've done a good job so far. But this time I think we'll crank up the pressure. Jack, you sit in as well, throw in a few questions from left field, see if we can rattle him a bit into saying something inadvisable.'

'Good cop, bad cop, sir?' Jack asked him.

'Okay, everyone. Jack, I know that was just a light-hearted remark, but let me make something abundantly clear. I'm not pointing the finger and I don't want to dwell on the past. But this team hasn't got the greatest track record in the force. You could say it was like a decent rugby team which got the tries but never the conversions. There've been too many cases that have fallen at the last fence because of sloppy paperwork.'

The DCI went on with his motivational address, seemingly unaware of mixing his sporting metaphors.

'I'm SIO on this case and I expect better. And just so you're all fully in the picture, DS Gregson is stepping up as Acting DI for now, assisted by DS Darling who is a stickler for paperwork. Believe me, I've seen his idea of how a report should be presented and it's high standard. Rightly so. Get sloppy with anything you hand his way and he's going to jump all over you, with my blessing. And get used to it because it's likely that before too long, he's going to be your new DI.

'You're all individually good coppers. I've got the go ahead to bring in two more DCs to increase the team's strength. We have the potential to be a cracking good team. The best in the division. So let's prove that by nailing Mann and presenting CPS with absolutely all the bullets we can find for them to fire at him.'

Chapter Twenty-eight

The DCI had been right about DC Hughes. After Ted had pulled him up a few times over late paperwork, poor procedure and his general attitude to people, especially suspects, he'd put in for a transfer to another division. The team went through the motions of giving him a send-off with drinks in The Grapes and a card signed by them all, as they'd done for the departing DI. But Hughes's shoes had already been filled by two new officers.

DC Dennis Tibbs had joined them, fresh from doing undercover work in a unit specialising in gang-related crime. He was perfect for such work. He didn't look much like most people's idea of a policeman, with his finely honed body-builder's physique and designer clothes. He was in a new relationship, planning to settle down, and his girlfriend had been pestering him to find a less dangerous post.

He told everyone he preferred Virgil to Dennis, a reference to the Sidney Poitier character in the film *In the Heat of the Night*. His sense of humour quickly endeared him to everyone. Whenever he was asked to do anything when he first joined them, he would respond with, 'Is it because I is black?', always with a broad smile.

DC Tina Bailey was young, keen and ambitious. She came with glowing references and had certainly earned her place on merit from her record. She was an ideal fit for the team as she'd come from working on Missing Persons. She was far from being the token female member and from the start she asserted herself, quick to stamp on any hint of a sexist remark. It was usually Maurice Brown who could be relied on to make one, but Tina was more than a match for him.

Ted was quickly realising that Maurice never meant any harm or offence. He just had a bad habit of opening his mouth before engaging his brain. Ted had found that out working with him on Missing Persons' files whenever they had a spare moment.

'There's this one here, Sarge. I think I might have spotted a reason behind this lad disappearing.'

He put the file in front of Ted who had pulled up a chair to sit next to his desk.

'Lad's first name is Bentley. Bentley Logan. I mean, who does that to a kid? He's going to go through life getting called Bent and I'm wondering, from what I've been reading about him, if he's maybe gay and that caused a rift at home.'

'And what are you basing that idea on?'

'Well, look at his list of friends. He hangs round with a bunch of lasses all the time. The only lad in the group. He's got girlie interests, from what his mam said about him. He likes going shopping with them. He's in a drama group with them. Stuff like that. It's all a bit too girlie for a lad of his age.'

'Do you think I'm girlie, Maurice?' Ted asked.

'Well, no, Sarge. You're a bit different to your lot. SFO, martial arts, that sort of stuff. Not like your average gay bloke.'

'Maurice,' Ted told him patiently, 'there is no average gay bloke. No more than there's an average straight bloke. You put on sparkly nail varnish to play with your daughters. Does that make you girlie? Trev and I have gay friends who would clearly surprise you, they're so far from the stereotype image you have. You really can't judge people like this, not if you want to be a good copper.

'But you may have something here. It's certainly worth looking into. Something else occurs to me as a possible reason for him going. If he's so popular with the girls at his school, there's a good chance that the other lads are jealous of him so he might be getting bullied about it. It could be as simple as that.'

Ted picked the folder up and looked at the face in the photograph. A fifteen-year-old boy. Good looking. Strikingly so. A touch of sensitivity about his expression. His was a recent file. He'd been missing for a month but with no sightings of him or news from him since, the file was under review so Ted had put Maurice onto it.

There was no trace of Bentley Logan's mobile phone having been used since his disappearance. It was switched off so there was no way to find its current whereabouts.

'Let me have a read through the file, then I'll decide if it's worth us taking a look into it. We could do worse than go and talk to the parents again. Make sure all your paperwork is up to date so you're free to come with me if I do decide to go.'

The team was working well with Ted and Jack in charge together to sharpen things up. The Big Boss was noticing a vast improvement in efficiency. Even the CPS prosecutors were commenting favourably on getting files on time and in good order. Ted was taking advantage of any quiet moments to go out with individual members of the team following up lines of enquiry and evaluating them at the same time. Having a closer look at the Bentley Logan case would give him a reason to work some more with Maurice.

The parents had done a televised appeal for news of their missing son. The father was in the Merchant Navy, often away from home for long periods of time. The mother worked part-time in a local shop. Bentley had a twin sister, Olivia. There were no other children.

Ted found the televised interview and watched it through, several times, sometimes frame by frame. He leaned close to the screen, looking at body language, for the smallest tell which might indicate anything was not as it should be. Then he went to find Maurice again.

'Maurice, I may be wrong, but I think there's something we don't yet know about this case. I think we should go and talk to the parents again. Preferably to the mother. I've got a strong feeling, from watching their appeal on TV, that she knows more than she's said so far. I'll give her a ring, find out if she's at home and more importantly, if the husband is. I don't want to scare her by just turning up on the doorstep and her thinking it's the worst kind of news.'

The Logan's home was a pleasant semi-detached in Reddish. Mrs Logan came to the door when Ted rang the bell. He and Maurice produced their ID as Ted told her, 'As I said on the phone, Mrs Logan, I'm afraid we don't have any further news of Bentley. We just wanted to ask you a few more questions to help with the enquiry.'

'I can tell it's not bad news. You'd have brought a lady officer if it was. Come through to the kitchen, I can put the kettle on. And he likes to be called Ben. He never liked Bentley. That was my husband's choice.'

The interior of the house was spotlessly clean, almost obsessively tidy. There appeared to be air fresheners everywhere, giving it a sickly, cloying, floral scent. Ted strongly suspected there would be no pets in a house like this. The kitchen was bright and almost surgically clean.

'Please take a seat. Would you like some tea, or some coffee?'

Ted seldom said no to a cup of tea and he knew Maurice was the same. They made inconsequential small talk until they were all sitting down around the white-painted table. Ted wasn't surprised the tea was served in delicate bone china cups.

'I'm fairly new to Stockport police, Mrs Logan, so I'm just taking a look at the file on Ben. Fresh eyes. May I ask you a direct question?'

She looked a little taken aback.

'Please do.'

'What do you think happened to Ben?'

'I ... er, well I don't know,' she bought time by fiddling with her teaspoon. They were silver apostle spoons. They reminded Ted of some his grandmother had had long ago. He's lost touch with her, too, when his mother had left home. He noticed Ben's mother had put one on her own saucer even though she didn't take sugar.

'Mrs Logan, we really do want to help. To bring Ben safely home. But I have a feeling there's something you're not telling us. You know Ben's alive, don't you?'

'Well, I hope he is, of course. I'm his mother.'

Ted's voice remained quiet and calm as he went on, 'No, Mrs Logan. You know, don't you?'

She looked from him to Maurice and back again, her eyes filling with tears.

'Will he get into dreadful trouble? I mean, we've been wasting police time. Will we be arrested?'

Maurice got up to get her some kitchen roll.

'Here you go, pet. Don't worry. Just tell us what you know and it'll be fine. We'll sort it.'

'It started with just one little lie. Then I couldn't stop. When the lady officer came to ask me what Ben had been wearing when I last saw him. I told her jeans and trainers and his bomber jacket. But it wasn't true. I couldn't tell the truth, I just couldn't. His father wouldn't have it known in public. He was that ashamed.'

Her look from one to another of them now was pleading. Maurice patted her hand gently, murmuring encouraging words.

'Mrs Logan,' Ted said gently, 'we can only help you if you tell us the truth. If it doesn't need to go any further, it won't.'

She hesitated a long moment before she began to talk.

'Ben was wearing his sister's clothes when he left. He likes to dress as a girl. With a wig and make-up and everything. Has done for a long time. His dad only just found out. They had a blazing row and Ben walked out, still dressed like that. I couldn't let everyone know that. I just couldn't.'

'And you have heard from him since he left, haven't you, Mrs Logan?'

She was crying now, noisy sobs. Maurice had stood up and was patting and rubbing her back. It may not have been politically correct, but he could never stand by and see anyone suffer without wanting to comfort them.

'Not directly. One of the girls he's friends with came into the shop where I work. He's been staying with her. She lives in a big posh house in Poynton Her parents are out most of the time. She has her own suite, away from the main house. They wouldn't notice if she had a load of boys up there. And if they see our Ben, dressed like he does, they'd just think it was a girl from her school. They wouldn't recognise him as the missing boy they may have seen on telly or in the papers.

'She comes in from time to time. The girl. She's called Tiffany. I give her a bit of money to give to Ben, and some of his own things. Some comfy shoes. His feet are bigger than Olivia's. Her shoes must have really hurt him to put on. I'm so sorry. I should have told you the truth but my husband wouldn't hear of it. He doesn't know where Ben is. He really does think he just went missing. I thought I'd give him time to calm down. He's gone back to sea, just this week, so I got word to Ben and he was going to come home. I was going to tell the police then. Honestly I was. Will he get into terrible trouble? Will I?'

'This is a serious matter, Mrs Logan, and I'm afraid it's not up to me to say whether or not further action will be taken. What I suggest you do now is to give us the address where Ben has been staying so that we can go and pick him up and bring him safely home. I'll go in person, so you have my assurance that it will be done discreetly and Ben will be treated correctly. After that I will have to hand the file over to my senior officer to see what will happen next.

'It might be a good idea if you give us some gender neutral clothing to take with us for Ben, just so that he arrives back home dressed as the neighbours are used to seeing him.'

'Well, I never expected that,' Maurice said as they went back to the car, carrying the bag of clothes Ben's mother had sorted out for them. 'So he's a bit of a Lily Savage, eh, the lad? A tranny? Does that mean he's gay? Or that he wants to be a lass? And how did you know?'

'Maurice, first off, tranny is offensive. It sounds, from what his mother said, as if Ben enjoys cross-dressing. Dressing in female clothing doesn't mean someone is gay. Have you ever seen me come to work in a dress?'

'Sorry, Sarge. I honestly don't know anything about this sort of thing. So he wants to change sex, is that it? To be a lass?'

'Possibly not even that. There are cross-dressing men who are in stable relationships with women. It's just a shame his father reacted as he did. And I knew from watching the appeal. When the mother was asked to describe what Ben was wearing when he left home. She was uncomfortable. Because she was lying, and lying clearly doesn't come easily to her.'

'Must have come as a bloody big shock to the dad, eh, though? Seeing his lad in a frock. And him a sailor an' all.'

'You've got two little girls, haven't you? How would you react if one of them came to you to say she wanted to become a boy? Or there was a girl at her school she fancied and wanted to kiss?'

'I'd never stop loving my lasses, whatever they did,' Maurice said fiercely.

'Precisely. That's what my dad said when I came back from a party and said I didn't want to kiss any of the girls there, only a boy, who thumped me when I tried. He told me he loved me then asked me what I wanted for tea.'

'So have you never ... you know, with a woman? Sorry if

that's too personal, Sarge. I'm honestly just trying to understand. So I don't keep putting my foot in my big gob every time I open it.'

Ted chuckled.

'It's fine, Maurice. I don't mind talking about it. No, I've never been with a woman.'

'Bloody hell,' was all Maurice could find to say to that.

'I know you're trying to join the twenty-first century, Maurice. But I think you can probably see why, when I go round now to find Ben, I'd prefer to take Tina with me, rather than you. It's going to be a delicate enough operation, without risking you saying the wrong thing.'

'Aye, fair enough, Sarge. I can see that.'

Ted waited in the service vehicle outside the station while Maurice went in to find Tina. Ted had phoned ahead to tell her she was required and to outline the situation. He was happy to let her drive to their destination in Poynton. He found he could tell a lot about people by the way they drove.

The house was certainly impressive. And secluded. The grounds must have been a couple of acres. Ted could well imagine that with a layout like that, the girl could have had Lord Lucan stashed away there without anyone knowing.

'Blimey, Sarge, this is a bit posh,' Tina remarked, looking round her as she parked the car and got out. 'How does our lad know the girl who lives here? They're surely not at the same school?'

'They're both in the same theatre group, his mum told me.'

'He's almost certainly not just going to open the door to us, though? What if there's nobody there to let us in?'

'We'll just have to try calling through the letterbox, trying to sound non-threatening. And if all else fails, come back when there is someone to open up, with a warrant if necessary.'

Ted could be persuasive when he needed to. After a few minutes of him speaking through the door, assuring Ben that they were there to help, a leaded window high up under the eaves opened and the face of young Ben Logan looked out at them.

'Ben? I'm Detective Sergeant Darling, from Stockport. This is DC Bailey. It's time to come back, Ben. This has gone on long enough. We can help you. But it's not right to be tying up police resources looking for you. Can you come down and let us in, please? I promise you we won't hurt you. I've got a change of clothes here for you. Your mam sent them.'

'And he let you in? Just like that?' the DCI asked, sloshing the coffee jug towards Ted in invitation.

'No thanks, sir, I've just had a green tea.'

The Big Boss made a face.

'What are you drinking that shite for? That'll not put hairs on your chest.'

'It was a Christmas present. From Trev. And no, it wasn't quite just like that with Ben. Tina and I had to be patient and persuasive but he did eventually come down.'

'And was he, you know, wearing girls' stuff?' Jim Baker seemed to be as uncomfortable with the whole idea as Maurice had been.

'He was wearing a track suit belonging to Tiffany, the girl he was staying with, and a pair of his own trainers his mam had sent for him via her.'

The DCI shook his head in disbelief.

'He was there in that house all the time and the girl's parents never knew he was there? It just goes to show that stuff can be going on in your own household, right under your nose, without you knowing a thing about it.'

241

Chapter Twenty-nine

It wasn't always such plain sailing, bringing runaways home safely. Ted was to find that out through bitter experience over the coming months. In between working the serious crimes the unit was designed for, whenever there was a lull, Ted would return to the Missing Persons files. He usually worked with Maurice or Tina to try to find out what was behind the disappearances and bring the young people safely home. When they could.

Sometimes they were successful and it felt good. Other times they were too late in their efforts. After a bad result, Ted would often go to The Grapes with Jack to talk things through before he went home. He tried to keep to his resolve of not taking his troubles back to the house.

On a day which had been a crap one for the whole team, to put it mildly, Ted was almost tempted to swap his customary Gunner for a snakebite. But he stuck to his promise to himself. He knew that if he weakened, he wouldn't be able to stop at one.

He'd had to appear at an inquest into the death of a young girl he'd been trying to find. He'd been called as a witness as he'd been the first CID officer responding to a report of a suspicious death, which had turned out to be the missing girl. She'd left home after a row with her parents over a boyfriend they didn't approve of and had been living rough. With a serious eating disorder and no means of heating the empty house where she was squatting, she'd easily fallen prey to a sudden cold snap.

The father was still at the blaming stage of his grieving process. Verbally abusive to Ted while he gave his evidence, then waiting for him outside to continue to harangue him after he'd been ordered out of the coroner's court with a threat of being charged with contempt of court. Ted had done his best to remain calm and not let the incident get to him, but it had affected him deeply. He found it easier to talk to Jack than to Trev about such things. Jack had been there himself on previous occasions, had the abuse, got the T-shirt.

'Don't beat yourself up about it, Ted. We can't win 'em all and we're already doing a lot better than we were before you joined the team. Why don't you and Trev come out with me and the wife for a meal this weekend? A curry maybe? Relax a bit, let our hair down.'

'That would be good. I'll ask Trev. How are things going between you two?'

Jack made a face.

'You're lucky your Trev is still at the understanding stage. I get nothing but earache whenever I'm late back, or I have to work on a day she has other plans. The curse of the copper's marriage.'

He took another large swallow of his pint before he went on, 'D'you know what's going to happen to Bill Baxter now?'

Bill was the Charge Office sergeant who'd taken Ted under his wing when he'd first arrived at Stockport. He'd recently suffered a serious assault by a prisoner in the cells. Because of a previous injury, he wasn't as quick on his feet as he had been. The incident had left him traumatised and, unusually for him, he was on extended sick leave. He usually grabbed every shift going as he was lonely at home and the nick was his sanctuary, among colleagues who were more like family.

'The Big Boss was saying they're looking at breaking with tradition and putting him on the front desk. Everyone knows Doris doesn't do much of a job there. Her timekeeping is lousy, for one thing. Bill would be a godsend. Because he knows the job inside out, he could be like triage, first point of contact. Making sure the serious stuff got straight to the best person and filtering out the timewasters. They certainly can't just pension him off, not with a bravery medal to his name.'

Some years earlier, Bill had witnessed a child abduction taking place. He'd jumped on to the front of the car which was speeding away with a frightened little girl in the back seat and clung on by the windscreen wipers whilst radioing for help. He'd been flung from the vehicle when an area car had managed to stop it, sustaining serious fractures which had left him with a limp.

'I was wondering if I should go and visit him. Phone him, at least. He's on his own, isn't he?' Ted went on.

'Good luck with that. You're a braver man than I am, Gunga Din. He's a right miserable old sod. Doesn't take much to company of any kind. And he's not entirely alone. He's got Father Jack.'

In response to Ted's questioning look, Jack laughed.

'That's his parrot. Almost as bad-tempered as Bill can be. Swears like a trooper, and worse. That's why Bill named him after that drunken priest on the telly.'

He finished his drink and stood up to go.

'Right, I'd best get home to the trouble and strife, see what sort of a reception I get tonight. Will it be the cold, silent treatment or the full-on bollocking, I wonder?'

Ted's own homecoming couldn't have been more different. The kitchen was full of the aroma of good food, Trev paused in his laying of the table to give him a hug, and the six cats started weaving their way round his legs, purring loudly.

Then Ted looked again and counted aloud.

'Seven? Who's this little person I spy hiding in the corner looking as if I'm some sort of a monster who's just invaded the house.'

'Oh, that,' Trev replied airily. 'That's Barcelona. She's a

bit nervous still. She's been hanging around at work looking hungry. I know Barcelona is your favourite Freddie song, so I thought that suited her. You don't mind, do you?'

'No, I don't mind, if it makes you happy. But do you perhaps think that seven is enough now?'

He crouched down near to the small black cat, not making any move to touch her while she was clearly still wary.

'Hello, Barcelona. Welcome to your new home.'

'What's up with the Big Boss?' Ted asked Jack.

They were about to start Monday morning briefing, expecting the DCI to join them. Instead Jim Baker had just lurched through the main office and into his own, hurling the door shut with such ferocity that it shook the partition wall and made the glass rattle alarmingly in its frame.

He'd looked shocking; unshaven, hair wild and unbrushed, his suit crumpled, looking like he'd slept in it. Since Ted had stopped drinking he had an acute sense for the smell of alcohol, although he suspected everyone present could detect the stench of stale Scotch as the Big Boss went past.

'No idea and frankly, with him in a mood like that, I'm not going to volunteer to find out. Shall we just start without him?'

Ted hesitated, looking across at the closed door.

'Perhaps I should just go and ask if he's going to be joining us.'

'Seriously, Ted? I'm not sure four black belts is enough to protect you from the reception you're likely to get. I've never seen him look so rough. Let's just crack on and then if there's no sign of him and you're still feeling brave – or reckless – perhaps you could go and take a look in the lion's den.'

There was still no sign of the DCI when they'd finished briefing. Ted went over to his door, knocked quietly, then went straight in. Jim Baker's enraged bellow must have been heard halfway round the nick, never mind just in the main CID office.

'How bloody dare you come marching into my office without waiting for permission!'

Ted could immediately see the cause for his angry outburst. There was a glass on his desk, next to an open bottle of whisky which was half empty.

Ted stood his ground obstinately, shutting the office door behind him.

'Sir, are you all right?'

'Mind your own bloody business, Sergeant. And shut the door on your way out.'

'Excuse me for saying, sir, but should you be at work? There's clearly something wrong. If the Chief Super sees you like this ...'

'Don't bloody patronise me, you jumped up little shit!'

As soon as the words were out of his mouth, sounding like the howl of a wounded animal, the DCI's face crumpled in shame and his voice dropped, broke as he tried to speak again.

'God, I'm so sorry. That was inexcusable. I should never have said it.'

'What's wrong, sir? Can I do anything to help?'

'It's my daughter. Rosalie. She's just joined the ranks of your Missing Persons. She's walked out. Left home. Left me a note, but I have no idea where she is. She's not answering her phone and I'm going bloody frantic here.'

He raised his head to look directly at Ted. There were tears in his bloodshot eyes.

'I should never have spoken to you like that and I apologise. It's just that my little girl has gone and I don't know where she is or if she's safe.'

'Right, sir, first things first. Let me drive you home. You're probably best off there today. There's just a chance she'll come home or make contact with you there. I'll get a statement from you, then I'll come back here and we'll start up an enquiry. But let me get you home first, sir.'

The DCI nodded meekly. Before Ted took him out of his

office, he first went to find Jack Gregson. He spoke quietly to him so no one else heard, although the other team members were looking at him, curious to know what was going on with the Big Boss.

'Big Jim's daughter's gone missing. Can you take everyone into the DI's office just long enough for me to get him out of here. He wouldn't want anyone seeing him the state he's in. He hit the bottle as soon as he arrived and he looks ten times worse now. When I've seen him home and got his statement I'll bell you and get you to send someone to pick me up.'

'Christ, the poor sod. I can imagine what I'd be like if it was one of my daughters.'

Ted drove the Big Boss's car to Didsbury. Baker was quiet on the drive, apart from repeating his earlier apology for his outburst.

Ted had to help him unlock the front door and turn off the alarm, then he followed him as he lurched his way to the kitchen. There was no sign of his wife or anyone else in the house. Ted started to make coffee, three times stronger than he would ever make it for himself, while Jim slumped dejectedly down at the table.

He put a mug in front of Jim and served himself half of one topped up with plenty of water, milk and two sugars. Then he sat down opposite the Big Boss, taking out his pocket book.

'Are you happy talking to me, sir, or would you like me to call someone else?'

'Jim, Ted. Jim. You're in my house, not the office. You're seeing me at what I hope to god is the lowest ebb of my life. Call me Jim.'

'All right, Jim. In your own time. Tell me everything.'

'I'm sure you've heard the rumours about my wife. Your Trev experienced a bit of what she's like, at Christmas.'

'I try not to listen to gossip, boss.'

'It's an open secret. Margery has certain ... appetites. They're not easily satisfied. I do my best, god knows. But it's never enough. I've let her know that as long as she's discreet about it, I'll turn a blind eye, as long as she stays with me and doesn't publicly humiliate me.

'Rosalie knows what she's like and she hates what it does to me. The two of them are always having screaming rows about it. But what can I do, Ted? I married her. I took vows. They're important to me, even if they aren't to her.

'Two nights ago, it was very bad. Part of the agreement was that she never brought any of her men to my house, certainly never when me or Rosalie were here. I was out at the Lodge but Rosie was here when one of them called to pick my wife up. I imagine the two of them had quite a fight. When I got home, Margery was still out with whoever it was but Rosie had gone. She'd left me a note.'

'Could I see the note?'

Big Jim nodded towards a piece of paper on one of the kitchen work surfaces. Ted went over to read it without touching it and took a picture of it with his mobile phone.

'Daddy, I can't stand it any more. That tart my mother had one of her fancy men round to pick her up as soon as you left for the Lodge. It's disgusting. I can't bear what she's doing to you. I can't stay in the same house as her any longer. I'm not asking you to choose between us. That would be too cruel. I love you, Daddy, and I always will. If ever she goes, I will know and I will be back. Please try not to worry. Rosie xxx'

'Try not to worry,' Jim said scornfully. 'I've been going out of my mind. I stayed in all day yesterday. I rang round all the family and all the friends she knows. Her own phone must be switched off, it just goes straight to voice mail. I really hoped that she would come back when she'd calmed down, or at least phone me. When she didn't, I opened a bottle. And yes, I know that doesn't help anyone.'

'I'm not judging you, boss. I don't have children. I can't imagine how you must be feeling.'

'Thank you for that. Is there any more coffee? It's a bit

weak but it's better than nothing.'

Ted got up to serve him some then asked, 'And Mrs Baker? Does she know yet?'

'I haven't seen hide nor hair of her since Saturday evening, early on, nor heard from her. But that's not unusual. Ted, look, I'm telling you stuff that you need to know to help you find my daughter. I'm hoping I can count on your discretion ...'

'Boss, like I said, I don't listen to gossip and I certainly don't engage in it. I've been talked about enough all my life to know what it's like. I wouldn't do it to anyone else. And you really have no idea where she might be?'

'If I did don't you think I'd have gone straight round there to bring her home?' the Big Boss asked testily. 'I may be her dad but I am still a copper, don't forget.'

'Sorry, sir. Just routine questions. Sorry if it was tactless.'

'No, I'm sorry. I shouldn't bite your head off. You're doing your job. Look, I'll make you a list of all her friends and contacts that I know. You'll want a photo too, of course. I've got plenty. I'll find you the most recent one, the one that looks most like her. You know what teenage girls can be like for changing their look. I can't tell you how many different colours she's dyed her hair.

'I can tell you more or less what she was wearing when I saw her last, although I'm a typical bloke, it won't necessarily be a hundred per cent accurate. I can give you details of her finances, too. It's me who's in charge of them. We should be able to track her that way, at least.'

He was visibly perking up now, switching into policeman mode. He was clearly still worried but he was thinking more like a detective than a father.

'Boss, she says in the note that if her mother goes, she'll know. So that must mean she's in touch with someone who would keep her informed. Someone in the family? Maybe someone at the nick she's close to?'

'I can't think of anyone in the family who'd hide her

without telling me where she was. They'd know I'd be going frantic. And god help anyone in the nick if I find out that they know something and they're not telling me.'

'Had you better give Mrs Baker a call, boss? Let her know what's happened? She might perhaps give a more accurate description of what Rosie was wearing, for instance.'

The Big Boss snorted.

'I'll tell her if and when she finally drags herself back here.'

Then he reached out a hand the size of a bear's paw and took hold of Ted's arm.

'You will find her for me, won't you, Ted? Find my little girl and bring her safely home.'

Chapter Thirty

'Sorry I'm so late. Only I couldn't really leave Big Jim on his own tonight so I went round there with a takeaway.'

The newest cat, Barcelona, sprang off the sofa and dashed across the room to hide behind the armchair as soon as Ted came in. She was still wary. The other cats merely yawned and stretched and had to be persuaded to move up to give him room to sink down next to Trev, who used the remote to turn off the French film he'd been watching. Ted had at least made time to text him to warn him he would be late.

'I can't imagine how he's feeling. And as I'm always saying one of the things I love most about you is how kind and compassionate you are, it would be the worst kind of hypocrisy to complain when you've been out demonstrating those qualities.

'I take it there's still no news from Rosie? Not even a phone call?'

'Nothing. I can understand her being furious with her mother but I can't understand why she would treat her father so badly. Not even a word.'

Trev draped his arm round Ted's shoulders and pulled him close.

'You're thinking of your mother, aren't you? That's what she did to you, so you understand Jim's pain, better than most people could.'

'I shouldn't. It's selfish of me.'

'You're the least selfish person I know. Something like this is bound to stir up bad memories for you, though.'

'It's because it's so similar to what happened to me. I came home from school one day and mam was gone. She never said anything, there was no note for me, and I never heard from her again. If she'd wanted to leave my dad, I could understand that. He wasn't easy. But she never even sent me a birthday card or a letter from time to time.'

'D'you think you can find Rosie?'

'I don't know. You know it's not always that simple. She said something in her note about how she'd know if her mother left home and she'd come back then. That makes me think she's in touch with someone who knows the family situation. I'll ask round the relatives, as discreetly as I can. But it also makes me wonder if it's someone at the station. I can't think who, though. They must realise this is destroying Jim.'

'I suppose there's still a chance she'll simply calm down and come back of her own accord.'

He paused to rearrange cats a bit more to make things more comfortable for both of them.

'You must have some good memories of your mother. Before she left? Tell me something nice about her that you remember.'

Ted hesitated. He was still bitter about his mother. He'd pushed most of the memories well below the surface.

'Welsh cakes,' he said finally. 'She'd often have Welsh cakes, fresh out of the oven, when I got home from school.'

'I can make you Welsh cakes. They're easy enough. She taught you some Welsh when you were little, didn't she? Can you remember any of that?'

'You know I'm rubbish at languages.'

He thought a moment then looked round at the cats, pointing to each in turn.

'*Un, dai, tri, pedwar, pimp, chewch, saith. Saith cathod.* Seven cats.'

'She taught you to sing in Welsh, too, didn't you say? Sing

me something.'

Ted shook his head.

'Too tired. And not really in the mood, after the day I've had.'

'Please. Just a short piece. I'd be suitably grateful.'

Ted sighed. He never could refuse his partner anything. He started to sing quietly.

'Calon lân yn llawn daioni,
Tecach yw na'r lili dlos:
Dim ond calon lân all ganu–
Canu'r dydd a chanu'r nos.'

'That was absolutely beautiful. Now, I promised to show my gratitude. You'll want a nice hot soak before bed, after a hard day at work. So why don't I come up and scrub your back for you. Then we'll see where that takes us.'

'Do you think this could be Rosalie, Sarge?'

Ted and Tina were on their way to a nearby shopping centre. A member of the public had phoned in, having seen photos of Rosalie posted up around the town and in the local papers. The Big Boss had so far stopped short of doing a televised appeal. It wasn't the first time his daughter had gone off, but she'd always returned previously. Until this time. And it was the first time she'd left a note saying she wasn't coming back until her mother left.

The person who rang in had reported being served with coffee in a shopping centre by a young woman he said looked like the picture in the papers.

'Impossible to say. You know how many of these sightings turn out to be false alarms. We have to check them out, though, because the one we ignore will be the real one.'

'And will you recognise her? Rosalie, I mean?'

'It depends how much she's changed her appearance. I'm usually not bad at face recognition.'

'Well, at least it's not a big place. Not like the Trafford

Centre or Meadowhall. If she's here, you may well be able to spot her and talk to her.'

Tina was just turning the car off the road to head for the car park when they spotted blue flashing lights and police activity.

''ello, 'ello, 'ello, what's all this then?' Ted asked ironically, just as his mobile rang. Jack Gregson calling.

'Ted, if you're on your way to the Mall we've just heard that there's a major incident going down there. Might be a good idea to turn round and come back, go again another day.'

'What sort of an incident? Have you got any details?'

'An armed nutter with a couple of big knives. Early reports are suggesting several injuries and one possible fatality, as yet unconfirmed.'

Ted hesitated for a moment before replying.

'Jack, there's a chance the Big Boss's daughter's in there. How do you think it would look to him if we turned tail and came back without at least checking?'

'It's not your call any more, Ted. This isn't our operation and you're no longer in Firearms. If Rosalie's in there and unhurt, your enquiries will keep until another day. If anything's happened to her ...'

'And you're saying this in what capacity, Jack?' Ted asked him.

He was testing boundaries. Seeing if Jack was issuing him with an order as Acting DI or just giving him advice as a friend of equal rank.

'I can come the heavy and make it official if you like, Ted. I'd just prefer you to listen to the voice of reason.'

'How about this, by way of a compromise? Even if Firearms are here, there's a strong chance I'm the only SFO on site. What if I go and find the Tactical Firearms Commander and offer my services? I promise to do as they say, but don't you think I should at least offer? It's what I'm trained for, and my training is still up to date.'

Jack sighed.

'On your head be it, then.'

A PC who was busily directing traffic away from the shopping centre, seeing their car hovering, came striding across, looking officious. Tina let the window down.

'No entry for now, folks. Drive on.'

Ted got his warrant card out to show him.

'DS Darling, from Stockport. I'm an SFO. Are Firearms on site? I could offer my services.'

The constable hesitated.

'Look, I may be able to help. Tell me where the Command Post is and at least let me go and ask them. I'll take full responsibility for entering the scene. But make sure you inform Firearms that I'm coming in. Tell them to look out for a skinny little blonde bloke in a brown leather jacket and not to shoot him.'

He turned to Tina as he said, 'You go and park the car somewhere, Tina, and stay with it.'

'Not flippin' likely, Sarge. If anything happens to you, I'm not going back and telling the Big Boss I didn't at least try to keep an eye on you. I'm coming with you.'

'Where is the CP?' Ted asked the constable.

'In the centre manager's office, Sarge. Just inside the entrance on the right. I can radio ahead to say you're coming in. Just leave the car over there so it's not blocking access for any more emergency vehicles they need to bring in.'

'Right, Tina,' Ted told her as they ducked under the tape and walked towards the entry to the mall. They'd both put on vests from the boot of the car. 'You stay behind me at all times and you go no further than the manager's office. Clear? And when we get back to the station, we'll have a long talk about following orders.'

'Yes, Sarge. Like you're following the ones DI Gregson was clearly trying to give you just now, over the phone?'

They both had to show their ID again before passing a second cordon at the entry doors. Uniformed officers were ushering frightened shoppers out of one doorway, keeping the other clear for authorised entry only.

Ted tapped briefly on the office door before he went in. He was pleased to see the Tactical Firearms Commander was a Superintendent he'd served under before and not had any problems with. The man looked up, smiled in surprise and said, 'Well, I thought I'd lost my faith. But there I was, just offering up a prayer, and who should walk through the door but Sergeant Darling. I thought you'd left Firearms?'

'I did, sir. I'm a DS at Stockport now, here following up a MissPers lead. But while I was here anyway, I thought I'd see if I could do anything to help.'

'Your specialist training is still up to date?' Superintendent Paddy Kelly asked him.

'It is, sir. What's the situation here?'

Kelly and the other officers present were looking at a bank of monitors which covered various parts of the centre's interior. The Super filled Ted in rapidly.

'A guy's come into the centre carrying a holdall. No reason to be suspicious particularly. He's started out quietly enough just browsing round. Then he's pulled out two bloody big machetes and run amok, hacking at anyone who got in his way.

'He's currently holed up in a shop on the top floor, surrounded by frightened shoppers. Any time any of them try to make a break for it, he starts rushing round waving his weaponry again. It's a nightmare for my shooters. There are too many panicking people milling about, and far too much plate glass for them to even try getting off a shot.

'We've got a negotiator trying to talk to him over the centre's address system. We're also in phone contact with one of the people inside. There's some confusion as to what his nationality is. No one can make out enough of what he's saying to be sure. Some are saying it could just be gibberish. It's going to take someone with close-up skills to take him down. Can you do it?'

'Is there any footage of him in action that I can watch, sir, to evaluate the situation?'

'As much as you need to. At the moment, as long as nobody is putting any pressure on him he's not doing much, other than just saying whatever it is he's saying.'

Kelly instructed one of the technicians to play the footage through while Ted watched.

'He's very unsteady on his feet. Have we any intel from anyone in there as to why? Drink? Drugs?'

'The chap on the phone to us, who's right at the back of that bunch of people, talking quietly, so our assailant doesn't seem to be aware of what he's doing, says he doesn't smell of drink. Looks like it could be drugs, then.'

Ted was studying a monitor closely, looking at replayed tape from moments when something pushed the assailant into action. Times when he lurched about, wielding the big knives.

'Or lack of medication, perhaps? Maybe he's supposed to be on pills and has stopped taking them. That might also explain why he's moving like he is. His movements look uncoordinated.

'The good news, sir, is that he's no knife expert. Look at his posture when he goes on the attack. He has one machete hanging down by his side, so the business end of the blade is facing the rear. Then he holds the other one up high and cocked back, so again, because of the way he's holding it, he would waste precious time bringing it into play.'

'Don't underestimate him, Sergeant. I'm waiting on confirmation but we think there's one fatality and several quite serious injuries so far.'

'I'm not underestimating him, sir. Just assessing him. He's dangerous. Very dangerous. But he's not combat trained.'

'So could you take him down? I daren't risk moving the shooters in any closer without a good distraction and I'm fresh out of other ideas.'

'Taking him down isn't the problem, from what I've seen,

sir. Getting me in there without spooking him into doing something serious is worrying me more at the moment.'

'And me. We can't do too much in the way of distraction technique because as soon as he sees anything happening, it triggers more of the violent behaviour.'

'It's a mobile phone shop he's in? What about the doors? Automatic opening?'

'We've managed to override that system from in here, so they're fixed open. We thought that would be safer, so if we can gain entry, it would be instantaneous.'

'That might be my way in, then. If I come walking along with my mobile in my hand and earphones in, as if I'm listening to music, I could wander straight in and look as if I hadn't noticed what was going on round me. That would at least get me inside.'

'He's never going to fall for that. For a start, you're wearing a police vest.'

'What if I wasn't ...'

'Don't even bloody think of it. Who's your new gaffer?'

'DCI Baker, sir.'

'Well, I'm not being the one to tell Big Jim I let one of his officers walk in there unprotected and get himself killed. Risk assessment. I'll need clearance from my Chief, and I ought to clear your involvement with Big Jim, as a courtesy if nothing else.'

'Sir, I'd be really grateful if you didn't tell my boss I'm here. You've heard his daughter is missing? We got intel that she might be here, but I didn't want to tell him in case it's just a false alarm. If he knows I'm here, he'll only want to know why and he might even come roaring over here, if he thinks Rosie's inside.'

Kelly weighed up what Ted was saying.

'All right, here's the deal, and it depends on my boss agreeing it. I won't tell Jim Baker anything at this stage. You put your vest on under your own jacket so it doesn't show and you try walking in. I move some of my shooters as near as I dare without risking him seeing them so you've got armed cover if you need it. You carry out a full risk assessment of what you see and if it's too dangerous, to you or to any members of the public, you abort. Understood?'

'Understood, sir. And don't worry – I can run away very fast when I need to. I'm not going to put myself or anyone else at risk.'

It felt good to Ted to be back doing the job he was trained for, as he made his way up the curved staircase to the upper floor. He could see the AFOs moving quietly along the walkway, two from each direction, keeping low down and close to the shop fronts. Ted was walking in the middle of the alley, trying to look nonchalant. His leather jacket, zipped up high, hid the Kevlar vest underneath which would hopefully protect him from serious injury if he got his timing wrong.

He wasn't too worried, from what he'd seen on tape. The man he was going in to face was dangerous, especially because he was so unpredictable. But it was clear from watching him that he had no proper weapons training. Ted had spent many hours with Mr Green learning any number of effective ways to disarm an assailant. He just needed the element of surprise on his side.

Strolling along as he was, earphones on attached to his mobile phone, nodding his head as he walked as if listening to some music, he shouldn't look too suspicious. There was no music playing; he had a line open to the Command Post so they could keep him appraised at all times of any new developments in the shop.

He knew that his biggest challenge was somehow to separate the knifeman from the throng of shoppers around him, so that it would effectively be just him and the assailant, facing off. Officers in the CP were explaining to the man on the phone inside the shop to remain calm and not react, but as soon as Ted made his move, to call out to everyone present to get out of the way. The negotiator would do the same over the public address system.

Ted didn't doubt his martial arts skills. He'd spent some time doing stretching exercises before he began, so he would be up to the task in hand. He couldn't afford to be let down by tight hamstrings. His main concern was his acting skills. He knew he didn't look anything like a police officer. But would the knifeman perceive him as a threat? In a way, he hoped so. He needed the man to focus all his attention on the new intruder. Perhaps even to make a run at him.

Only then would Ted know if he really possessed the skills to take him down.

Chapter Thirty-one

When Ted sauntered in through the open door, trying to look casual, the attacker had the frightened group of shoppers huddled towards the back of the building. He was pacing up and down in front of them, still holding both machetes, like an obsessive collie dog having penned his flock and waiting for the shepherd to close the gate.

The way he was holding the weapons confirmed Ted's assessments from the security cameras. He was dangerous because he was unpredictable but he clearly didn't know much about handling knives professionally. Just before leaving the Command Post Ted had been told that the fatality, now confirmed, had probably been the result of a heart attack rather than a knife wound, although the victim had received a few glancing blows with the machete which could well have caused it.

All the time the man was prowling to and fro he was talking to himself. Ted had no idea what language it was. It sounded harsh, guttural. It reminded him of the Orcs speaking in the *Lord of the Rings* films he'd seen with Trev. He couldn't be sure but it sounded as if he was repeating the same phrases over and over.

Ted was relieved, too, that his assessment of the man's height had been about accurate. He was not tall, so Ted didn't have to revise his planned attacking moves.

A woman's voice, calm, measured, was talking over the public address system. The trained negotiator, assuring the man that the situation could still be resolved with no need for further bloodshed. Occasionally she would add another phrase in what sounded like different languages. The man was taking no notice. He didn't even seem to be aware yet of Ted's sudden presence in the shop. He hadn't even glanced in his direction.

Now came the most dangerous part. Ted needed to get himself noticed. He had to draw the man away from the bunched shoppers, out into the open space in front of them, so he could deal with him effectively without him harming anyone else.

Or so he hoped.

He knew there was armed back-up right outside the door now, but he needed to take the man down first. There was no way they could risk a shot at him with so many people about in such a confined space.

The best way to provoke an attack was usually to launch one. Ted had to get his timing exactly right, to get the attacker to come to him. The nearer to the door he was, the easier the situation was to manage. Ted had handcuffs in one jacket pocket, a CS spray in the other, should he need it. He was hoping his martial arts skills would be enough. He was about to find out.

'Hey! What are you doing?' he shouted.

The man seemed to notice him for the first time. His eyes appeared unfocused as he tried to make sense of what this short intruder was doing there, speaking to him. Then, as Ted had hoped, the man lowered his head, raised the big knife in his right hand and charged forward. His movements were clumsy, uncoordinated.

Ted pivoted on one foot. This was the fleeting moment when he left himself open to serious injury in parts of his anatomy which weren't protected by the vest. If the man moved fast enough to bring that lethal blade in his left hand up and into play, Ted was in serious trouble. He'd based his judgement on the man's evident lack of skill and coordination. Now was the time to find out whether his risk assessment had been an accurate one.

His other leg shot up high to hook round the back of the man's neck, pulling him forward and down, before he was able to do anything with either knife. Swiftly, Ted straddled him, shouting loudly for the benefit of the Firearms officers just outside, 'Man down!'

The first AFO through the door kicked the machete away from the man's left hand. Ted had already dealt efficiently with the other one, pulling the man's hands behind him and reaching for his handcuffs. The whole thing had taken seconds.

The Firearms officer was someone else Ted knew.

'Nice one, Ted. You can safely leave him to us now, thanks.'

'Be gentle with him though, eh? I don't know, but he looks to me like he's having some sort of psychotic episode.'

Paramedics were appearing now that the all clear had been given. A lot of the shoppers were looking on the verge of hysteria with the relief of knowing they were safe. One or two of them approached Ted to thank him, some of them with telephones out to capture his picture. He politely asked them not to do that. He didn't want Trev to see his picture appear anywhere in public. He wasn't planning on telling him too much about what had happened.

He walked out of the shop, his job done, apart from a debrief with the Super. As he went back down the stairs, officers coming up paused to congratulate him on a job well done. A few shook his hand or clapped him on the shoulder. Ted hated all that. He was just doing what he was trained for.

When he went back into the Command Post, there was a spontaneous round of applause from all present, including Superintendent Kelly.

'Well done DS Darling, good job. Let me have your report

as soon as you can.'

'Brilliant, Sarge,' Tina told him enthusiastically. She'd watched the whole thing on the monitors. 'That kick-trick was amazing.'

'Not a trick, Tina. It's a Taekwondo hook kick,' Ted started to correct her. He hated inaccuracy.

'Well, whatever it was, it was incredible.'

'Sir, before we go, can we have a look at any security camera footage of the cafés, to see if we can get sight of our Missing Person? No point trying to talk to anyone until it's all calmed down, but it would be nice to follow the lead up while we're here.'

'Be my guest. I hope you can find the lass. I can imagine how frantic your DCI must be.'

They looked through all the available footage but there was no sign of anyone who remotely resembled Rosalie. Despite his success with the attacker, Ted was subdued as Tina drove them back to Stockport. He'd been so optimistic about getting a lead on Rosie's whereabouts to put the Big Boss out of his misery, but they were going back empty-handed on that score.

Once again, when Ted walked into the office, he was greeted with a round of applause from the team members, who got to their feet. Nothing stayed a secret for long in the Force. Jack came over to shake his hand then to hold it aloft like a winning boxer.

'Here he is. The man of the moment. Stockport's very own Mr Miyagi – the Karate Kid.'

Ted pulled his hand free, looking uncomfortable.

'It wasn't karate, it was a Taekwondo move ...' he started to say.

Jack leaned closer and breathed in his ear.

'Just watch out though. Not everyone was thrilled to hear what you've been up to.'

Right on cue, the Big Boss's door burst open and the DCI

stood there, almost filling the door-frame. He certainly didn't look amused.

'DS Darling, a word, please.'

Jack gave Ted a pat on the shoulder and a murmured, 'Good luck,' as he headed for the office, wondering what was in store for him.

'Shut the door.'

The DCI sat back down heavily, his chair creaking in protest, and looked up at Ted.

'Would you like to explain to me what the bloody hell you were doing going off playing cowboys without even consulting me?'

'Sir, I just happened to be somewhere where there was a serious incident in progress. I was the only SFO on site so I thought it only right to offer my services.'

'Oh, you did, did you? Without consulting me? Why was I not kept informed of any of it, including the reason for you being there in the first place?'

'I'm sorry, sir. We'd had a reported sighting of someone looking like Rosie. I took the decision not to inform you until I'd checked it out, rather than get your hopes up ...'

'Don't you bloody dare!' Big Jim's sudden bellow was so loud it almost made Ted jump. 'Don't you dare use my daughter as an excuse for you to start playing the maverick. I expect you to keep me informed at all times of any and all case developments. And that includes the one involving my daughter.'

'Sorry, sir.'

'And was it her?'

'No, sir. I went through all the CCTV footage of the café where she was supposed to have been seen working, but there was no trace of anyone who looked like her.'

'Right. Well, you need to make your bloody mind up about what you want to do. What role it is you want to play. I brought you into this team because I thought you'd make a good DI. I still think that, most of the time. But I can't have a DI who does their own bloody thing, without consulting me. For whatever reason. That's not how it works. It's not what I expect from you.'

'Sorry, sir. I made an error of judgement. It won't happen again.'

'It bloody better not, because I was getting ready to move you up to acting DI fairly soon, until you did this. Are you on the rota this weekend?'

'No, sir.'

'Well, you spend the time asking yourself some serious questions. Are you still hankering after the Special stuff, or are you happy carrying on with us mere mortals in CID? Talk it over with your Trev, see what he thinks. Because I don't like mavericks. There's no place for them on my team. I don't want you suddenly racing off somewhere all guns blazing when you're supposed to be following up other lines of enquiry. Not without at least clearing it with me first. I want a DI I can depend on to work by the book. It may not be all that exciting, but it's how I like things done.'

'Sir.'

'Before you go, it's only fair I tell you. You know something like this gets round the whole Force in seconds. I had the ACC on the phone, saying I should put you forward for a Chief Constable's commendation for bravery.'

Ted's face was anguished.

'Please don't, sir. I'd hate anything like that.'

A flicker of a smile passed over Big Jim's face.

'Now you've shown your underbelly. I'll know what to threaten you with if it ever happens again. And it bloody better not. Make sure you have a long, hard think about your future, then let me know on Monday morning. Now go on, piss off back to work.'

Ted hesitated at the door.

'Sir, can I ask, does Mrs Baker have any idea where Rosie

might be? Have you discussed it with her at all? Is it possible that it's her Rosie's in contact with?'

He wasn't sure if he was about to get his head ripped off for being too personal. But he felt he needed to know.

The DCI sighed and ran a big hand over his face.

'She graced me with a few moments of her presence last night. She just came back for a change of clothes. I told her there was still no sign of Rosie. She didn't seem all that bothered. I'd put money on her not being in contact. They don't get on at the best of times.

'She said she'd done it before and come back, so she'd be back again, probably when she needed to make a withdrawal from the Bank of Dad. Then she went off again to see whoever it is she's seeing at the moment. I've lost track, although I bet almost everyone in this nicks knows who it is.'

'Will you be all right, sir? I could come round this evening...'

'You've got your own life. Get off home to Trev, and your moggies.'

'If I tell Trev I'm taking him away for the weekend, he'll be fine about me going out again tonight. Indian or Chinese, sir?'

'You're home early.'

'I am, but I'm not staying. Sorry. Big Jim's not in a good place today. I said I'd go round with a takeaway. You don't mind, do you? Only in exchange, I'll take you away for the weekend.'

Trev's eyes lit up at the prospect.

'That sounds like a fair exchange. Where are you taking me? The art galleries of Paris? The fashion houses of Milano?'

Ted hesitated, never sure with Trev whether he was having his leg pulled or not.

'Er, I was thinking of Snowdonia. A nice little B&B, some

hill walking, that sort of thing. We can go to Paris if you'd prefer?'

Trev laughed.

'Silly sod, you'd hate it. But to what do I owe the honour? Not that I'm looking a gift horse in the mouth, or anything like that.'

'I had to do something today. A bit outside my current remit. More like the old SFO days. Big Jim wasn't best pleased. He's told me to have a long, hard think about my future and decide where it lies. I need to talk to you about it and you know me, it's easier if I do that out in the open.'

'I'm not best pleased either,' Trev said, looking worried now. 'You've been up to something dangerous? Ted, seriously? You know I've said all along I wouldn't ask you to choose between me and your job. I thought you were settled in CID? Happy with your new role?'

'I am. It's just something came up, I was there, I had the training. Look, can we talk about this at the weekend? Please?'

'I need a spy on your team,' Trev told him. 'Someone to keep me informed of what you're getting up to. It's nice going out with Jack and his wife but I'd like to meet more of them, to pick myself a mole. Why don't you have them all round for drinks or something?'

Ted made a face. He preferred to keep his home life separate from work whenever he could.

'There isn't really the room here ...'

'All right then. Next Christmas. Talk to Dave at The Grapes about using that small room of his. I'll make food. Mince pies. The works. Get all the team together. Big Jim too, and Bill, perhaps. Then I can pick myself an informant, and you'll never know who it is.'

Ted agreed, kissing him on the cheek. He went upstairs and quickly changed out of his work clothes into something more comfortable Then he headed back out to his car to go and pick up a takeaway before driving round to see the Big Boss.

Trev's words had made him think once more about the possibility that someone inside the station was in contact with Rosalie. And of what that knowledge would do to Big Jim if he ever found out who it was.

Epilogue

Six months later - Christmas Eve

DCI Jim Baker tapped a spoon against the side of his whisky glass.

'All right, everyone, a bit of hush, please. Now I don't want to bore you all rigid. I just thought that as the senior officer present, I should say a word of thanks to DI Darling ...'

A cheer went up from the team members. Ted had had the acting role for a couple of months now and he was proving to be a popular boss. This was the first official confirmation of his promotion. Jack knew already, of course. The DCI had taken the two of them aside a couple of weeks earlier so they were both in the picture.

'I'm grateful to you, Jack, I couldn't have done it without you,' Ted had told him candidly.

'I know you couldn't,' Jack had laughed in reply. 'So in exchange you can help me with all the insider knowledge I'm going to need to catch you up.'

'So who's the boss now, then?' Maurice Brown called out. 'It was bad enough calling you both Sarge but I'm thoroughly confused now.

'I'm the Big Boss on this team, DC Brown, and don't you forget it,' Jim Baker growled, but his tone was good-humoured. 'But I think DI Darling has finally shown us all he deserves the title of Boss. It's in no small measure due to him that Ray Mann is now enjoying an extended stay at Her Majesty's pleasure. A good result, and one of many.'

There was another shout from the team members at the mention. Despite his not guilty plea, Mann had been convicted and sent down for life with a recommended minimum of twenty-five years.

'And of course I'd also like to thank Trevor, who's very kindly put on this spread for us all this evening,' the DCI went on. 'Not to mention looking after Ted so he can do a good job on the team.

'I'm going to shut up now and get stuck into those mince pies. But first, can we all just lift a glass. Merry Christmas to all of us, and our thanks to Ted and to Trevor.'

They were all off duty. It was informal, a convivial gathering of friends and colleagues. Just how Ted had hoped it would turn out when Trev had first suggested it.

Ted was keen to have a quiet word with Jack. He knew he couldn't have got where he was now without his constant help and support. Jack could have made his life difficult but they'd become good friends as well as work colleagues.

'No hard feelings that I leapfrogged over you?'

'Just as long as we're clear who the real boss is,' Jack told him with a wink. 'You deserve it, Ted. You've worked hard, proved yourself. You've shaken the team up better than I ever could.'

'When you're ready to go for inspector, you know I'll back you all the way. So will Big Jim.'

'Thanks. I'll hold you to that. This was a great idea of your Trev's,' Jack said, looking across the small room to where Trev was chatting with Rob O'Connell and Virgil Tibbs with their partners. He was in his element. Always the party animal.

'I certainly couldn't have got there without his support. Goodness knows why he stays with me when he could have anyone he wanted, but I'm glad that he has so far.'

'Are you kidding? You're supposed to be a detective. Good at reading people. If my missus had ever once looked at me the way your Trev looks at you, I'd be well happy.'

As if he sensed he was being talked about, Trev suddenly looked across at them, smiling fondly at Ted.

'See what I mean? I probably don't want to know what your secret is but anyone can see how good you are together.'

'How are things between you and the wife now, Jack?'

Jack Gregson's wife was talking to Maurice Brown's, over by the buffet table.

'Not brilliant. She's talking about a trial separation. If we get another shout this Christmas, it could turn out to be a bit more permanent. She wants me to leave the force, but I don't want to.

'Do you regret leaving Firearms to be with Trev?'

The look on Ted's face as he returned Trev's smile across the room said it all.

Big Jim made his way over to talk to Ted, his plate piled high with festive treats. He and Ted were becoming not just work colleagues but friends too, outside the office. It was usually to Ted he turned when he was feeling down, with still no word of his missing daughter.

'If you're at a loose end any time tomorrow, Jim, you know you're very welcome to pop round and have a drink and some more mince pies with us.'

Ted was being tactful, trying to sound out whether the Big Boss would be on his own for Christmas or whether his wandering wife might put in an appearance, even if only briefly. Jim Baker had become a not infrequent visitor to their home, whenever he was at a low ebb. He always skilfully dodged Trev's hugs. Trev was tactile, with everyone. It took Jim too far outside his comfort zone, although he appreciated the warmth and kindness he always found from them both.

'That's a kind offer, Ted, thanks. But Margery usually pitches up some time over Christmas and plays the dutiful wife for a few hours. Until the novelty wears off and she's gone again.'

'You're very welcome to bring her too, of course.'

'Thank you. I appreciate the offer. So, you've no regrets about deciding to stick with us and give up the exciting stuff?'

'None at all, really. If it makes Trev happy, then it's fine by me. We had a long discussion about it, that weekend I took him to Snowdonia. He knows it's never easy being in a relationship with a policeman. But he's happier with me in CID than in Firearms. And if he's happy, I'm happy.'

Ted was looking round the room, watching Trev, ever the perfect host, move from one guest to another with offers of more food and drink. He wondered if he'd been successful in finding himself a mole among the team members and who it might be.

'Don't blame yourself, Ted, that we've not found her yet.'

The DCI was perceptive. He knew Ted hated the fact that he'd not been able to reunite the Big Boss with his missing daughter. He put every one of the few spare moments he had into trying to.

'She's a copper's daughter, don't forget. She knows a thing or two. If she doesn't want to be found, she knows all the best ways to stop it happening.'

Ted was about to reply when his mobile phone rang. Kevin Turner. He was duty inspector for the evening, Ted was duty CID inspector. He knew instinctively that this was not going to be a call to wish him season's greetings.

At least he'd warned Trev in advance this time that he was on call. And booked a surprise trip away for him on his next days off.

'Sorry to interrupt your little do, Ted. We've got a suspicious death for you. A man, no ID, no further details yet. Just been fished out of the river near Merseyway. Not a very appetising one, by all accounts. Can I show you as attending?'

'A choice between Trev's mince pies and a rotting corpse? That's a tough one, Kev. Yes, I'll get Jack and we'll go over there now, find out what's what, and keep you informed. And a

Merry Christmas to you too. I hope you get something a bit more exciting than a dead body in your stocking.'

'A shout?' the DCI asked him as he ended the call.

'The Mersey just spat out our Christmas present. A man's body, and not too fresh, by the sound of it. I'll take Jack and we'll go and take a look. See if it's one for us or not. Would it be selfish to hope that it isn't, so we can all get a decent Christmas?'

'Natural thought rather than selfish I would say. Keep me posted.'

Ted went to let Trev know first.

'Get a taxi home. Don't drive if you're had a few,' Ted warned him, taking out his wallet to make sure his partner had enough for the fare.

Trev had used Ted's car to bring the food to the pub, while Ted had gone into work on the motorbike. He'd go with Jack in a service vehicle to the site where the body had been found.

'I've no idea until I get there how late I'll be.'

Trev bent to kiss him. Nothing too full on, he knew that would have embarrassed Ted in front of the team.

'Just take care and get back when you can. We can do our celebrating whenever you've finished being a policeman.'

The look Jack's wife gave him when Ted went over to tell him they had to go was a world away from Trev's reaction. She looked tight-lipped, disapproving. Ted hoped that, despite what Jack had been saying earlier, it wouldn't prove to be the final nail in the coffin of their marriage.

'You and me on a shout for Christmas, Ted?' Jack said as they went out of the pub and over to the station to collect a vehicle. Ted had agreed at the start of the evening that he would do the driving, if it became necessary, as he wouldn't be drinking anyway.

'Isn't that where it all began?'